X3 4116

D0160476

A DEATH ALONG
THE RIVER FLEET

A DEATH

— ALONG THE —

RIVER FLEET

Susanna Calkins

MINOTAUR BOOKS ✼ NEW YORK

This is a work of fiction. All of the characters, organizations, and events portrayed in this novel are either products of the author's imagination or are used fictitiously.

A DEATH ALONG THE RIVER FLEET. Copyright © 2016 by Susanna Calkins. All rights reserved. Printed in the United States of America. For information, address St. Martin's Press, 175 Fifth Avenue, New York, N.Y. 10010.

www.minotaurbooks.com

The Library of Congress Cataloging-in-Publication Data is available upon request.

ISBN 978-1-250-05737-2 (hardcover)
ISBN 978-1-4668-6113-8 (e-book)

Our books may be purchased in bulk for promotional, educational, or business use. Please contact your local bookseller or the Macmillan Corporate and Premium Sales Department at 1-800-221-7945, extension 5442, or by e-mail at MacmillanSpecialMarkets@ macmillan.com.

First Edition: April 2016

10 9 8 7 6 5 4 3 2 1

To my family

ACKNOWLEDGMENTS

So many people have made this book possible:

First, I would like to thank my beta readers—Maggie Dalrymple, Heidi Janitschke, Mags Light, and Mary Schuller—for your gentle feedback and guidance. As always I would like to thank the wonderful team at Minotaur—Kelley Ragland, Elizabeth Lacks, India Cooper, David Rotstein, Sarah Melnyk, and the others who helped along the way—for the care you have taken with my books. I also feel grateful to my agent, David Hale Smith, for helping bring this book into existence.

I'd also like to thank those friends who are always so supportive of my writing, including Muveddet Harris, Greg Light, Erica Neubauer (who may or may not have a namesake in this book), Lori Rader-Day, Clare O'Donohue, Lynne Raimondo, Steve Stofferahn, and Sam Thomas. I also greatly appreciate the friendship offered by fellow Sleuths in Time authors: Tessa Arlen, Anna Lee Huber, Anna Loan-Wilsey, Alyssa Maxwell, Christine Trent, Ashley Weaver, and Meg Mims and Sharon Pisacreta (D. E. Ireland).

I would also like to acknowledge my readers, especially the ones who take the time to send me an e-mail. Your questions and ideas keep me motivated and excited to write, and I very much appreciate your enthusiasm about Lucy and her world.

Finally, I'd like to thank my family, especially my wonderful children, Quentin and Alex Kelley, for inspiring me each and every day. In particular, too, I must thank my husband, Matt Kelley, who, as my alpha reader and in-house cognitive psychologist, ensured that my descriptions of memory and cognitive impairment were all plausible. He also took care that the thousand monkeys typing on the thousand computers were fed and cared for—without his taking on those extra family responsibilities, this book would never have been finished. So, to Matt, I offer you my deepest love and appreciation for all that you do to support this crazy pursuit.

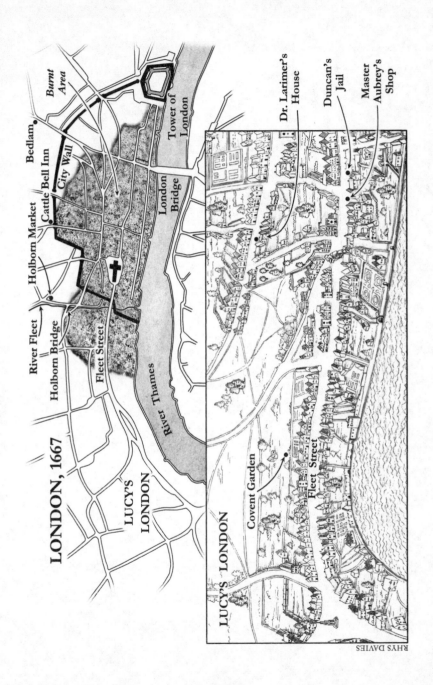

LONDON

———

April 1667

· I ·

Lucy Campion slipped toward the vast wasteland where London's busy markets had once bustled. Since the Great Fire some seven months before, the region was silent, lifeless—the ash-covered rubble and charred tree stumps were a grim reminder of all the city had lost. The mumpers and beggars who had sought refuge in the area had been removed before the winter had come, and the burnt ruins had been steadily cleared away by soldiers and conscripted Londoners.

As the sleet-filled wind picked up a bit, Lucy shivered. The winter that had just passed was the coldest anyone could remember—even the Thames had frozen over in January—and there were many times throughout that winter when Lucy had wondered if she would ever be truly warm again. Spring had not come easily to this region; there were no trees, and the chill morning air was strangely silent from the lack of birds trilling.

Far off in the distance she caught the crunching sound of a cart making an early delivery somewhere. It brought to mind the strange journey by cart that she herself had made, just two weeks before, on a wild search to locate a dear friend who was caught in the grip of a murderer.

Without thinking, Lucy rubbed her knee, which had been hurt most dreadfully during the encounter, and still pained her from time to time. Master Aubrey, the printer who had taken her on as an apprentice after the Fire, had bid her make several deliveries this early morning. *Best get used to walking again, Lucy,* he had told her in his usual gruff way. *I have no place for you in my shop otherwise.* So she was up before dawn to make her deliveries, even before the other printer's devil, Lach, had got up to piss in his pot. Several books had come for Mr. Oldham, a private tutor who lived just beyond the northwestern part of the burnt expanse. Indeed, his home had been spared, having been just beyond the Fire's reach.

Unlike most of the books they sold, which were made of a flimsy paper, these three books were hefty, clad in leather, and— to Lucy's disappointment—written entirely in Latin. Although she had learned to read and write when serving in the household of Master Hargrave, a London magistrate, she had never learned a foreign tongue, let alone a language of the ancients.

As she neared Holborn Bridge, the wind shifted and the nau-seating smell of the old Fleet River assaulted her. Master Hargrave once had told her that, long ago, the river had flowed easily, allowing barges and ships to move without difficulty through its winding course. Such a thing was hard to believe; it was now more ditch and drainage than a true river, full of excrement and animal parts from the Smithfield markets, decaying in ill-flowing streams. The houses and sheds that had long lined the river—an open sewer truly—had been pulled down and cleared to keep the Fire from spreading farther west. Just beyond the bridge, civilization could be viewed again—lanes and paths leading north and west, with church steeples and markets just beyond.

Now holding her nose with her free hand, Lucy mounted the three steps on the ancient stone bridge, her eyes averted from the muck and squalor that lay beneath. She peered across the bridge, trying to see through the gray mist that swirled above the rubble. Even in the early dawn light, it was hard to see much more than shadows in the mounds of debris.

As she reached the end of the bridge, for a moment the fog parted, and she froze.

There, looking unearthly and strange, a specter of a woman in white was moving toward her. Clad in a long white gown, her hands pressed to her head, the specter was approaching with a strange and jerking gait. Dark hair streamed wildly past her waist, and her face was as pale as her gown.

Her heart pounding, Lucy stepped back. *A ghost?* She had never seen a ghost, but tales and stories abounded of the mischief and evil that some might bring upon earthly inhabitants.

She looked about. Was she near a crossroads? She'd heard tell how the Ghost of Dorchester had gotten confused at the crossing of two roads, not knowing which direction to turn, and had simply disappeared forever. But the rubble from the Fire made it impossible to discern the original roads. Perhaps if she moved back across the bridge?

The apparition continued to advance. Lucy pressed against the stone wall of the bridge, hoping that it would pass her by. A ghost could not harm her, surely that was true.

Then, as her heart beat even faster and she felt a cold chill snake along her neck, the apparition sneezed.

An everyday, common sneeze, nothing otherworldly about it. The sneeze of a human.

Relieved, Lucy chuckled, even as she admonished herself. *Such a fool you are, Lucy. She is of flesh and bone, same as you.*

Still, though not a specter, there was something very odd about this woman. Clad only in a torn white shift, the woman seemed oblivious to her bare feet and wild hair, which Lucy could see was full of burrs and ashes. Her hands, still pressed to the side of her head, were filthy, as if she had been digging in mud. Her eyes, fearsome and dark, were unfocused, as if she were looking into another world.

Feeling goose bumps rise all over her body, Lucy took another step back, and then another. Since her eyes were fixed on the woman, she did not realize she was stepping on a patch of unstable rocks, which caused her to slip.

"Oh!" she exclaimed, then clapped her hand over her mouth.

But the damage was done. At her voice, the woman whipped her head toward Lucy and stared directly at her. "Has the devil come?" she whispered to Lucy in a harsh, strained voice, before looking frantically behind her. "Did he follow me?"

"Em-m—" Lucy gulped, peering out into the sprawling wasteland that lay before her, half expecting to see a horned figure in black striding forward on two cloven hoofs, pitchfork in hand, his pointed tail waving behind him. Such was the image of the devil she would set in the penny pieces back at Master Aubrey's.

But there was no dark figure. Indeed, no movement at all could be discerned on the barren landscape. "I see no one," Lucy whispered.

"You lie!" the woman hissed. Then, without warning, she grabbed Lucy's arm. "Are you in consort with him?"

"Let me be!" Lucy cried. She shook her arm free with a violent move, causing the woman to fall heavily to the ground, far harder than she expected.

Lucy turned to run back across the bridge, but before she had taken two steps a bright flash of pain in her knee stopped her from fleeing. Grimacing, she put her hand on the edge of the bridge, still trying to move away as fast as she could.

From behind her, Lucy heard the woman start to weep, loud desperate cries. "Please, miss! Please!" the woman called out to her. "Please do not leave me."

Against her instincts, Lucy turned back around to face the woman. She was still crouched on the ground where she had been pushed.

It was then that Lucy noticed something new. What she had assumed to be mud on the woman's shift and hands was, in truth, the deep reddish-brown stain of blood.

After a cautious look around, Lucy knelt down a few steps away, still keeping a little distance between them. She had heard of thieves and highwaymen pretending to be ill so they could catch a victim unawares. Yet this woman looked genuinely distressed. "Miss, please," Lucy said. "What is wrong? Are you injured? Did someone hurt you?"

Without speaking again, the woman began to sway back and forth, murmuring to herself, a great dullness to her expression.

For a moment, Lucy was reminded of another dull-witted person of her acquaintance—a gentle soul named Avery who had been injured by an exploding gun in Cromwell's wars.

Edging closer, Lucy looked again at the woman's bloody hands. She had small cuts all over them, but the blood was no longer flowing. Her wrists were covered with purple and yellow bruises. Lucy sighed, looking at the woman's blue lips and ashen face. She knew she could not in good conscience leave her on her own. What injuries she had sustained surely would only be worsened by lying on the hard frozen ground.

Lucy picked up her book-filled sack. "Come with me. I will take you to someone who can help you."

The woman made no move to stand. Lucy took off her own warm cloak and flung it around the woman's frail shoulders. She extended a hand, half expecting her to rebuff the gesture. To her surprise, the woman put her hand in Lucy's own, allowing Lucy to pull her to a standing position, like a docile child with her mother.

"The physician Larimer is a good man. He will help you," Lucy murmured to the woman, more to assure herself than the other. To be honest, she did not know what Dr. Larimer would think. Good man or not, he might not appreciate being asked to attend to a woman who had no coins to cover the cost of his service. But Lucy could not just abandon her. She felt that in her bones.

The wind picked up as they walked, the woman clinging tightly to her arm. Shivering, Lucy berated herself for her folly. Why had she given the woman her cloak? Indeed, why was she helping this odd woman at all? This was the kind of impetuous act that always got her into trouble. *No matter now,* Lucy thought.

The gesture has been made. I will have done my duty when I leave her with the physician.

As they passed through the edge of Holborn Market a few moments later, she could see the merchants eying them suspiciously. No wonder. The woman looked quite frightful indeed, with her wild hair and stricken features. Lucy feared she looked little more presentable herself, without a cloak to keep her tidy.

The woman began to move more sluggishly, now fully clinging to Lucy as if she were unable to move without the support of her strong young arm. "They are all staring at me," she whispered. "They think I have done something dreadful."

"No, no," Lucy murmured. "Let us keep moving. The air is too cold, and we are not dressed for such a chill." She began to pull the woman more forcefully. "Come on, now. We should not dally."

But the woman stood stock-still and began to mutter to herself.

"What is it? What are you saying?" Lucy asked, putting her ear closer to the woman's mouth. "I cannot understand you."

Then, unexpectedly, the woman began to jerk her head to one side, her dark eyes once again taking on that fearful unseeing look.

"M-miss?" Lucy said, taking a step back. "I fear something is wrong."

A few steps away, a boy tugged on the sleeve of his mother's brown cloak. "Ma, look at that woman there!" he said loudly. "What is wrong with her?"

His mother turned away from the stall of vegetables. "Dunno, Tim," she said to her son, yanking him away. "Nothing good comes from crossing paths with them sort."

But Tim continued to stare at the woman. "Got a wild look to her, don't she?"

Lucy glared at the boy. Unfortunately, her response drew an equally baleful look from his mother. "Devil has her!" his mother hissed, looking at the vegetable-seller, who nodded in agreement.

"Witch's eyes, she has!" the vegetable-seller said loudly, planting her hands on her plump hips. "Off with you now! We're godly folk in this market. There is no business for the devil here."

"No, no!" Lucy cried out, putting up her hands. "She is injured, she needs help! She is not accursed! Please, I am bringing her to a physician! The good Dr. Larimer. He lives near here! Pray, let us pass!"

She pulled at the woman, who still stood as if her feet had frozen to the ground. "Miss," she whispered urgently. "We must leave here."

Other people who had been milling about at the small market began to gather around them as well. "Devil got her!" they began to call and jeer. "Cast her from the market!"

"No, please!" Lucy pleaded, above the growing din. "We are just passing through the market. A stone's throw away, I tell you. That is where we are going."

Suddenly a potato glanced off Lucy's cheek, and she turned angrily to face her assailant.

"There is your stone's throw!" The vegetable-seller cackled. "Take that cursed woman away from my goods, lest she draw down the hex!"

Although Lucy desperately regretted having taken charge of the pitiful woman, there was no way she could leave her to this frenzied crowd. "Come with me," Lucy said, putting her arm around the woman, trying to steer them both away from the market and away from the cruel chants and jeers of the crowd.

At that moment, the woman, who had not moved for the last two minutes, suddenly seemed to leap back into her senses. "What is going on? Where am I?"

She stared in fear at the taunting faces around her, digging her nails hard into Lucy's uncloaked arm. It was all Lucy could do to keep from crying out herself. Lucy did not want to rile the crowd any more. She pulled the cloak up around the woman's head, hiding her wild hair again. "Please, miss," she said again, more urgently. "We must keep moving."

The woman began to sob quietly but allowed herself to be led. Her change to a more piteous creature did not pass unmarked, and Lucy could feel the mood of the Londoners around her changing as they continued through the market. Thankfully, the crowd did not follow them, and they soon found themselves away from the busy stalls, in an old abandoned cow pasture.

Lucy let go of the woman and looked at her. There was a time when she might have feared the woman as one beset by the devil. Her years living in the magistrate's household, though, had taught her to be suspicious of those who spoke too easily of witchcraft and magical doings. Still, had she not seen, with her own eyes, the movement of God working among those who called themselves Quakers? So who was to say that the devil could not move those weak of heart and faith? She shook her head.

At the edge of the dusty road, Lucy spied a well. Fortunately, when she pulled up the bucket, the water was not frozen and seemed clean enough, aside from a few dead bugs floating around. Using the little tin cup that she always carried in her pack, Lucy scooped out some water and bid the woman to drink.

Her hand now clutching the side of the well for support, the woman drank a bit, sputtering at the taste. Ignoring the shouts still ringing in her ears, and the still-rapid beating of her heart, Lucy regarded the woman critically. Between her wild unkempt hair, the bloodstains on her clothes, and the dirt and blood on her hands, they would likely be barred entrance to the physician's home on sight. No, the woman's wild beggarly state required attention.

Dabbing her handkerchief into the pail, Lucy washed the woman's hands and face, scrubbing away some of the dried blood, before drying them with her own cloak. Then, reaching under her white cap, Lucy carefully untied a ribbon from her hair. Before the woman could resist, Lucy created a quick knot so that it lay at the nape of her neck, securing it with the ribbon. Though her hair was still untidy, the woman looked a shade more respectable.

"He will see us now," Lucy murmured to herself.

A few minutes later, she tiptoed to the tradesman's entrance at the back of the physician's house.

"What is this place?" the woman asked. "Where have you brought me?"

"Dr. Larimer's," Lucy said. "Now, hush."

When Dr. Larimer's housekeeper swung open the door, she took in their bedraggled appearance and immediately began to close the door. "Off with you," she said. "The doctor don't do charity."

"Please," Lucy said, sticking her foot in the door so that it would not close. "I have a delivery for Dr. Larimer. From Master Aubrey, the printer." Lucy crossed her fingers behind her back, hoping that the small lie would pass unnoticed. "My master did tell me to get the payment before I left."

"What about her?" the servant asked, flicking a finger toward the woman. "She has a sickly look to her."

"I do not know her," Lucy said. "Truth be told, I found her nearby. There is something amiss with her. I *do* think she requires a physician. I thought since I was coming to see Dr. Larimer anyway—" She broke off, hating to lie. She spoke more quickly. "Please tell your master, I beg you. I cannot in good conscience leave her on the streets. My name is Lucy Campion. I sell books for Master Aubrey, and was employed with Master Hargrave before that. He knows me." She pushed against the door a bit more firmly. "And I think you know me, too."

Something about Lucy must have stirred the housekeeper, for she opened the door and allowed them entrance. "Come with me," she said. "Do not let her touch anything, though. I do not want her muck all over my clean floors."

Lucy had started to step in when she realized that the woman was hanging back, a fearful look on her face. " 'Tis all right," Lucy said taking the woman's hand again. As they entered, Lucy saw a young girl about seventeen years of age, wearing a servant's cap and apron, peek out at them, taking in their appearance with a mixture of fear and curiosity.

The woman seized Lucy's hand then, so tightly it hurt. Together they followed the servant to a room near the front of the house. "Wait here," the housekeeper said tersely. "Both of you. I will fetch Dr. Larimer."

· 2 ·

Awkwardly supporting the strange woman with her left arm, Lucy looked about the physician's office with interest. Like Master Hargrave's study, the physician's had several shelves of old leather books, like the three she had lugged all the way from the printer's shop. He had a desk with writing implements—quill, ink, paper, sealing wax, and a seal—and sheaves of paper everywhere. There the resemblance stopped. Unlike the magistrate, the physician had instruments hanging from one wall, most of which Lucy did not recognize, as well as shelves of vials and jars. All the while the woman paced anxiously beside Lucy.

Dr. Larimer walked in then, scowling. "Lucy, what is this nonsense you told my housekeeper, Mrs. Hotchkiss, about a delivery from Horace Aubrey?" He eyed the woman. "I do not think that even he would find it humorous to send me such a sickly piece."

Despite his jest, she could hear the annoyance in the physician's voice. The woman backed up against the wall.

Though a flush of shame passed over her, Lucy kept her head up. "I am aggrieved that I told that story," she said. "It is just that I encountered this woman on my travels this morning. I do not know who she is. Indeed, she seems unable to explain anything for herself." She paused. "Please, sir. I think something terrible has happened to her. I was hoping you could help her."

"Lucy, I do not take charitable cases," he replied sternly. "If she is injured, you should have brought her to St. Bartholomew's. That hospital would take her, as they do all the indigent." He turned to go. "Please remove her from my home at once."

"Wait, sir," Lucy cried. "If you could just look at her. I dread taking her to the hospital, and I should hate to simply leave her on her own. I think she is wounded; I saw blood on her hands and body. She might grow worse, unattended."

At her last words, Dr. Larimer raised a fist heavenward. "Oh, Hippocrates!"

"Sir?" Lucy asked, confused.

"Blasted Greek. *I will use my power to help the sick to the best of my ability and judgment; I will abstain from harming or wronging any man by it.*" He glanced at Lucy. "Never mind, Lucy. Though some of my fellow physicians may disagree, I am obligated to seek to preserve life, no matter how lowly." Still a few steps away, he scrutinized the woman, raising an eyebrow when he noticed her feet. "No shoes? But a cloak?"

" 'Tis my own cloak wrapped around her, you see," Lucy explained. In a softer voice she added, "She wears no frock either. She is only in her shift. This is how I found her." She chose not to add that the woman had claimed that the devil had been chasing her. *All in good time,* she thought.

"I see," he said. "That she is standing, and was able to walk from where you found her to here, makes me suspect that her injuries are not substantial. I shall examine her." The physician leaned over to open her cloak.

At his touch, the woman began to scream, great terrible shrieks that made the hairs on Lucy's neck rise up.

Unexpectedly, Dr. Larimer reached out and slapped the woman smartly across her mouth. She stopped screaming abruptly, though tears filled her eyes. "That is better," he said. "Now, let us continue."

Lucy hesitated. "Shall I leave, sir?"

But as she turned to go, the woman clutched Lucy's hand, a mute plea evident in her anguished eyes.

"She does not seem to want you to leave her," the physician said drily, observing the gesture. "She is showing great suffering of the womb. The *hystericus* is evident upon her, which I will treat most appropriately with a tincture of opium. Surely, for that alone, my dear Hippocrates will allow that I have done all I can before I turn her loose. At the very least, I can seek to redress her obvious humoral imbalance."

Opening the door, he called down the corridor. "Mrs. Hotchkiss! A white wine posset, if you would." He began to crush some ingredients with a mortar and pestle. Both women watched him.

Shortly after, Mrs. Hotchkiss entered the room, with a mug of warmed wine. Dr. Larimer stirred in some crushed ingredients and held it out to the woman. "Drink!" he commanded.

When she did not take the mug, he brought it to her lips as

if he were going to force her to swallow the warm liquid. Clenching her teeth together, the woman shrank back and began to flail her arms, trying to bat away the drink.

Dr. Larimer scowled. "I do not have time for this nonsense." He gestured to the long bench. "Sit down, woman."

"Let me try," Lucy said hastily, taking the fragrant drink from his hands, before he could cast the woman out of his house. She had dealt with sick and frightened people before. "Please, miss," she said, patting the long bench. "Sit here beside me."

To both their surprise, the woman stopped struggling and sat down.

"That's right," Lucy said, keeping her eyes steadily on the woman. "You must drink this. It will help you feel better." She wrapped the woman's now docile hands around the warm mug. "Take a nip."

Obediently, the woman took a small timid sip. Evidently finding the posset to her liking, she took a few deeper sips, and then a few mouthfuls, before draining the cup.

"She had blood all over her hands and feet when I found her," Lucy said quietly to the physician. The woman's eyes were already starting to flutter. The wine and the opium were no doubt working quickly on her emaciated body. "Perhaps you could start there?"

Together they eased the woman back on the bench, and Lucy slipped an embroidered pillow under her head.

Carefully, the physician grasped the woman's hands. She moaned and tried to pull them free, although her movements were slow and lacked power. But he would not let them go.

"Hold there, miss!" Dr. Larimer said, examining the palms and backs of the woman's hands. "Sanguine? No, cold and dry. Full of black bile. Likely melancholic." He released the woman's hands and touched her face. "No fever, at least. That is a blessing, to be certain." He scowled when he examined her feet. "Why was she wearing no shoes?"

"I do not know, sir."

The physician frowned. "I am not liking this," he said. "Her legs and feet are bruised and bleeding, and the scratches are all recent." He pointed to the purple marks on the woman's wrists and ankles. "Then there are those marks, too."

"What are those marks, sir?" Lucy asked.

"I would surmise this woman has been bound in rope."

"Bound?" Lucy gasped. "How awful!"

Still frowning, the physician began to examine the gashes on the woman's right hand. "These cuts will need to be bandaged before the great pus sets in." He paused, holding her limp hand up to the light. "Strange."

"What is it?" Lucy asked.

"The nature and position of this cut." He pointed to the long slash that cut across her palm from below the smallest finger on her right hand. "If I had to guess, she inflicted this herself."

Lucy stared at him. "Whatever do you mean, sir?"

"I mean, as if she had been holding a knife in her hand. Like so." The physician gestured with the knife, making a quick cutting movement in the air.

"Might she work for a butcher? I did find her not too far from the markets," Lucy said. She doubted it though. The woman looked scarcely strong enough to be involved in such a profession, at least not in the capacity where she would be butchering the beasts herself.

The physician did not answer. His eyes, trained on the woman, were speculative. "I need to see if she has been further injured or," he said briskly, "otherwise violated. Remove her cloak."

Lucy stepped forward and carefully loosened the cloak from around the woman's neck, all the while murmuring soothing sounds. The woman squirmed, but allowed Lucy to remove the cloak. As she lay there in her flimsy undergarments, the long streaks of blood and mud across the front of her shift were obvious in the brighter light of day.

The woman closed her eyes, and at last her breathing began to slow. Her tight hold on Lucy's hand finally began to loosen, as the opium and wine took effect. Without encountering any more protest, Lucy helped the physician pull the dirty shift over the woman's head.

Hearing the physician click his teeth, Lucy glanced at the woman's naked form. Startled, she could see that the woman had more bruising around her upper arms and shoulders. There was something tied to her neck with a bit of black string as well, which fell atop her chest. Lucy pulled a blanket over her while the physician examined the woman's private parts, a serious look on his face. "No sign of the bloody flux," she heard him mutter. "But nothing of the whore upon her either."

For a few minutes more, he examined her body, before he began to bandage the cuts on her feet and hands.

As he wrapped one hand, Lucy pointed to the cloth object hanging around the woman's neck. "I wonder if that could tell us anything about her."

The physician slipped the filthy piece from around her neck and passed it to Lucy with a grimace. "I doubt it," he said. "Best burn it."

Taking the object, Lucy glanced at it. She could see it was covered in muck and grime. She placed it on the table and stood up then. She had heard the church bells ring a while back, and it was high time for her to return to Master Aubrey's. She looked down at the woman, who was now sleeping. Her hair was spread wildly about on the white pillow, and she still looked dirty and unkempt. Unprotected.

Though she might have to take on extra chamber duties for a month and be banned from setting type or, worse, selling books, Lucy knew she could not leave. "Shall I bathe her a bit?" Lucy asked, spying a porcelain ewer and basin on a side table. "She could do with some clean clothes as well." She bit her lip. She did not want Dr. Larimer to ask one of his servants to give the woman a dress to wear, as it was likely that they only had one or two spare garments, and one would be for Sunday church-going.

To her surprise, Dr. Larimer seemed to understand the dilemma, or more likely did not even think to ask his servants for an unused dress. "My wife surely has an old frock on hand that she could at least loan to this misfortunate soul. She is visiting her family outside London but should be back for our evening meal. I shall send in Mrs. Hotchkiss to assist you." For a moment, he stared at the woman lying on the bed. "With any luck, her agitation will have subsided when she awakes, and her memory will be restored. Surely then we will be able to return her to her family."

After he left, Lucy began to smooth the long tangled hair from the woman's face. She recalled the streaks of blood on her face and hands. *What happened to you?* she wondered.

· 3 ·

Not too long later, the door opened and Dr. Larimer's maid came in, carrying a heavy metal tub full of hot water. Someone had probably been boiling the water for soup in the kitchen, for Lucy caught the smell of boiled onions. Dr. Larimer's housekeeper strode in behind her, holding a plain gown over her arm and a lump of soap in her hand.

"Set it there, Molly," Mrs. Hotchkiss instructed the servant, who was gaping at the woman in the bed. After the girl complied, the housekeeper all but pushed her out of the room. "We shall call you if we need you," she said, shutting the door firmly behind the maid.

Lucy took the soap that Mrs. Hotchkiss handed her and sniffed appreciatively. "Lavender," she said.

The housekeeper only grunted in reply. The perfumed soap probably belonged to the physician's wife, and Lucy thought it better not to say anything else about it.

After dipping a small cloth into the hot water, Lucy began to gently wash away the light grime that covered the woman's face.

The housekeeper stared down at the sleeping woman. "The Lord's will be done," she said, clucking her tongue. "Though it hardly seems likely that a bit of soap will wash off this woman's sins."

How easily we pass judgment, Lucy thought. She was about to say as much when Mrs. Hotchkiss spoke again. In a decidedly different tone Lucy heard her whisper, "Oh my." She had seen the bruises around the woman's wrists, and the other marks across her body.

The two women exchanged a look. That something terrible had happened to this woman could not be denied. They continued to bathe her with care, so that they would not bring her pain, toweling her off and pulling the dress over her head. "An old one belonging to Mistress Larimer," Mrs. Hotchkiss whispered. "She only wears it on wash-days, when she oversees the laundering of the linens."

Though she tried to sound certain, Lucy caught a note of hesitation in her voice. Not every woman would take too kindly to seeing one of her frocks being worn by another woman, particularly without her say-so.

Lucy sought to reassure her. "It is warm and serviceable, and I cannot imagine that your mistress would begrudge the loan. Besides, I know that, like her husband, she would take care of another in need." At least she hoped that to be the case. She did not know Mistress Larimer all that well. Sometimes the Larimers had dined at the Hargraves', and Lucy remembered her as a gossipy woman, but not an unkind one.

Together, they pulled the blanket over the woman so that she would not develop a chill. Studying her, Lucy could see that the woman's features were delicate and well formed, although a little drawn, probably from sickness or hunger. She was a bit puny of frame as well.

Mrs. Hotchkiss gazed down at the woman, too. "Did she say nothing at all?" she asked softly. "Who is she? What brought her to this state?"

In her mind, Lucy could hear the woman's terrified whisper. *Has the devil come? Did he follow me?* She shivered at the thought.

"No," Lucy replied, her voice a bit shaky. "She's spoken so very little."

Molly came back in then with a straw basket. "Doctor says I am to burn all her clothes," she said, gingerly picking up the woman's shift. "Dirty as a beast, ain't she?"

"Wait!" Lucy said. "Pray, let us examine them first."

Both the physician's servants stared at her. "Whatever for?" Mrs. Hotchkiss asked.

"We might learn something about her. Some clue to her identity." Lucy looked down at the shift, rolling a bit of the dingy white material in her fingers. "What do you make of this?" she asked the housekeeper.

She half expected Mrs. Hotchkiss to turn away with the garment, but instead she felt the cloth expertly in her hands. "Linen," she said. "Of a fine quality." Taking it from Lucy, she held it up to the light. Her eyes widened, taking in the intricate tatting at the bottom. "Lace?"

She looked back at the woman. Lucy could guess what she was thinking. This was the undergarment of a noblewoman.

"Likely stole it," Molly interjected.

"Or someone gave it to her," Lucy said. "Her mistress?"

"Be a shame to burn it, then," Mrs. Hotchkiss said. "A good dosing of lye-soap will get those bloodstains out. The master must have thought it was ridden with mites, but I don't see any, do you?"

Lucy shook her head. Gently, she picked up one of the woman's hands, turning it this way and that. Although the woman's fingernails were ragged and torn, and her hands were a bit scratched, her palms were soft and devoid of calluses or other indicators of hard work. "This is not the hand of a servant," she said. "Or of a woman who must ply tools in a trade. Who is she?"

"She's a madwoman, she is," Molly offered, unhelpfully. "'Tis easy enough to see! Don't know why we haven't just sent her on her way."

Lucy frowned at the maid. "Dr. Larimer wouldn't do that."

Molly sniffed. "Well, maybe he should." She poured the dirty water from the basin into the larger tub she had carried in earlier. Picking it up in both hands, she looked at the housekeeper. "Got to start cutting potatoes and carrots for dinner," she said, making a big show of leaving. "Master will not like it if the stew's not on the table when he asks. I've enough on my plate to do without tending to this one."

The housekeeper nodded in agreement, but seemed a bit more reluctant. "Yes, I've got duties to attend to myself." She hesitated, looking down at the woman. "She needs looking after, she does."

"I could sit with her for a bit," Lucy offered. Something about the woman made her so curious. And her vulnerability made Lucy wish to protect her. "If she wakes up, she may be less startled if she sees me again."

"Does your master not expect you back?" Mrs. Hotchkiss said a bit suspiciously.

"Yes, of course. But he knows I was making a delivery and that I would be selling near Holborn Market after that. I am a bookseller, you know." As always, when she told people that, a bit of pride had crept into Lucy's voice. "Of course, I should not like to be away very long. I can manage, though."

When Mrs. Hotchkiss and Molly left, Lucy poured a little more fresh water into the basin. After wiping the woman's face, she pulled a stool over to the bed, to be close to the sedated woman.

Lucy picked up the dirty object that had been tied around the woman's neck. Examining it closely, she could see that a bit of cloth had been wound around a hard object. Carefully, she unwound the dirty cloth, until she was staring down at the object in her hands in amazement.

It was a beautiful talisman of some sort. A polished reddish stone, shaped liked a teardrop, had been inlaid into an elaborate silver setting. The stone was smooth to her touch, and she could see that it had flecks of pinks, taupes, and whites deep within it. She had scarcely seen anything so lovely.

The physician came back in then. "What is that?" he asked.

"This is what was around the woman's neck," Lucy said, still staring down at the remarkable object in her hands. A line ran along both sides, and she could see a hinge at the teardrop's base. "I think it is an amulet."

With great care, she undid the clasp and opened the amulet. Inside, there were two chambers, each filled with a familiar dried herb.

"Rosemary," she said, sniffing. She handed the amulet to the physician.

"*There's rosemary, that's for remembrance: pray, love, remember,*" Dr. Larimer said, taking the piece from Lucy.

"Pardon, sir?"

"Ah, a line from the Bard. The poor mad lass Ophelia says it to the Dane."

At their voices, the woman began to revive. "Please," she murmured, her voice still drowsy. "I must continue on my journey. Pray, let me leave. At once!"

Lucy and Dr. Larimer looked at each other. Now that the woman was no longer weeping and carrying on in that insensible manner, her voice sounded cultured and genteel, and her words were those of a lady. Indeed, there was no trace of her earlier lunacy in her speech.

"Madam," Dr. Larimer said, using his most soothing tone, "would you be so kind as to tell us your name? I should very much like to contact your family."

"My name?" she asked. She sat up straight, the sleepiness leaving her body while the earlier fear returning to her eyes. "I-I do not know!" She searched their faces. "Why do I not know who I am? What have you done to me?"

"We have done nothing to you!" Lucy burst out. "I found you wandering about in the ruins, by Holborn Bridge. I brought you here!"

"Lucy, please," Dr. Larimer said. He turned back to the woman. "You cannot remember your name? What about that of your family? Your surname?"

"I tell you, I do not know that either!" she said, her voice rising. "I know the words you say, but there is no sense to be made in my mind."

She looked around at the physician's study, for the first time taking in her surroundings. Her eyes lingered on a large print depicting a man's body, half with flesh and half just a skeleton. "What is this place?" she whispered.

"This is my study, where I see my patients," the physician replied, uncorking a vial. "You seem to have suffered some sort of shock, although of what nature I cannot say for certain." Carefully, he poured some of the liquid from the bottle into a smaller cup. "Drink a little more of this tincture. It will help soothe you."

Lucy half expected the woman to struggle, as she had done earlier, but this time she drank the liquid quickly.

"I should like to diagnose the source of your affliction," the physician said. "Perchance you have sustained some type of blow. That might account for your loss of memory, although I must say it is a most odd phenomenon. Have you struck your head recently?"

"I do not believe so," the woman replied, reaching up to feel her head. She put her hand at the base of her neck. "I can feel a sharp pain here."

"Let me see," Dr. Larimer said. He pushed the woman's heavy hair off the base of her neck. When he did that, he exposed another scar that they had not previously noticed, which ran vertically along the woman's neck. He inhaled sharply.

"What is it?" Lucy asked.

"A surgeon has been letting her blood," he said, probing the scar with gentle hands. "The skin here is just healed. See how it is scabbed over?" he said to Lucy, who nodded.

He turned his attention back to the woman. "For what condition has the surgeon been at your neck?"

The woman shook her head, wincing a bit at the movement. "I cannot say! I do not remember!" she replied, anxiety rising in her voice. "Who would do that to me?"

"Such bloodletting from the vein of your neck tells me that you have had a disorder of the head that someone has been seeking to correct," the physician explained. "It may explain why you do not remember. Your memory loss may have been what he was trying to alleviate when he performed the bloodletting."

"Can you tell how long ago the bloodletting occurred?" Lucy asked Dr. Larimer, in a low tone.

"Recently. The skin is pink and new where the scar has formed," he replied, still examining her carefully. "Within the last few weeks, of that I am certain."

"Oh, why can I not remember?" The woman's voice caught in a half sob, and Lucy could hear a bit of hysteria rising once again. "I can scarcely think."

Dr. Larimer resumed his questions. "What is the last thing you do remember? Do you know why you were at Holborn Bridge?"

"Holborn Bridge? Where is that?"

"It crosses the River Fleet. Just beyond the great expanse where the Fire laid waste," Lucy replied. "It is where I found you, before I brought you here. I washed your hands—do you recall that?"

The woman blinked, trying to remember. "Washed my hands?" A flicker of recognition. "By a well, was it not?" Her brow furrowed. "There was a crowd, was there not? They were shouting." She looked at Lucy. "Someone threw potatoes at us!" She looked scandalized, which would have made Lucy smile if she were not so concerned.

"Do you remember anything before that? What brought you to Holborn Bridge?" Dr. Larimer continued to press. When the woman did not answer, he pointed to the bruises on her wrists. "Do you recall how you received these injuries?"

He touched them gently, and she flinched. "I do not know." The woman pulled back, taking on the stance of a trapped animal. She put a hand to her chest and neck, frantically feeling for the object that had hung around her neck.

"Where is it?" she cried. "Where is my amulet? Give it back to me!" she demanded. "I need it!"

Hastily, Lucy handed her the amulet, and the woman put it back around her neck.

"It's beautiful," Lucy said. "Where did you get it?"

The woman looked startled, and afraid. "I do not know! I just remember the feeling of the amulet around my neck." As she stroked the gemstone, her rapid breathing began to slow, and she pulled the blanket up to her shoulders. It was clear that she had no wish to continue the conversation.

The physician coughed then, still regarding the woman's form in a puzzled way. "Such extreme memory loss is very uncommon," he said to Lucy. "I wonder—"

She did not know what he would have said, for just then James Sheridan, Dr. Larimer's assistant, strode into the room. He was a thin man with glasses, with the haughty manner of a gentleman who was completing his medical studies at Cambridge. He was residing in Dr. Sheridan's home while he assisted him with his patients, before he would be accepted as a physician in his own right. He and Lucy had met a few months prior when Dr. Larimer had conducted an autopsy of a murder victim. Mr. Sheridan had been quite annoyed when the physician had seemed to hold Lucy's opinion in good stead.

"I was informed that some riffraff had been brought here," he said. His scornful gaze encompassed both Lucy and the woman huddled in the bed. He looked at the physician. "You are charitable indeed, sir."

"Lucy found this woman in a delicate state," Dr. Larimer replied. "I cannot in good conscience go against our sacred oath." His tone was mild, but Lucy could hear the slight chastising. Mr. Sheridan simply shrugged, clearly less mindful of the admonitions of the ancient Greeks.

As the two men were talking, the woman pushed back the blanket that had been covering her face and gazed up at Mr. Sheridan, a fearful expression on her face.

He glanced at her, and then his gaze deepened. From her vantage point, Lucy saw something flicker in his expression, the faintest sign of recognition.

"Do you know her?" Lucy asked Mr. Sheridan, startled.

"Of course not—" he began to say, before he stopped and stared at the woman. He took a step closer, and then a step back. "By Jupiter! No, it cannot be!"

Dr. Larimer looked at his assistant in surprise. "Good God, man. *Do* you know this woman? Who is she?"

James Sheridan, looking more human than Lucy had ever seen him, was still staring at the woman. His gaze, at first shocked, had turned to fury and something worse. Disgust.

"I thought for a moment that—" He broke off, gulping. "No, I do not know this woman. A trick of the light. If you'll pardon me." With that, he turned and walked quickly out of the room.

Lucy and Dr. Larimer stared after him and then at each other. The woman still stayed huddled, the blankets again drawn up to her chin.

"Miss?" the physician asked, his voice gentle. "Did you know that man?"

The woman shook her head and then rolled back in the bed. "No, I think not. Please, I beg you. Leave me to my slumbers. I find that I am too weary for further discourse."

For a moment, Dr. Larimer seemed at a loss. "Well, well." He gestured for Lucy to follow him out of the room. In the hallway, he put his hand to his head.

"I am deeply troubled by all of this, Lucy," he said, his voice low. "Who is this woman?"

"Sir," Lucy whispered, "she sounded like a lady, did she not?"

"Though her trappings are not fine, the grace of her bearing and her voice suggest to me a lady of quality." He frowned. "I cannot cast her out now, not at least until we can confirm this to be true."

Lucy nodded. Had she spoken with the voice of a pauper, the woman would likely be getting the heave-ho after a long nap and a spot of bread to eat. Her cultured voice had given her a second chance that would have been denied to a woman of a clearly lesser station.

"What happened to her? How long has her memory been lost?" He sighed. "What a predicament, Lucy. I do not quite know what to do with her. There have been cases where a memory remains lost for years, while other times it all comes back in just a day or two. Truth be told, I do not even know how to treat her. We can only hope that her memory returns to her quickly."

A thought nagged at Lucy. "Could she be a player, sir? Perhaps she is performing for us." She had, several times in her life, met others who pretended to be something they were not. Outwardly kind and gentle people, but scoundrels all.

The physician shook his head. "I do not think so, Lucy. I have seen such hysterical women before. Her distress and terror are real. That woman has been through a trauma, of that I am sure. I must find a way to locate her family." He was speaking now to himself rather than her. "I shall draw upon the authorities to assist me. After all, someone must be looking for the wretched woman. For now, I am going to start with Mr. Sheridan. I think he knows something about that woman, and I intend to find out what."

· 4 ·

Lucy regarded the blurred page, fresh from the printing press, with some irritation. This would make the fifth time she had adjusted the type that morning, and the print was still coming out smudged. Master Aubrey would be none too pleased when he saw the wasted paper. Lucy had learned the hard way that he would make them re-ink and reprint dozens of sheets, at a cost to their own wages, if he thought the print looked smeared or blurry. He'd be even less happy when he learned that his apprentice had not finished printing *The True Account of a Most Barbaric Monster Who Did Push His Own Sister into a Boiling Pot,* which he had intended to sell at St. Mary's that afternoon. To make matters worse, she had developed a bad cold during the night and had awoken that morning sniffling and with a voice that came and went. Certainly, she would not be of much use selling if she could not speak.

She was already a bit on the outs with Master Aubrey. After she had left Dr. Larimer's yesterday and delivered the books, she had returned home rather later than expected and with a nearly full pack of broadsides left unpeddled. Truth be told, she could have just lied and said that few were in a buying spirit, but she had told Master Aubrey the truth of what had occurred. "Sounds like a demon was upon her," he said. "Best be rid of the woman." Thankfully, he was not the sort to whip his servants, but he did lightly box her ears for not doing as she was told.

Now, Lucy stepped back and considered the printing press sternly. Ink was smudged all over her hands, and she suspected across her face as well.

"Kick it!" Lach recommended from the table. He was carefully setting type for another ballad. "Teach it who is the master."

Lucy rolled her eyes. "I suppose, Lach," she said in her hoarse, painful voice, "that it never occurred to you that kicking the press may be why it's not working properly now?" Surveying the machine, she added, "See, 'tis at a slant. It looks like it's been jarred." She began to push the press back into place, angry that she had wasted her voice on Lach.

"Watch it!" Lach warned, as the box of metal type began to topple to the floor. Lucy managed to steady it, but not before twenty or so of the tiny metal letters flew out. She cried out, only to realize that her voice was completely gone.

Lach crowed. "Hoo boy! You will be in for it now!"

Lucy was about to throw something at him when they heard a quick tap at the door. Being closer, Lach opened the door, disclosing a young man in livery.

"I have a message," he said smartly, holding up a letter. "For Lucy Campion."

Lach shut the door behind him, so that the blustery April wind would not blow all their papers about, or bring dirt, feathers, and other debris from the street into the shop. "Is that so?" he asked.

Lucy scrambled up from the floor, brushing her skirts. She held out her hand. "I am Lucy Campion," she said. Or that was what she tried to say. What came out was an odd squeak. The little croak she had mustered before was now completely gone.

The messenger looked doubtfully at her, taking in her smudged hands, mussed skirts, and tousled hair. Seeing this, Lach grinned broadly and stepped between them, before the man could hand her the letter. With a quick mocking look toward Lucy, Lach said, "I will make sure Miss Campion receives the letter."

Lucy stamped her foot in indignation and held out her hand again. With a squawk, she tried again to say who she was.

The messenger looked even more confused, looking at her outstretched hand. "Is this her?" he asked Lach.

Lach laughed. "Her? Oh, no. This wanton miss is our chambermaid, and a dumb one at that." He made a twirling gesture with one finger that referred to an addled soul. With feigned sorrow, he added, "A bit touched in the head."

With that, Lach ushered the messenger out and held the letter up to the sunlight, well out of her reach. Lucy could only see that it had been sealed with red wax.

"Give it to me," she tried again to say, to no avail.

Lach was still looking at the letter. "Which of her two suitors seeks to see her now? The young laird of the manor?" he said, deliberately thickening his brogue. "Or," he continued with flatter tones, "the 'cozened constable'?"

Lucy rolled her eyes. As the son of a magistrate and a lawyer who had trained at the Inns of Court, Adam Hargrave was certainly no Scottish noble with a manor house, even if he was a member of the English gentry by dint of his profession. Nor was Constable Duncan, a member of the King's Army and currently running a jail on Fleet Street, anything like the figure of ridicule and mockery that so often described the local constable in the penny press.

Whether either was truly a suitor was difficult to say. She had seen little of either man these last two weeks. Adam was still helping with the newly installed Fire Court, which had been created at Clifford's Inn, to resolve landlord disputes after the Great Fire. He spent his days collecting testimony and examining documents, and more recently was accompanying the surveyors who were mapping the new streets of London out of the charred earth. Surely he was too busy to see her, or—and she hated to voice this thought even in her own mind—he did not wish to see her. *Duncan is in love with you,* he had told her, *and I am not certain where your heart lies.*

Duncan had stopped by once or twice to see her, usually near suppertime to have a chat, but he never inquired about her days off. If he were indeed in love with her, he certainly was doing little to show it, which annoyed her more than she cared to say. And truth be told, both men quickened her senses and stirred her heart. She had long adored Adam from afar when she was working in the magistrate's household, but it would be a match that everyone—including herself—would view as unequal. Her feelings for Duncan, though, were of a different sort. The easy friendship that had bloomed between them these last nine months had made her more thoughtful about the partnership between man and woman. With Duncan she could still work with Master Aubrey, but with Adam, such employment would be unlikely.

With her hands on her hips, Lucy planted herself straight in front of Lach. Heaving a dramatic sigh, he gave her the letter, starting to hum one of the many tunes about the ineptness of constables. As she took the note, she stepped hard on Lach's foot.

"Graceful, aren't you, lass?" he said, snickering.

Nervously, Lucy glanced at the note. It was addressed simply to Lucy Campion, and it was written in a fine script that was similar to Adam's elegant hand, but completely unlike the constable's crooked letters.

"Just open it already," Lach said. "Or I will."

With that, Lucy broke the seal. A quick glance at the signature revealed it was from Dr. Larimer. Slowly, she read the note.

Lucy,

    I must see you about the devilish matter that you left upon my threshold yesterday morn. I shall stop by Master Aubrey's at ten o'clock this morning. I expect that you will ensure that you are in attendance when I arrive.

                          Yours,

                        Dr. Larimer

She put the message thoughtfully back down on the tray with the metal type. Lach snatched it up and read it out loud.

"Devilish matter? Have you the green sickness, then?" he taunted. "Need a provoker of your monthlies?"

Lucy frowned. Everyone knew about the malady that struck

young women, and it was nothing to jest about. "Not that it is any of your concern, but I do not."

Why did the physician want to speak to her again? Maybe the woman had recovered her memory. But if that were the case, why would he think to inform Lucy of such a thing?

As if he heard her, Lach continued in his taunting way. "Well, what does the physician want from you, then? Why is he calling on you this morning?"

The door opened as he asked the question, revealing Master Aubrey. As always, the rotund man looked a bit red-faced and out of breath.

"Who is calling on you this morning? Another suitor? I will have him out on his ear. I cannot have my apprentices being wooed in my place of business!" he grumbled as he took off his coat and hung it on a peg on the wall. Though his tone was gruff, Lucy could hear the teasing underneath. This was what Lach would be like in twenty years, she thought. It was also why they all managed to get along so well. He pulled on his apron.

After placing a steaming mug on the table for him, she stood before him. Hands on her hips and her head shaking, she waited for him to finish his little speech. " 'Tis bad enough we have the constable dropping by in the evenings for a bit of supper. I only abide him because he always has strange news to tell." Sitting down, he looked at her hopefully. "Is it the constable?"

"No, it is Dr. Larimer!" Lach intervened before she could speak, placing the note before the printer. "He is the one who is calling on her. This morning at ten o'clock!"

"Hmmm," the printer said, pulling out his pocket-watch. "Any moment then, I should think." He turned to his apprentice. "Lach, go fetch some of the medical books that came to us. The good physician might be needful of an anatomy. Or even an Aristotle."

Sure enough, a few minutes later, Lach had just laid a few medical books down on the table when they heard a sharp rap at the door. The physician entered.

Master Aubrey stepped forward, vigorously greeting the physician. Years of selling tracts made his voice boom, even when speaking in regular conversations. Lucy stood still, her hands clasped behind her back.

"Come sit down, good sir. Lucy will bring you something hot to drink." Master Aubrey gestured to the table by the kitchen, just outside the workroom. "Lach, get back to work."

As Lucy set the cups down, she asked after the woman. Or at least she tried to speak, but she could only manage a squeak.

"Lost your voice? Even Culpeper can be consulted for such a minor sickness, Lucy. What is it that that herbalist's adherents all say? Every man his own doctor, and all that," he said, a slight dismissiveness creeping into his voice. Most physicians were a bit skeptical of the "people's doctor," as they called Nicholas Culpeper, claiming him to be no more than a gardener who knew his roots and flowers. Still, in a pinch, his home remedies might be referred to for the most common of ailments. "Honey for the soreness, and chamomile to relax your vocal cords. A bit of garlic or ginger will clear it up." Here he frowned at Master Aubrey. "This lass may be hurting her voice by all the shouting you have her do."

"Is she my apprentice or not?" Aubrey growled.

Hastily, Lucy pushed a steaming cup toward Dr. Larimer. "The lady," she managed to croak.

"How does she fare?" Dr. Larimer asked, interpreting her question correctly. "A difficult question indeed. She has mostly remained asleep. On the few occasions she awoke, neither I nor my housekeeper could get any more sensible words from her, beyond what she told us yesterday in your presence. Her memory of her identity is completely gone, as though someone took a bit of lye-soap to a dish and wiped the whole thing clean."

"How can that be?" Master Aubrey asked, wiping the sweat off his own face with an ink-stained handkerchief.

The physician shook his head. "A rather odd thing, to be sure. I have seen several such cases, and usually with soldiers—men who had waged war in the most difficult of straits. There is no accounting for it, to be sure, but at times they believe they are still at battle, shrieking of cannonballs and wheel-locks, or believing they are under the barber-surgeon's knife."

Master Aubrey nodded, his jovial demeanor disappearing. "I know of what you speak. Some men were so broken in spirit and health by war that they seem to have lost something of their natural mind." He looked back at Dr. Larimer. "And you think this lass suffers the same malady of war?"

"Not exactly," the physician said. "But last night, she woke us all a number of times, with terrible sobbing that set us all on edge. I believe she is reliving an attack of some sort."

Lucy thought of the blood on the woman's hands, the clear disarray of her clothes, the bruising on her arms. She was afraid that the physician was right. She wondered if the woman had said anything more.

As if he were privy to her thoughts, Dr. Larimer continued. "It is quite clear, to be sure, that she is from a family of quality and breeding." He took a slice of apple from the plate Lucy had laid before him and crunched it loudly.

Lucy nodded, stirring a bit of ginger and honey into her own cup. "What about Mr. Sheridan?" she asked. In her raspy voice, only parts of each word were audible. "Did you speak with him?"

The physician frowned. "Yes, I did press Mr. Sheridan. After some questioning, he gave me a name."

"What did he say? Who did he say she was?" Aubrey asked.

The physician leaned forward and looked up at Master Aubrey, who nodded. A sudden conspiratorial silence fell over the group.

"He thought—and mind you, he was not sure—that she might be Octavia Belasysse."

"Belasysse? As in—?" Master Aubrey asked.

"As in daughter of Lord Belasysse, most recently captain of the Gentlemen-at-Arms and governor of Tangier."

A baron's daughter. Lucy nodded. The woman's manner was certainly that of a person used to ordering about servants and having her bidding done. That she might be a member of a noble family with political connections did not seem at all far-fetched.

"Would she be related to Henry Belasysse, member of Parliament?" Master Aubrey asked. "I remember *that* affair—" When Dr. Larimer coughed, Master Aubrey changed direction. "Why was she wandering about, then? Was she cast off?" Master Aubrey mused.

"Probably with child!" Lach chimed in from the table where he was just about to start composing a piece.

Master Aubrey threw a quoin at him. Nonchalantly, Lach picked it up from the floor and began to measure out the pamphlet.

"No, not with child," Dr. Larimer replied. "Nor has she ever been in such a condition. Even if she were only in her first few weeks, there would be other signs." He took a deep gulp of his hot drink and continued. "This brings us to the devilish predicament and why I am here. What to do with the lass. Mrs. Larimer and I are in agreement. We cannot throw her into the street—no matter that she plagues us with her shrieks. My oath precludes from causing her harm. Nor can I leave her at a local parish."

"What about St. Bartholomew's?" Master Aubrey asked.

Dr. Larimer shook his head. "The young woman is clearly from a family of quality. Such a place would not do. If she is indeed a Belasysse, well, it would behoove us all to see her carefully attended."

"Quite so," Master Aubrey said, still looking puzzled.

Lucy took another long sip of her drink. The honey was already soothing her throat, and when she gave a little cough, a bit of phlegm arose obediently, helping coat the scratchy parts.

The physician continued. "I thought to hire a nurse. On a temporary basis. Someone who could look after her for a short spell. At least as long as it takes to locate her family." He looked up at Lucy. "Will you do it?"

Lucy was too startled to speak, but Master Aubrey was not. "Hire my apprentice? Out from under my nose? Sir!" His scandalized tone sounded real.

Dr. Larimer held up his hand. "Hear me out, my good man. For the next few days, no more than a week. Well, ten days at the most, I assure you. I would like to buy out Lucy's service so you are suitably reimbursed for your loss of her labor. Clearly, with that voice, she cannot be out selling books right now anyway. To

Lucy, I will provide a room and a small wage." Turning back to Lucy, he named a sum. "This young woman needs another woman to care for her. I cannot ask my housekeeper to take on the extra responsibility, and my maid Molly"—he hesitated—"does not have the temperament to look after someone in such distress." Lucy thought of how the maid had spoken in an unkind manner, and privately agreed.

"But why Lucy?" Master Aubrey asked. "Surely there are other women who could handle such a task?"

"I cannot hire a stranger to do this. I need it to be someone I trust, particularly if this young woman does turn out to be Octavia Belasysse. I will not be the one to bring scandal upon the baron's home. Besides, for whatever reason, Lucy has had a calming effect on this woman."

Dr. Larimer pressed his thumb against the plate so that he could get the last crumbs of cheese. "I know that Lucy is well respected by the Hargraves, and I have seen her nursing skills myself." He turned back to Lucy. "I know that you are a discreet and loyal companion. Indeed, I just need someone to sit by, make sure she eats and takes her medicine, and that her other needs are tended to. That she is taken out for walks, to revive her spirits, for I fear a deep melancholy will follow her present frenzy. Her sickness is of the mind, not of the body, so there is no chance that Lucy will grow sick from their increased acquaintance."

Seeing Master Aubrey's face, Lucy could tell he was undecided. She knew he did not like to turn down the request of a member of the gentry. She also knew that he was always unsure about how to deal with her, since she did not completely fit into the traditional role of an apprentice.

"May I speak to Master Aubrey for a moment, sir?" she whispered to the physician.

At his nod, she and Master Aubrey went back into the main workroom. He looked at her warily. "You are not going to start weeping, are you?"

She crossed her arms. "Certainly not."

"Then what is it?"

"Remember I told you that there was blood on her hands and shift when I found her?" she asked her employer in a painful whisper. "Why do you suppose that was?"

Whatever he had expected her to say, this was certainly not it. "How in the name of God would I know that?" he asked.

"Well, I don't know either!" Lucy replied. "But it is rather strange, do you not think so?"

"Well, yes, I suppose the circumstances of how you found her are all rather odd," Master Aubrey replied. "Perhaps she was involved in a crime of some sort?"

Lucy nodded emphatically. Now he was catching on. "That's what I was thinking. I think it would make for a good story, don't you think?"

Seeing Master Aubrey's expression grow speculative, she continued more hastily, "I could write a short piece. Maybe you could include it with a recent gallows speech?" It was commonplace for Master Aubrey to sell last dying speeches of criminals at the Tyburn Tree near Newgate prison. The bloodthirsty crowds who would gather for the hangings were always willing to purchase a penny piece while waiting for the executions to start.

"You think you can figure out what happened to her?" Master Aubrey asked, sounding both doubtful and hopeful at the same time.

Lucy shrugged. "I don't know. But I'm determined to try," she declared. "Of course, this means you have to let me attend to her."

The printer began to stroke his chin, while Lucy grinned inwardly. She knew that the printer was always up for a good story, Belasysse family or not. "All right! You may attend to this woman." He wagged his finger at her. "This true tale had better be worth it!" He called out to the physician, "All right, Lucy may tend to this beleaguered woman. But I need her back in one week's time."

· 5 ·

Around one o'clock that same afternoon, Lucy followed Mrs. Hotchkiss up the stairs of the physician's home, an old leather satchel clutched in her hands. The patient, it seemed, had been moved into a private bedchamber on the third floor.

"Moaning and lamenting, she was. Dr. Larimer thought that she would scare off all his patients," Mrs. Hotchkiss said, pausing to look at Lucy over her shoulder. "Worse than a babe stricken with the sickness, the way she wailed. You would have thought we were torturing the poor girl, for all her fretting and crying. Kept me awake half the night, she did."

Clearly, the housekeeper did not take kindly to seeing her orderly household turned upside down. "Only after she took some soup with a smattering of ale did she begin to quiet down. Just curled up in a ball, silent as could be." She lowered her voice. "I have half a mind to call in the astrologer myself, if I did not think the master would throw me out on the street!" She guffawed when she looked at Lucy's face. "Follow me, then."

They entered the room. The young woman was lying in the bed, fast asleep, her rich black hair loosened about her face. It was still a bit wild, although it looked like someone had attempted to get a comb through her thick locks. "Your room is just beside hers," Mrs. Hotchkiss whispered, whisking Lucy through a second door. "You may put your satchel there," she said, pointing to a small table.

Lucy looked about. The room was finer than what she had had at Master Hargrave's. There was even a small stack of kindling.

"This used to be the nurse's room," the housekeeper said, "and next door, where that miserable woman is lying, the nursery. We have not used these rooms in some time. I am on the other side of you," she continued, "should you need me." A bit of steel had entered her voice. It was clear that she did not expect Lucy to need her for anything. "Molly will be in at seven to bring you some water and take your pot."

Lucy nodded as if she had not been doing those very duties herself for the Hargraves just a year before.

The housekeeper looked at her curiously. "Sitting with the woman is a bit of a dull task, is it not? Unless she wakes up, I think the time will pass by slowly." She patted the Bible on the table. "The Good Book, of course, is here." The housekeeper turned to go. "I will have Molly bring you a small bite to eat."

"Thank you," Lucy replied. Fortunately, the herbal mixtures she had been drinking for the past few hours had done much to relieve the soreness of her voice. She dared not speak any longer, for it still hurt her throat, but for now she could at least be understood again. Then, before the housekeeper left, Lucy asked, "Are there some other books I might read?"

"Other books?" Mrs. Hotchkiss looked taken aback. "That you might read? Whatever do you mean?"

Having seen the physician's study the day before, Lucy knew Dr. Larimer possessed fairly far-reaching reading tastes. Her tone firmer, she said, "I think a bit of lighter fare to start. Something of the Bard, perchance?"

Mrs. Hotchkiss raised an eyebrow. "I shall have to confer with the physician, of course."

After she left, Lucy opened the door to the sickroom. The woman was still sleeping deeply, though her cheeks were flushed. Pouring a bit of water into a small ceramic bowl, Lucy began to bathe the woman's forehead, trying not to disturb her. She peeked inside the wardrobe and was surprised to see three dresses hanging there, one of which she remembered seeing Mistress Larimer wear in the past when she had dined with the Hargraves. Clearly, Mistress Larimer was not taking chances. If this woman was indeed a lost noblewoman, as Mr. Sheridan suspected, then Mistress Larimer would make sure that she was well dressed while recovering in their home. She would hardly have done such a thing for a pauper, of that Lucy was certain.

As she continued to move around the room, Lucy felt restless. In the drawer of the dressing table, she found a few combs and some dust balls but little else. Clearly, no one had resided in the room for some time. There was a trunk as well, and lifting the lid, she found a few spare blankets, an old kerchief to wear to bed, and some clean hand towels obviously meant for use alongside the pitcher and basin on the table.

Lucy peered out the window then, into Dr. Larimer's courtyard far below. There was a large apple tree right outside and she could see tiny buds already starting to sprout. Soon the buds would grow into lovely pink and white blossoms along the great branches that stretched across and shaded the ground below. There was a small stone bench, where someone might go to do embroidery or sketch. What would it be like to own a fine home like this, she wondered.

She wandered back through the connecting door to her own chamber. The room was fairly similar in layout, though smaller, again with table, mirror, and Bible beside the bed.

Unused to sitting about idly, Lucy picked up the Bible and returned to the woman's room, leaving the door between the rooms open. Taking the chair in the corner, she sat down with the Bible on her lap. After reading a few passages here and there, she set it aside.

She half wished the woman would wake up, so that she could ask her some more questions. But the woman continued to sleep, breathing deeply, making odd gulping and grunting sounds from time to time. Lucy watched the woman's eyes move rapidly under her lids, and she could see her fingers begin to twitch.

Why did I bring nothing of my own to read? Lucy thought, sighing. Then she remembered Lach, looking unusually impish, tucking a tract of some sort into her satchel before she left. "Might come in handy," he had said, and winked in a knowing way.

Passing back into her own room, she reopened her satchel and withdrew the piece Lach had given her. Glancing at the title, she groaned. *The Daimonomageia: A small treatise of sicknesses and diseases from witchcraft, and supernatural causes.* Hardly light reading, but it looked worth the effort.

Returning to her chair in the corner, she examined the tract.

Written by a man named William Drage, it looked to be one of the ponderous tracts that Master Aubrey hardly ever tried to sell. Many of the words were beyond her, and slowly she worked out the difficult subtitle: *Being useful to others beside physicians, in that it confutes atheistical and skeptical principles and imaginations.*

At a cumbersome pace, Lucy began to read the tract, intrigued despite the difficult language. Drage mostly described how to help those who were afflicted by demons or otherwise touched by witchcraft. *Hold the head of the be-witched over a pot of boiling herbs. When the fit approaches, be mindful of what might leap forth from the mouth of the afflicted.*

Lucy frowned. Whatever could that mean? Fortunately, Drage explained in the next line: *Master Gibbson of Hatborough cured a serving girl just so, and a mouse leapt forth of her mouth. Thus, the girl was absolutely freed of the demon. A deep glimpse into her eyes proved this to be so.*

Lucy shuddered and continued to leaf through the long tract. Her eye was caught by another passage: *All diseases that are caused by nature, may be caused by Witchcraft; but all that are caused by witchcraft, cannot be caused by nature.*

She continued to read, occasionally glancing at the woman lying on the bed. As if sensing her appraisal, the woman began to stir, anguished lines appearing on her forehead. "No, no!" she murmured. "Devil take you!"

Lucy felt a tingling on her skin. Who could say for sure that the woman was not possessed? Setting aside her jangling nerves, Lucy grabbed her by her shoulders and shook her hard. "Miss!" she cried. "Miss, please wake up! You are having a nightmare."

The woman's eyes flew open, and she pulled herself away from

Lucy. "Where am I?" she asked, her eyes darting around the bed-chamber. She stared at Lucy. "You. I remember you." She looked at her bandaged wrists. "You brought me to the physician who tended my wounds."

"Dr. Larimer asked me to tend to you, for a short while," Lucy explained, her voice still a bit hoarse. "I am staying in the chamber next door. You have been asleep for much of the day." She hesitated. "You were speaking in your sleep. Do you remember who you were dreaming about?"

"Nothing that concerns you. My head pains me, and I am hungry," she said, a bit petulantly. "If you are indeed here to nurse me, as you say, then I require some victuals and something for my tender pains. If you cannot provide me with such relief, then pray, leave me be." She sank back into her bed, clearly spent by her outburst and the general fatigue that had not yet lifted. She began to stroke her amulet.

Seeing that she would not get any further with the woman, Lucy edged out of the room and headed down to the kitchen. There was a great kettle in the hearth, and when she peered inside, she could see that a venison or rabbit stew was bubbling away.

Molly looked up from chopping vegetables. "Hungry?" she asked.

"Would you please take a bowl of the stew to the woman upstairs?" Lucy asked.

Molly's smile fell away. To Lucy's surprise, the maidservant crossed her arms. "No," she said.

"Of course she will," Mrs. Hotchkiss said, frowning at Molly.

"Something not natural about that woman," the maidservant

sputtered. "Her shaking and contorting, not to mention all that wailing. There's a demon inside her, trying to find its way out. Don't want it finding its way into me!"

"You are paid to tend to Dr. Larimer's guests," Mrs. Hotchkiss reminded her. "Do not forget that, lest you are thrown out on the dusty road, with no coin in your pocket! Do you understand that, Molly Greenbush?"

Molly stretched her lips into a smile, though her manner remained sulky. "Yes, Mrs. Hotchkiss."

When Lucy left to go speak with the physician, the maid came trotting down the corridor after her. "Lucy, a she-devil she is! Did you not see her eyes? She is accursed, likely by the devil himself!" Molly looked around, and took a step closer. "What if she puts the curse on *me*?"

Lucy thought of the tract she had just read. With a tug of her lips, she said, "Yes, but according to the *Daimonomageia* such a thing cannot pass." Seeing Molly's eyes grow wider, she could not help herself. "If she be be-deviled, then she may not be the be-deviler. Or perhaps she is be-witched, not the witch herself. We must look elsewhere for such a being and rout it out—"

"Lucy Campion!" came a roar behind her. It was Dr. Larimer. "Such words I should never hear in this household! I thought you knew better than to spew such nonsense. Be-deviled and deviltry indeed."

To her chagrin, Constable Duncan appeared from behind the physician, looking fine in his customary red coat. From his slight grin, she could tell that he had heard every word she had just spoken.

"Nay, sir, I was just teasing the lass. Pray forgive me, Molly,"

Lucy said contritely. "The poor creature upstairs is not be-deviled or accursed, though sickly she may be."

"That will be all, then, Molly. Please take the bowl up in a few minutes' time. Miss Campion will spoon it to our patient herself."

The physician gestured that Lucy should follow them both back into his study. "I asked Constable Duncan to come around, to speak to the woman," he said. "Maybe there is more he can learn about her." He gestured to a bench against the wall. "Go talk while I prepare another tincture. The other did not calm her as I would have liked. I should not like people to think the woman is bedeviled, especially the servants in my own household!"

"Yes, sir," she said, catching Duncan's eye. He winked at her.

The physician began to mix different ingredients in a small stone bowl. "Any illness she has is natural, I can assure you. Not brought on by deviltry and foolishness." He wagged his finger at her.

"Yes, sir," Lucy said again, more sincerely this time. Although she knew that the physician was not actually angry at her, he did care about his patients, and he did not like to see them mocked. He also cared greatly about the dignity of his profession, and she did feel a bit ashamed about the teasing he had overheard.

"Enough of that," Dr. Larimer replied. "Now tell the good constable how you came to find her."

Taking a seat on the bench, Lucy related to Duncan how she had come across the woman and everything the woman had said.

"Has she truly forgotten everything? Her name? Her family?" Duncan asked in his Yorkshire dialect. "Could she be lying?"

Lucy sighed. "I do not know. I do not think so. She seemed

genuinely agitated and confused when I met her. If you had seen her as I did—" She broke off, recalling the woman's distraught and undressed state, her amulet her only possession. "I know it sounds foolish, but when I found her, she told me the devil had been chasing her."

Duncan did not laugh. "Do you think someone *was* chasing her?"

Lucy closed her eyes, imagining how the woman had drifted toward her, in and out of the fog, like an apparition in a dream. "She did not move with the haste of one being followed," she said. "She moved through the rubble as one in another world. Her eyes, I thought, seemed without vision, and it looked as if an unseen force were working upon her." When Duncan raised an eyebrow, she gave a short self-mocking laugh. "Heartily, I do admit this. I did believe her to be a ghost, and I hoped to trick her by leading her to a crossroads."

She saw Dr. Larimer roll his eyes at her words, and she continued. "But then she sneezed. It was all quite strange, to be truthful."

Duncan nodded. "It is all very strange indeed," he agreed. "I wonder what it was that frightened her so?"

Lucy could not help but think of the cuts on the woman's hands, the rope burns on her wrists. What had the woman gone through? "You believe that she sustained a fright so great that she lost her memory?" Dr. Larimer had said something similar.

Duncan considered her question. "Yes, she may well have experienced something that has destroyed the natural balance of her mind. I have witnessed this deep loss of memory for myself, usually after a terrible battle." For a moment, a shadow passed in front of his eyes. Lucy knew he had fought in the King's Army, from a regiment outside York, but she knew little else about that part of his military experience. She touched his arm, and he smiled down at her.

"What do you make of her amulet, sir?" Lucy said, looking back to the physician. "You mentioned before that rosemary was for remembrance. Could someone have been trying to help her regain her memory? Maybe someone gave it to her?"

"That may be so. The ancients were convinced that convulsions, hysterics, and vertigoes were caused by mischievous—even evil—spirits and demons," Dr. Larimer explained, still carefully grinding something with the pestle. "So they tied amulets with such herbs as rosemary, along with rue, birch, and peony, about their necks, with the hopes of keeping such malice at bay."

"And there is nothing you can do for her?" the constable asked. "Nothing that may be administered to revive her memory?"

"I am certain that we shall hit upon some concoction in time that will stir her mind. For now, this tincture will have to do. If you will excuse me, I must confer with Mr. Sheridan about another matter." The physician left then, the aroma of herbs still filling the air.

"He is a generous man," Constable Duncan commented. "To do all of this for an unknown woman, brought to him under such circumstances."

"This woman puzzles him," Lucy said. "I think that he feels responsible for her, too, even if he does not yet know how to make her well. Being that she is a woman of quality, he cannot just take her to the local parish as he would someone of my ilk—or yours."

Duncan turned back to her, his hazel eyes intent. "What makes you think she is a woman of quality? After all, this would not be the first time that we have seen others try to pass themselves off as someone they are not." Indeed, she had written of this in a recent tract that she had titled *The Masque of a Murderer.*

"I know," Lucy said. "I suggested as much to Dr. Larimer. When I first met the woman, I was of a different mind altogether. She seemed wild and strange, and more than a little touched by poverty. Her speech was so odd, I scarcely understood her. But later, after she calmed and the fervor left her words, her speech was that of a gentlewoman." She laughed. "Not like me or mine, that is certain. A woman of Quality."

He shrugged. "There is *Quality* and there is *quality*," he said. "Some may not understand that distinction, but I do. I can assure you, I am not so impressed by the former, especially when unaccompanied by good sense and a courageous spirit."

Lucy coughed. He had taken her far more seriously than she had intended, and the conversation was bringing them along a path upon which she did not wish to tarry, at least not at this moment. "There were other things, too, that made us suspect that she is gently born. Not just her voice."

"Such as?"

"The amulet she was wearing is surely dear, and her shift was of a fine linen. And the lace was of a superior nature."

At his interested look, she continued. Although she should have felt embarrassed speaking about the woman's undergarments with the constable, she found she was not. She explained about the nature of the stitches, and the kind of tailor who must have made them. Despite not having been employed as a lady's maid for overly long, she had learned much about such things in the Hargraves' employment.

"Mrs. Hotchkiss agreed with me as well. The most telling thing, I find, is that she seems to carry herself as a woman of quality," Lucy said, thinking of the woman's haughty and arrogant tones. "She knows how to give orders, as if she was born to it."

The constable listened carefully. "I should speak with her now," he said. "I hope she will be more forthcoming with me."

A few minutes later, the woman balked when Lucy explained that the constable had come to ask her questions, and was now waiting outside in the hallway.

"I do not think so, Lucy," she said, accepting the tincture that Lucy handed to her. "It does not seem proper for me to speak with a constable." She took a long sip and then frowned. "How can I remember this feeling, but I cannot know my own name?"

"I cannot tell you," Lucy said as pleasantly as she could. "I do assure you though, that Constable Duncan wishes to help you. He might be able to help discover what happened to you. He is a good man, committed to his work." Spying a bright wrap on the chair beside the bed, Lucy pulled it around the woman's shoulders. "There, that looks nice."

The woman began to rub the bandage that covered the cut on her hand. "Maybe I do not want to remember," she whispered. *"The memory of the just is blessed: but the name of the wicked shall rot."*

Lucy shuddered. She had heard the minister at St. Andrew's say those very words before, standing righteously at his pulpit, but never had Proverbs 10:7 sounded so ominous.

Soon the mixture of opium and wine had its desired effect, and the woman waved her hand at Lucy. "You may summon him."

Opening the door, Lucy found both physicians waiting with the constable. "She does not quite think it proper that she speak to you," she said, giving Duncan an apologetic glance, "but she has agreed to do so nevertheless."

"I see," he said. "Let us proceed."

When the men entered the room, Dr. Larimer presented the constable to her.

Constable Duncan gave her a clipped military bow, the likes of which Lucy had rarely seen him do. The woman inclined her head graciously, much as Lucy had seen other gentlewomen do to acknowledge a gallantry. The gesture had seemed natural, not forced, and indeed, the woman drew herself up to full stately bearing. There was no evidence of yesterday's downtrodden state, or even the terror she had shown a half hour before.

Dr. Larimer pulled the chair away to the edge of the room and gestured for the woman to sit down. "If you would, miss."

"Constable," she said, sitting down grandly. "You have questions for me, I presume. I am doubtful that I have answers."

At her voice, he looked at her in surprise. "You speak as someone from my own region. Have you lived near York, miss?"

"How can I know?" She shifted impatiently. "I knew there was no use speaking to you. Until I remember who I am, there is nothing I can do."

"Octavia! I know it is you!" Mr. Sheridan burst out. "I am certain this is true." He knelt by her bedside. "Can you not remember me? James Sheridan?" When she continued to stare at him blankly, he said again, "You *are* Octavia Belasysse!"

The woman gulped. "That name! I do not know. Am I she? I do not know! I do not know!" Tears began to stream down her face, and she pressed her hands to her head. Suddenly, her eyelids began to flutter. "Help me!" she whispered. "I beg of you—"

"What is happening?" Duncan asked. Lucy did not reply, watching as the woman's eyes rolled back into her head.

"She is convulsing!" Mr. Sheridan cried, grabbing the woman as she slumped to the ground, her body still contorting and shaking wildly. Gently, he laid her head atop a pillow that he pulled from the bed.

"Grab that comb. Place it between her teeth so that she does not bite off her tongue," Dr. Larimer instructed with absolute calm.

Seeing where he was pointing, Lucy grabbed the short wooden comb from the table and handed it to Mr. Sheridan, who inserted it between the woman's teeth.

"Roll her on her side, with her knee out like so," Dr. Larimer said to the younger physician as he positioned the woman's legs. "This way she shall not choke on her spittle or bile, should her mouth grow filled."

For a moment, they all watched the woman shake uncontrollably. At last her terrible shaking subsided, and her cheeks were no longer so sallow.

"Let us get her back into her bed," Dr. Larimer instructed.

Before anyone could step forward, Mr. Sheridan scooped the woman into his arms and, with a great grunt, managed to pick her up and lay her heavily onto the bed. The gesture was protective, intimate even. "I will tend to her," he said, without meeting anyone's eyes.

Dr. Larimer gave his assistant a curious look as he sat beside the woman on the bed, but only said, "As you wish."

"I shall take my leave as well," Duncan replied, moving toward the door. Lucy found herself accompanying him down the hallway.

At the front door, the constable stopped and looked down at her. "If she is indeed Octavia Belasysse, we should know that soon enough. If she is not, well, I scarcely know where to start. I hope to know something soon, although a bootless errand I fear this may be."

·6·

The rest of the afternoon passed painfully for Lucy. Miss Belasysse, as Lucy had taken to calling the woman in her mind, barely slept. When she was not weeping, she would rage around the room until she grew unnaturally calm. Underneath the woman's rage, however, Lucy could sense a great despair and frustration at her inability to remember, and a great fear that underlay everything else. Finally, the woman's fatigue overwhelmed her, and she seemed to drop off into a great sleep once again.

Around seven that evening, Molly tapped on the door. "If you would, miss, you have a visitor. Mr. Adam Hargrave." The servant's eyes were wide with curiosity about the magistrate's son coming to call so late in the day, and seeking the company of a nursemaid at that.

Lucy took off her apron and smoothed her hair. She knew she looked tousled, but she did not wish to keep Adam waiting. *He has seen me look worse,* she thought to herself.

Fortunately, the Larimers were dining at a friend's house, and Mr. Sheridan seemed to have retired for the evening, so she did not need to explain Adam's presence to anyone else.

Not feeling comfortable greeting him in Dr. Larimer's drawing room, she drew him out into the courtyard, ignoring the curious eyes of Molly and Mrs. Hotchkiss as they passed through the kitchen. She pulled her cloak on as they went.

They sat down on the bench under the apple tree. It was a little chilly, but the garden smelled sweet, no doubt from the herbs that Dr. Larimer kept on hand.

"What are you doing here?" she asked, smiling up at him. She could still remember the first time she looked into his deep blue eyes, when she was still a servant. How he had wiped away the blood from her nose—an unexpected gesture that always reminded her of his sense of compassion and justice for those less fortunate than himself.

"I could ask you the same thing, Lucy," he replied. Though he returned her smile, there was a serious note to his words. "I stopped by Master Aubrey's earlier this evening, hoping to see you, and that printer's devil told me that you were living here." He paused, looking slightly hopeful. "Have you left Master Aubrey's employment?"

"Oh, no!" she exclaimed. A quiver had pierced her heart at the thought of leaving the printer's shop permanently. "I do love printing books. I should never wish to leave my employment. Master Aubrey has been ever so good to me."

Seeing the slight shadow that crossed his face when he heard her words, she began to hastily explain all that had transpired over the last two days.

"How curious," he said when she was finished. "Why did you not tell me sooner?" Then, before she could answer, he touched her hand. "Never mind about that. It's all very strange, is it not?"

She nodded. "Do *you* know Octavia Belasysse? Have you met her? Or maybe her brother?"

He shook his head. "No. I have met Lord Belasysse, who would be this woman's father, if her identity is true. But he is in Tangier now, from what I understand." He furrowed his brow. "Although he might have returned. Has anyone sent word?"

"I imagine that Dr. Larimer and Constable Duncan have thought to do so. I believe they have sent messages to the family, here in London and at the family seat," Lucy replied.

"Duncan? You have spoken with him about all this, have you?"

"Yes," she said hurriedly. "He was summoned here this morning."

Molly opened the door that led out to the courtyard. "If you would, miss, the woman is awake again. We need you." She darted back inside the house, leaving the door open.

"I am sorry, Adam, I must leave."

He nodded. "Please let me know if there is anything I can do in this matter. Other inquiries I could make." He seemed about to say something else, but did not. "You must go. I shall show myself out."

As Lucy approached the bedchamber, she wondered if she would be met with another dramatic hue and cry. Instead, when she opened the door, she found the woman lying on her stomach on the floor. She was not suffering from convulsions; she was just tracing a crack on the floor with her fingernail, her eyes gleaming with unshed tears.

"Miss," Lucy said, kneeling beside her, "may I help you back into the bed? It is too cold to lie here."

When the woman did not reply, Lucy sighed and began to tug the straw pallet from the bed onto the floor. The woman's eyes flickered over to her, but she seemed otherwise wholly disinterested in what Lucy was doing.

Without saying anything more, Lucy rolled the woman on top of it. After covering her with a blanket, Lucy finally crept back into her own room, keeping the door open between them, so that she could listen for the woman's breathing. Finally the woman began to breathe more deeply and, except for some odd grunting and exclamations, soon fell into a mostly sound sleep.

Lucy, however, found it hard to grow accustomed to the strange bed, and could not keep from tossing and turning. Eventually she went over to the small window and unlatched the shutters so that she could peer out at the moonlit world below. For once, the fog was not rolling in, and she could see the shadows of houses and church pinnacles in the distance, beyond the branches of the apple tree.

She sighed. It was not just the strangeness of her surroundings and the oddly sleeping woman in the next room that were keeping her awake. Seeing both Adam and Duncan earlier that day had brought up feelings that she was still not ready to address.

By morning, the woman's lethargy had deepened, and she would answer only yes or no or shake her head. She seemed unable to eat or drink on her own, as if all the energies from the day before had been spent.

Even using the chamber pot became an ordeal, because the woman suddenly seemed completely unable to tend to even her most private acts. Dr. Larimer said that she was entering a melancholic state, which was common with those who had experienced great anxiety, trauma, and loss.

"We must tend to her carefully, Lucy," he said. "I fear now that her moroseness will weigh her spirit down so that she may not ascend again. I have seen such despondency precede the most wicked act, that of self-murder."

Lucy shuddered. The Church did not look kindly on those who took their own lives, refusing to bury them in sacred ground. She did not wish such a sorry fate to befall the woman in her charge. "I will be mindful, sir," she said. "You may depend on that."

At around eleven o'clock, the constable returned to the house. Lucy heard him at the door when she was ladling some stew into a bowl for the woman. Stepping into the corridor, she saw him disappear into the physician's study, a grim look on his face. A short while later he opened the door. He did not seem surprised to find her loitering in the hallway.

"I thought you might be out here," he said, beckoning her to join Dr. Larimer and himself inside.

"What is it?" Lucy asked. "Have you heard from her family?" She looked at Dr. Larimer. "Sir?"

The physician frowned. "In a manner of speaking."

"I do not understand, sir." Something about his demeanor

seemed unnatural. "Are they coming to fetch Miss Belasysse? Or were you unable to locate them?"

Constable Duncan coughed. "I was able to send a message from the physician to the Belasysse family. The reply came this morning."

Dr. Larimer held up a note. "These circumstances are dashed odd. I trust, Lucy, that you will be discreet about what we are about to tell you."

At Lucy's nod, he opened the note. *"Dear Dr. Larimer,"* he read out loud. *"I must say, we are quite puzzled by your note. My dear daughter Octavia entered the embrace of the Lord some Ten Months ago."*

"What? She is dead?" Lucy exclaimed. "They are saying Miss Belasysse is dead?"

With a frown, Dr. Larimer continued to read. *"She is buried in St. Paul's Churchyard. Or at least her poor body was interred there, before the Fire overcame us all. God rest her soul. Yours, Lady Belasysse."*

Lucy stepped back. A momentary remembrance of how the woman had emerged like a specter from the ruins flashed into her mind. "Oh!" she said.

"I see you have grown pale, Lucy," Dr. Larimer said, chuckling. "I hope you do not believe that the woman lying in the room upstairs is anything but flesh and blood?"

Seeing that everyone was regarding her with an amused air, Lucy giggled, too, though she was a bit embarrassed by how transparent her absurd thought had been to the others. "No, sir. I know now that she is no specter, but very much of this earth." She paused. "Does that mean, sir, that Mr. Sheridan was mistaken when he identified her?"

"That is a far more plausible resolution to this quandary,

I would presume," the physician replied. "Besides, it is not the first time that my assistant has blundered, although never before in such an issue as this." Though his last words were spoken in jest, there was a thoughtful look in Dr. Larimer's eye. Like Lucy, he had seen the start of recognition when his assistant had first seen the woman, as well as his protective manner around her later.

The constable sighed. "Well, if she is not Miss Belasysse, we will have to find a different way to determine this woman's identity. And for now, I am stumped. All we know about her—her fancy amulet, her undergarments, her manners—none of that is enough to identify her, as far as I am concerned. It seems cruel to have a member of the Belasysse family travel here to verify the woman is not Miss Belasysse, but that is what we may need to do."

"What about the servants who maintain the London home?" Lucy asked. "Could one of them identify her?"

"No," Dr. Larimer said, wagging his finger at them. "We owe it to the Belasysse family to keep this scandal suppressed, should she prove to be their missing member. We do not know who among the servants might be trusted."

Lucy and the constable exchanged a glance. Even Dr. Larimer, good man that he was, seemed to believe that servants were naturally of a less sturdy character than the gentry.

"Maybe," Lucy ventured, "someone was commissioned to paint her likeness?"

"A good thought," Duncan replied. "I shall check their London home. Discreetly, of course," he added hastily when Dr. Larimer gave him a warning look. Duncan frowned. "It is likely that their daughter is indeed dead, and I should hate to trespass on their grief. There might be others who knew her. I will make inquiries with the Lord Mayor, and approach only those individuals who might be discreet."

Dr. Larimer rubbed his nose. "Thank you, Constable. Perchance, though, there is another way to lift the fog from her memory," he said.

"How?" Lucy asked, cocking her head. She was always fascinated by what Dr. Larimer was able to do.

"If we had other objects of hers, that might possibly help," Dr. Larimer explained. "Objects, especially those that the woman may hold dear, may prompt a sensibility or other emotion that may help bring to the surface those memories that have been suppressed."

Lucy nodded. That made sense. But what other objects could she have? They had none, save the amulet and her undergarments. She thought about how she had first encountered the woman wandering around in the rubble by the River Fleet. She started to speak and then dropped off.

"What is it?" Duncan asked her.

"My suggestion is foolish. I thought we might bring her back to where I first encountered her. Maybe there are other objects of hers there. We might find something that might prompt her memory?"

"Splendid suggestion," Dr. Larimer said. "Even the location itself could be enough to spur memory. Familiar locations, like personal belongings, have been known to stir powerful memories. Smells, too."

"I should not like to re-create the smell by the River Fleet," Lucy said, wrinkling her nose as she recalled the horrid stench.

"Nevertheless, I think it is a good idea to take her back to where you first found her. Tomorrow," he added firmly, as he saw the constable about to speak. "She must rest today."

"I will accompany you," the constable said. "I do not think it is safe for you to go back there alone. I will be making inquiries in the morning, but would be free to join you later in the day."

"If I were not seeing patients all day tomorrow, I would accompany you myself," Dr. Larimer said. "Lucy, if you do take her over to Holborn Bridge, it is imperative that you ensure that she takes her tincture first and remains well rested enough for the walk. You must refrain from agitating her; we have seen how her spells are brought on when she is distressed." He paused. "There is something about this young woman that concerns me greatly, and the sooner we can sort it out, the sooner we may return to the more trifling matters that fill our days."

After the constable left, Lucy returned to the woman's bedchamber. There she discovered Mr. Sheridan sitting on the bed beside the sleeping woman, staring down at her. The room was dark; the windows were shuttered so that very little of the late-morning light could find a way inside. Lucy thought the physician might have been holding the woman's hand, but then saw that he was holding her wrist. The woman, breathing deeply, appeared to have fallen into a deep slumber once again.

"How is she?" Lucy asked softly, not wishing to disturb the woman.

Mr. Sheridan scowled at her. "She is much the same as she has been. I gave her another tincture to ease her mind—she was restless and full of terrors. Perhaps it has something to do with *this*." He ran his finger along the rope marks that encircled her wrist.

"These rope marks are quite deep in places," Lucy said. "Who would have tied her up like that?"

He flinched. "I do not know who would have done such a terrible thing."

"She told me the devil was chasing her," Lucy commented.

He looked disgusted. "Poppycock. Miss Belasysse was not one for such fancy."

Lucy pulled the chair closer to the bed so that she could keep her voice low. "So you still believe that this woman is Miss Belasysse? Do you believe the letter Dr. Larimer received from her family to be untruthful?"

"Of course I do not believe such drivel," he said. "I know without a doubt that she is Octavia Belasysse. I am quite certain of it. Unfortunately."

"How can you be so certain?" Lucy whispered.

"Because of the falling sickness," he replied, reaching down to smooth a hair away from the woman's forehead. "Known in the Latin tongue as *epilepsia* and in Greek, *epilepsis*. Octavia always did suffer from the malady. 'Tis a marvel she has lived this long." Then he pointed to the woman's wrist. "She has a birthmark here. Though I have not seen her in some time, I remember it clearly." He frowned again. "It seems like a lifetime ago."

"Did you know her family well?" Lucy asked.

"Yes. As one does, you know. Her brother Henry and my older brother, Dennis, went to university together. We moved in the same circles," he explained, seeming to have forgotten to whom he was speaking. "Sometimes her family would come visit and we would all take supper together. That sort of thing."

He dropped off then. The conversation seemed to be over, but Lucy would not be deterred. She thought she might not get the chance to ask her questions if she waited for him to speak again. "If you are certain that this woman is Octavia Belasysse, why then would her family say that she had died? What kind of grievous mistake has been made?" she asked. "Can you explain that?"

Mr. Sheridan shrugged. "The madness of the plague and the Great Fire no doubt resulted in many unmarked deaths." His manner grew more abrupt. "It may be, too, that they cast her off, when her sickness grew too great." He gently laid the woman's arm back along her side. "Is it any wonder that they will not extend familial accord to such a shameful and woeful creature?" he asked, his voice taking on its usual biting tone. Lucy did not know, however, whether his anger was directed at herself or at the Belasysse family, or even the woman stretched out on the bed before them.

"I will send another letter to her brother, and get to the bottom of this." He stood up and moved to the door.

"But if they cast her out, will they admit it?" Lucy asked, before he could leave.

"We will make them admit and acknowledge their sins," he said, staring back at the woman. "It is a grievous thing they have done, and an act not easily rectified."

When the door shut, the woman gave a deep sigh. "Leave me *be,*" she murmured fearfully, her voice heavy in sleep. Then, one last whispered word, more like a sigh. "James."

Lucy froze. "Miss? Miss? Do you know that man?"

But the woman just rolled back over, taking in the deep heavy breaths of one lost to the world.

·7·

I wager that creature is still sleeping as one dead," Molly whispered to Lucy the next morning around eight o'clock, as they passed each other in the hallway. " 'Tis not right, I tell you. Unnatural," she hissed.

"Dr. Larimer said that the melancholia which has gripped her spirits may make her too fatigued to move," Lucy replied, shifting the hot bowl of stew in her hands. "He said such deep sleep is not uncommon for one in such a state. Mayhap she's awakened by now, though."

"I doubt it. That's the devil working through her," Molly scoffed.

Lucy rolled her eyes and continued to the woman's bedchamber. When she opened the door, however, she found her lip curling when she saw that the woman was still sound asleep. Even though she had just defended her actions to Molly, it was hard not to be annoyed by such seeming indolence. Even her late mistress, who could be a bit flighty, had never slept so late into the morning. *Idle hands are the devil's tools,* she could almost hear the minister's voice intone.

Setting the bowl on the table with a loud thud, Lucy gazed down at the woman. She wanted to wake her up, ask her about the name she had uttered before she fell into her deep sleep. "James," she had said. "Let me be."

Did she mean James Sheridan? If so, why did she wish him to leave her alone?

"Miss!" she said.

The woman did not reply.

"Miss!" she said again, this time more loudly.

Still the woman did not stir. Sighing, Lucy was about to turn away when she caught sight of the amulet where it gleamed softly against the woman's throat. Where had the woman gotten such a precious piece? she wondered.

Then another thought occurred to her. Perhaps she could learn something about the woman if she learned more about the beautiful gemstone.

With a wary eye on the woman, Lucy grasped the amulet with three fingers and, holding her breath, slipped it over the woman's head, taking care not to pull her tresses.

Lifting her own skirts, Lucy placed the amulet in her hidden pocket so that she would not draw the attention of thieves. *Hopefully I am not the one thought to be the pilferer!* Lucy thought to herself, a bit guiltily. If she were caught, she would have a little trouble explaining to Dr. Larimer why she had taken the amulet.

Moving quietly into the kitchen, she encountered Mrs. Hotch-kiss, who was examining her besom. The cord tying the heather, broom, and other twigs to the handle had come apart, and little pieces from the bundle were all over the floor. "It seems I need a new besom to sweep up my old one," she remarked drily to Lucy. "And I cannot spare Molly today, for she will dawdle for sure at the market."

Lucy seized on the woman's words, seeing an opportunity. "By your leave, ma'am. I should very much like to see my brother, Will," she said. Truth be told, as a nursemaid she only needed Dr. Larimer's permission, but she did not wish to make an enemy of the housekeeper. "I promise I shall not be gone long. I should be happy to stop at the market to get a new besom. A good hag-gler I am, too."

With Mrs. Hotchkiss's grudging consent and a coin in her pocket, Lucy set out.

Instead of heading straight to the printer's shop, however, Lucy stopped first at the shop of a goldsmith she knew, to inquire about the amulet. Like many other guilds, the Worshipful Company of Goldsmiths had seen most of their members lose their shops and livelihoods during the Great Fire. Originally, all the gold-smiths' shops had been located near St. Paul's, to the south of Cheapside, but now they were spread throughout the city. Og-den Dalrymple had been the first to resettle on a side street off of Fleet. She knew him to be reputable and, as rumor would have it, quite knowledgeable in jewelry.

When she walked in, Mr. Dalrymple looked up. He was a short, rather sickly-looking man, who moved as if every joint pained him. When Lucy had met him before, she recalled, he always had a bit of a smile on his face, but now he looked world-weary.

"Good morning, sir," she said. She noticed then a huge man sitting in the corner, who opened his eyes when she walked in. He was dressed as a simple tradesman, but she suspected that he was employed by the jeweler to protect him from bodily harm and theft.

"Is there some trinket I may show you, my dear?" the jeweler asked gently, trying to smile. It looked like his jaw hurt him, though, for he moved his hand to his teeth.

"Are you all right, sir?" she asked.

"Must see the tooth-puller," he said rubbing his jaw. "I am very sorry to say that I am likely to have another cursed tooth. The perils of aging."

As he spoke, he ran his eyes over her in a professional way. She could see him taking note of her unfashionable sack and the mud splattered along the hem of her dress. "Or are you here on behalf of your mistress, perchance?"

"Well, not exactly either, sir," she said, turning away from him for a moment, and away from the probing eyes of the large man in the corner.

Swiftly, she pulled the amulet out of the pocket that lay hidden below her skirts. "There is something I should like to show you."

Turning back around, she faced him again, amulet in hand. The jewelry-maker did not seem nonplussed or taken aback by her brief lack of modesty. He must have seen women do this many times over his decades buying and selling jewelry.

Lucy held out the precious piece. "Sir, could you please tell me about the amulet?" She hesitated. "It belongs to my mistress, and she would like to know more about it."

"Looking to pawn it, I suppose? Well, we shall see," Mr. Dalrymple said, accepting the piece. "I am moving out of the trade soon, as my goodly years are leaving me at last. Still, I will examine the piece and let you know if it has any value. Since the Great Fire, I have had to turn away many pieces that rummagers unearthed from the scorched-out areas. Twisted and burnt beyond repair. I can do little for them."

He moved over to the light and picked up his spyglass so he could see more clearly. Lucy saw his eyes widen in delight. "Why, this is quite remarkable," he exclaimed.

First, he examined the outside, stroking the gemstone, running his finger over the hinge. He refrained, Lucy noticed, from touching the dirty cord that had been strung around the woman's neck. Finally, he pressed the clasp so that he could open the hinge. He examined the chambers, even holding it to his nose. He took a deep sniff. "Rosemary," he murmured.

Lucy nodded, even though he was not looking at her.

After a few more minutes, he finally looked back at her, speaking in a quick, excited voice. "This piece is quite fine indeed. Except for this bit of filthy twine, of course." Before Lucy could protest, the jewelry-maker took a knife and cut the cord off. "Ah, that is better. I could not abide such a hideous thing—something so profane should not come in contact with something so sacred."

He continued. "I have seen such pieces before, but they are rare. It is likely from Germany or France and is maybe fifteen years old." He pointed to the stone in the middle. "This is agate," he said, "which is a member of the chalcedony family. Specifically, bloodstone. Many people believe it to have healing properties." He opened the clasp and pointed to the two inner chambers. "Someone has put rosemary in here, but it was made to hold relics."

Lucy wrinkled her nose. "Like saint's bones?" She knew that was what papists did to commune with the Lord. It seemed a rather odd practice to her.

"Bones, or teeth, or bits of skin or hair, perhaps. Or even just a piece of a special shroud." He touched it. "So smooth to the touch. This gem was cut and polished by a great craftsman, and set by another brilliant artisan."

"Do you have any idea who the artisans may have been?"

He shook his head. "No, but I have seen such things on my travels through the Continent. After completing a pilgrimage, the devoted might have been able to purchase such a thing to hold relics from the shrines and churches that they visited." He looked at Lucy. "We English, of course, do not hold with such idolatrous practices. So I would suspect that it has lost any religious significance, although its original health-giving purposes may have been retained."

"I see," Lucy said.

"Does your mistress wish to sell it?" he asked. "I have some customers who might enjoy a piece such as this."

"Alas, my mistress is not well," Lucy said. "I am afraid, to be truthful, she is quite ill indeed. This amulet brings her great comfort in her illness."

"Ah," he said. "Well, please allow me to extend a small courtesy to the owner of this beautiful piece."

Opening a box, he took out a small silver chain and quickly

looped the amulet through it. He held it out to Lucy, who looked at him stunned.

"I-I have no money to pay for this gift. My mistress sent me no coin, either."

The man looked at her. "I am an old man. I have acquired many beautiful things in my lifetime. I will never sell everything I own, and I have no children to pass my life's work to. If your mistress is sick, maybe this will give her a little pleasure. It will give me pleasure to imagine someone enjoying my gift. Take it, my child, and bless you on this good Maundy Thursday. In honor of the King of Kings, if you would."

Lucy looked over at the huge man sitting in the corner. He nodded and jerked his head toward the door. As she walked out, the man followed her. "The old man is doddering a bit now. You must tell no one about what he has given you. And keep it to yourself. I do not want your friends coming around, sniffing about to see what they can take from him. He gave you a gift—which I hope will indeed go to *your ill mistress*"— he emphasized the last three words as if he did not believe her— "but do not take it into your pretty head to come back. Do you understand?"

Afraid of the way the man loomed over her, she nodded and stammered, "Th-thank him again, if you would," before she walked quickly to the printer's shop.

"Did not expect to see *you* for a while," Lach sneered when she entered the printing shop a few minutes later. He had just been getting the flames under the great pot going in the hearth at the

back of the main room. "How about you get our afternoon dinner ready for us? Master Aubrey is out selling, but he said he'd
be back before noon."

"Can't. I don't have time," she said breathlessly. "I said I would
be back to Dr. Larimer's shortly. Before I do that, would you be
so good as to locate some tracts?"

"What sort of tracts?" he asked, his eyes narrowing.

"Any that speak of Henry Belasysse," she said. "Do you not
remember what Master Aubrey said when Dr. Larimer was here?
He spoke of an affair, a scandal of some sort, from his tone, about
our patient's brother—well, assuming she is who we think she
is." Seeing the fleeting recognition in his eyes, she grabbed his
arm. "You know what the story is, do you not? Tell me!"

"I am sure I do not recall the particulars," he replied in his
teasing way.

"Argh!" Lucy cried. "Lach, it is clear that you know the story.
Tell me."

"I do recall a broadside, or a pamphlet, providing the ins and
outs of that particular scandal. But who is to say where they are?"
He began to whistle then.

"You know exactly where they are. I know it, you dreadful
lad!" Lucy cried. "You spend more time poking around down in
the cellar than anyone. Tell me where they are."

"Find them yourself, then, why don't you?" Lach replied. "I
do not have the time." He looked over at the type from a broadside he and Master Aubrey must have printed the day before. The
typeface still needed to be cleaned and sorted back into the mas-
sive trays of wooden boxes that lined the walls of the printer's
shop.

Lucy rolled her eyes. They both knew she would not be able to find the tracts in a timely way. She knew that Master Aubrey had a system of grouping different types of tracts and penny pieces into bags that hung on pegs in the cellar and throughout the shop, but, in her eight months as an apprentice, she still did not fully understand how they got grouped together or where the different groups were kept.

"All right, Lach," she said. "How about I break down this type, while you locate the tracts for me?"

"Deal," Lach said, sticking out his hand to shake. Lucy was just glad that he had not spat on it first or cut it with a blade to seal the promise.

Lach went down into the dark cellar with a lantern to look for the tracts while Lucy cleaned the typeface with a rag and began to nimbly sort the type. Long ago, when she had first started working for the printer, such a task had been quite arduous, for each piece of type was small, and she had to make sure that each piece was properly sorted. Gothic. Italic. Roman. But she had learned that there was a rhythm to be found in the dismantling of each quoin and the text held within, and her fingers flew as she tossed the type rapidly into the correct spaces in the tray.

After about fifteen minutes, though, she began to wonder where he was. "Lach," she hissed down the stairs. "Hurry up!" Had he tricked her? Was he even looking? This would not be the first time the printer's devil had convinced her to do something for him.

"I'm coming, I'm coming!" he called. A few minutes later, he came back into the main part of the shop with a grin. "It took me a while, but here you are."

From the broad grin on his face, it was fairly clear that he had stayed away so that she could do more of the tray in his absence.

Lucy snatched them from his hand and went upstairs to the third floor, to enter the rooms she shared with Will. She was not surprised to find him awake, munching on a bit of hard cheese and bread.

"Good morrow, Brother," she said, greeting him with a kiss on his cheek. "How goes the life of a master smithy?" She sat down at the table next to him, the printed pieces still in her hand.

Will stretched out, putting his arms behind his head, and preened a bit. "Quite well, actually. I have several orders to fill today, but I have a few moments to hear about this mysterious woman you are tending for Dr. Larimer." He looked over at her in mock despair. "Chambermaid, bookseller, nursemaid . . . what is next, I wonder?" He punched her softly on the arm. "Wife?"

"Not straightaway," she said, making a face. "You shall not be dancing at my wedding anytime soon. There's something I need to do right now," she said, pointedly changing the nettlesome subject.

She pulled out the tracts that Lach had found for her and spread them out on their low table. Her brother continued to chomp noisily on his food. As he ate, she told him quickly about the mysterious woman. "Mr. Sheridan is convinced that she is Octavia Belasysse. It seems that Mr. Sheridan's brother and her brother, Henry, were Cambridge chums or something of that nature."

She picked up the first tract, her eyes widening as she read the title out loud. *"The Strange and True Tale of Two Noble-born Men Who Did Most Ignobly Kill a Man."* She broke off, starting to scan the tract more quickly.

"Killed a man?" Will repeated. "Who did?"

Lucy kept reading. *"Henry Belasysse and Lord Buckhurst did kill a man after a night of tippling down in Waltham Forest."*

She stared at Will. "I can scarcely believe it," she said, before turning her attention back to the printed page before her. *"Upon leaving the local tavern, the two ignoble nobles did mistake a poor tanner as a highwayman and did kill him for fear that he had designs upon their wealth."*

"Were they hanged, then?" Will asked, touching his neck beneath his collar. Lucy did not need to see his face to know what he was thinking. There was a time when his own life had hung in the balance, before the fates had intervened and justice was restored. The noose had nearly brought an end to him, and only she knew the despair that he still sometimes felt when reminded of this bleak moment in his life. "Shame about the tanner."

She pressed his hand. "No, I do not think they were hanged for this crime." Lucy returned her attention to the other piece, this one a broadside. "Ah, the rest of the story. *The Murderers Pardoned,*" she read. Frowning, she added, "It seems that the case never went to trial." Skimming the page, she read, *" 'O! the folly of youth!' His Majesty lamented. 'A youthful mistake need not end with the hangman's noose.' "* She pushed the piece away. "It appears that King Charles pardoned them both. And Henry Belasysse ran for Parliament a few months later. He is now an MP for Great Grimsby."

"You mean they did commit the murder and got away with it?" Will's brows furrowed. "Ninny-hammers."

Lucy skimmed the rest of the piece. This one gave a little more information about the life of Henry Belasysse. It seemed he had been widowed at age nineteen and married his second wife a few years later. Here, she began to read out loud again. *"Having made some waste in his estate, he was compelled by his father to marry a lass just thirteen, but possessing great fortune—"*

"Yeah? How much?" Will asked, interested in spite of himself.

"She is said to be *worth £1,000 per annum and with vast expectations.*"

"Hmpph," Will grumbled, beginning to sharpen his knives.

Lucy read the final part to herself. *"Though of a very small proportion of beauty, she is said to have much life and vivacity and will soon do her duty by producing an heir."*

"Poor lass," Lucy said out loud. Thirteen was quite young to be married, but not for the nobles and gentry. That was one small blessing to being a servant and apprentice—no one expected a woman to marry until she had a dowry in hand. Few people of her social standing got married before they were twenty-five; there was not much use to thinking about marrying when there was no income or a place to live together. As for herself, she was quite content to live with her brother above Master Aubrey's shop, creating pieces both practical and strange. Or at least she thought she was.

Hearing the church bells toll ten times outside, Lucy grabbed all the tracts and stuffed them in her sack. "I must get back," she called to her brother, dropping a quick kiss on his cheek.

She raced down the steps and through the printer's shop. She was almost to the door when she collided with Master Aubrey as he walked in from Fleet Street.

"Oof," he grunted. "Lucy! What are you doing, running through my shop like this!"

"Good morning, sir. I was just here to see my brother," she said, giving a little teasing curtsy. "A pleasant Maundy Thursday to you."

He grunted. "It would be more pleasant if all my hard-worked wares were not in danger of flying away, due to the giddiness of my sometimes apprentice."

Behind her, she heard Lach snicker.

Seeing Master Aubrey's pack, she asked sweetly, "Out selling tracts, sir?"

"Smart, isn't she?" Lach asked.

Master Aubrey laid his pack down. "I sold a few. I went to Whitehall to see King Charles wash the feet of the poor people, but the Bishop of London did it on his behalf." The printer seemed a bit disgruntled. It had long been the custom for the monarchs of England to wash the feet of twelve men and women, as Jesus had washed the feet of the Apostles before the Last Supper. Having the Bishop of London take on the task instead of the king clearly irked him. Sometimes she suspected the printer had Leveller sensibilities and liked it when the royals took on more mundane responsibilities.

"Which pieces did you bring?" Lucy asked, changing the subject. In truth, she was always intrigued to know how the packs got decided. Master Aubrey had a knack for knowing what to sell, and to what crowd, that she desperately hoped to learn for herself one day.

"Could not very well sell murder ballads and monstrous births on Maundy Thursday, hey? Brought along John Booker's *Tractatus paschalis* and John Pell's *Easter Not Mis-Timed.* Too many of them, it seems. Only the sinners' journeys, like the one you wrote about that Quaker, sold today."

He kicked the still-full bag, looking in that moment a bit like Lach, causing Lucy to hide a smile. A rare miss for Master Aubrey. Most people did not care how the date of the movable holy day was affixed in the almanacs each year, or why Catholic nations celebrated Easter and Christmas on different days than they did in England.

He looked back at Lucy. "That reminds me—"

"I will have a great piece for you soon, sir! Just wait!" she said, darting past him, hoping he would not ask her any more questions.

"That had better be true," she heard Master Aubrey grumble as she scrambled out the door, anxious to find a besom-seller before it grew too late in the morning.

·8·

After triumphantly handing Mrs. Hotchkiss the new besom a short while later, Lucy headed upstairs to the woman's bedchamber, whistling a little tune.

When she opened the door, however, the woman turned on her with furious eyes.

"Miss, is something wrong?" Lucy asked, wary.

"Where have you been?" the woman demanded. "I thought you were engaged as my nurse, to attend to my needs." Despite the haughty quality of her voice, Lucy caught an underlying note of distress in the woman's tone.

Trying to soothe the woman, Lucy said, "I am sorry that I was not here when you awoke." She pointed to the bell on the table. "You might have rung for Molly. Though a maidservant, I am sure she could have rendered a tidy enough attempt to service you."

Unexpectedly, the woman's lips puckered and tears shone in her eyes. Like mercury, her mood had changed from that of an arrogant noble to a frightened child. "I was afraid to ring for her," the woman whispered, her shoulders slumping. "Afraid of who might come."

A chill went up Lucy's spine at the woman's strange comment. "Whatever do you mean? Molly would never hurt you."

The woman sat still. "I do not know. I can remember a bell and something else—" She shook her head. "I do not know. I do not know." Tears began to slip down her cheeks.

Remembering what Dr. Larimer had told her, Lucy began to speak in a more soothing manner. "I was a lady's maid for a short spell," Lucy said, picking up the comb, seeing that the woman had been attempting to put up her own hair. "If you will allow me, I can fix your hair in a manner that is more pleasing to you."

The task would surely be easier if the woman would just take advantage of the looking-glass, but it had been inexplicably covered with a cloth. Taking the brush from the woman's hand, Lucy swiftly undid the messy styling, letting the woman's dark tresses fall freely to her hips. Ever so gently, she began to brush the woman's hair, starting from the ends to remove the tangles.

The woman closed her eyes. "You said you were a lady's maid?" she murmured. Her earlier terror seemed to be dissipating. "For whom?"

"I worked for Master Hargrave, a magistrate," Lucy said. "I tended to his wife and his daughter, Sarah."

As she combed and pinned the woman's locks, Lucy told her a little about her life with the Hargraves. "That was all before the Great Fire," she said, remembering with a shiver the night that the inferno had begun. Things had happened that September night that still haunted her dreams. "I only lived with them a few more weeks after that. It was then that I took up rooms with my brother, Will, above Master Aubrey's shop, and became a printer's apprentice."

"A printer's apprentice?" the woman asked, her eyes flying open. "That is a rather unseemly occupation, is it not?"

Lucy pulled the comb through the woman's hair a little harder than she intended. "I suppose some would say so," she said, striving to keep her tone even. "Master Hargrave did not consider the occupation to be unseemly when I left his employ. Indeed, he equipped me with funds to keep myself on at the printer's, since I am not a true apprentice, licensed by the guild."

"Why ever did you leave the Hargraves, Lucy?" the woman asked, suddenly taking on a familiar demeanor, much the way a kindly mistress might inquire after the doings of a servant. "It sounds like they treated you well?"

Lucy's fingers, which had been flying through the woman's hair, slowed. Why had she left the Hargrave household? The question was simple, but the answer was far less so. The complication of living so close to Adam. The draw of the printer's world. What to say? Instead, she gave the simplest, most direct answer. "My mistress had passed away, and the master's daughter became a Quaker and left his home. There was no lady left to tend."

"And you have not married? Have you no suitor, then? You are comely enough."

Lucy shifted uncomfortably. The conversation was getting far too personal, and since she was employed by Dr. Larimer, and not by this woman, she decided she did not need to answer beyond what she had already revealed. "Miss," she said instead, "what do you think? Does this suit you more?" She reached to remove the cloth that was draped over the mirror.

"No!" the woman exclaimed, stopping Lucy's hand before she could remove the cloth from the glass. "I do not need to see for myself."

"Why ever not?" Lucy asked in surprise. Mistress Hargrave, though a good and kind woman, had spent many hours at the mirror, as had her daughter, Sarah, at least before she ran off with the Quakers. Lucy assumed that was what noblewomen did. "You look lovely," she said.

"Thank you, Lucy," the woman said, blinking back a sudden tear. "I do not know what has come over me." She slumped back in her chair, stroking the red lines that encircled her delicate wrists. Lucy recalled what Mr. Sheridan had said about the marks the day before.

"Miss," Lucy said softly, mindful of setting the woman off into another fit, or even of prompting her to return to her more haughty and imperious self. "Those wounds on your wrists, they look as if your hands were bound together by something . . . ?"

The woman looked down at her wrists then, her brow puckering. "I can scarcely remember anything."

"But you do remember something?" Lucy pressed. "What do you remember?"

"I do not remember being bound. But I remember someone untying me. Someone who put salve on my wrists." She touched her wrists again. "Someone kind and gentle."

"Was it Mr. Sheridan?" Lucy asked. "James Sheridan? Is that who you are remembering?"

The woman looked confused. "N-no. I do not think so. It was someone else."

"But do you remember Mr. Sheridan? From before, I mean."

The woman clutched her head. "I am telling you, I cannot remember anything. Fleeting things—like smells on the air. Nothing I can grasp! Nothing that can tell me anything for certain! Please!" She banged her fists against her head. "I need to remember!"

"Please, miss! Do not strike yourself!" Lucy said, trying to restrain the woman's hands.

Instead the woman broke away and began to pace about. She reminded Lucy of a cornered dog she had once seen, as it tried to find its way out of a penned-in yard. "I cannot breathe in here! I need air!"

There was a mad anxiety rising in her voice that Lucy sought to contain. "Miss, let us go outside, then. Let us breathe in some fresh air."

"Outside? Yes, I should like that."

Relieved, Lucy started to help her out, but at that moment the woman reached for her amulet, scratching at her throat. "Where is my amulet?" she said, growing agitated again. "Did I lose it? Where is it?"

"I have it here." Quickly, Lucy sought to produce the amulet from her pocket.

"Why did you take it?" the woman demanded, watching her remove it from her skirts.

She could read the suspicion in the woman's eyes. It hurt, truth be told. "I am no thief," Lucy said, and then hesitated. She did not want to say why she had gone to the jewelry-maker. The woman might not appreciate her trying to discover her identity.

"I thought the cord was dirty," she said instead, dangling the amulet by its gleaming new silver chain.

Seeing the chain, the woman's eyes welled up with tears. "How lovely, Lucy. Thank you for this. That was very kind." She paused. "I have no money to pay you. And that seems quite strange. Do I usually have coins?"

"I would imagine so," Lucy said, trying to smile. Uncomfortable with passing the jeweler's gift off as her own, she opened the door.

"We shall just take a short stroll," she announced to Mrs. Hotchkiss, who was looking at them both with a concerned expression. "We shall be quite all right," she said.

When they stepped outside, the woman just stood on the street outside Dr. Larimer's house, taking great breaths. Only when they started to walk did she begin to relax and move more easily.

They strolled slowly. The gentle breeze and unexpected warmth from the sun seemed to have a restorative effect on the woman. Indeed, after a little while, she even began humming in a happy, tuneless way.

"I am ever so glad to see spring return," she said, a wistful tone to her voice. "The buds on the trees. The life around us." She looked up at the sky. "I should very much like to be as a bird, flying from tree to tree. I would collect twigs for my nest, and hide from the world. Let me fly!"

To Lucy's surprise, then, the woman took off and ran across the small meadow that lay between them and the next road. Lucy stopped and watched her for a while. There was something both childlike and feral in the woman's movements, and Lucy did not know what to make of it.

Then, as she watched the woman, a hundred or so yards away, a man stepped out from behind a tree and began to speak to her.

Nervous, Lucy ran forward and stood close beside the woman. When she approached, the man held up his hands to show he had nothing in them. He wore the nondescript gray woolens of a tradesman, and he was mostly clean-shaven. He looked to be in his thirties. He was no one Lucy knew.

"Good morrow, sir," she said, pleasant but wary. "We hope we are not barring your path. Pray continue on your way, as we shall continue on ours."

The man smiled. "Ah, no. I have been looking for you. Or rather, her." He nodded to the woman, who shrank against Lucy.

"Miss, do you know this man?" Lucy asked, cupping her hands to whisper in the woman's ear.

"I do not know him!" the woman replied loudly.

The man cocked his head. For a moment he seemed to be studying them both. Then he smiled. "She is my wife. I heard tell that she was under the physician's care, and I have come to collect her."

"Your wife?" Lucy asked, glancing at the woman, who looked very alarmed indeed. She whispered again. "Is he your husband?"

Before the woman could reply, the man stepped forward, extending his hands. "Sweetheart," he said, "I have been so very worried. I have been looking for you, and only just heard tell of your whereabouts."

The woman looked stricken. "I do not know him!" she said, backing away. "Please, Lucy! I do not know him. Please do not let me go with him."

Though she was trembling greatly herself, Lucy forced herself to step in front of the woman. "What is her name? Can you tell us that?" she asked the man. "For she does not seem to know you."

His brow cleared. "Oh, I see. She is having one of her little spells again? That happens. Loses her memory and wanders off. My poor sweet dear. It will come back to you soon enough. It always does, you will see. Then we will have a hearty laugh."

His words startled Lucy. Indeed, he seemed familiar with the woman's ailments.

The man continued. "My wife's name is Erica. Erica Nabur. And I am Gunther." Again he held out his hand. "Come, dear, it is time for us to go home. Let me take care of you."

The woman was now clutching Lucy's arm, painfully digging in her fingers. "I do not know him," she whispered fiercely. "Please do not send me with him. I do not know him."

"Do not be ridiculous, my dear wife!" To Lucy he said, "She knows not what she speaks. We have been married these past five years." When his lips parted, she could see that he was missing a few teeth, and his grin looked a bit more feral. More menacing. "Come along, my dear," he said to the woman. "We have tarried here long enough."

Lucy began to pull the woman away from the man. "We were on our way to see the constable. If you would be good enough to show him your papers, then I am sure we can—"

She did not get a chance to finish her thought before the man grabbed the woman's other arm and began to forcibly pull her away from Lucy. "How dare you try to keep my wife from me!"

Without thinking, Lucy began to slap and kick him hard. In the months she had spent selling books, she had learned quite a bit about how to land a blow that would hurt. At first, the man held on, but under Lucy's relentless assault he broke away, stumbling a few steps back. Rather than running off, though, as Lucy expected, he just gazed at the women, leaving her oddly uncertain.

"Leave us!" Lucy commanded, fearful he might try to forcefully drag the woman down the lane.

At that, the man turned on his heel and strode away.

Lucy turned back to stare at the woman, both of them breathing heavily. "Are you all right?" she asked. When the woman nodded, Lucy took a step closer. "I do not believe for a moment that that growling cur was your husband. He was a charlatan, of that I am certain. But are you quite certain that you are not Mistress Nabur?"

The woman's face went blank again, but she didn't say anything. She began to rub her wrists as if she were cold. "I am not she," she whispered. "That is not a name I know."

"An odd thing, though, that he was so familiar with your fits," Lucy said as they began to walk again, more quickly now. She kept darting glances over her shoulder, in case the man decided to follow them. "And yet you say you did not recognize him."

"I cannot explain it," the woman gulped. Beads of sweat began to form on her forehead, and she had begun to breathe more rapidly.

Something else was bothering Lucy. "He also lied to you outright. He claimed to be your husband because—"

"Because he knew I would not recognize him," the woman concluded. "He knew I would have no memory."

Lucy frowned. "That must mean he knows you. But what he wanted with you is another question altogether." Seeing the woman's face blanch, Lucy took her arm. "Let us get quickly to the constable's. He resides just a small distance away, on Fleet Street."

Shortly after, they arrived at the constable's jail, Lucy having kept a tight hold on the woman's arm the entire time. She did not think anyone would try to tear the woman away again, but the strangeness of the incident made her wary.

The jail had been a candle-maker's shop before the Great Fire, and was just to the west of where the Fire had stopped. The owner likely succumbed to the plague that had decimated London, or fled when the Fire started, for there had been no sign of the former inhabitant in the eight months since the Lord Mayor had allowed Duncan to set up a temporary jail. They went straight inside.

"Lucy!" Duncan exclaimed in obvious pleasure when he saw her. "What brings you here?" When she coughed, he became aware of the woman's presence behind her. He flushed slightly, but drew himself up sharply. "Miss," he said, bowing his head. "Good day to you."

"I have just been assaulted," the woman said.

"What?" Duncan cried, looking at Lucy. "Explain, if you would!"

"We are fine," Lucy replied, hastening to reassure him. Quickly she explained what had just occurred.

"Are you certain you did not know him? That you are not his wife?" Duncan asked, repeating the same questions that Lucy had just posed.

"I am certain I am not his wife," the woman replied. But she did not claim again that she did not know the man, Lucy noticed.

Duncan might have had the same thought, because he glanced at Lucy. "Let me escort you ladies back to Dr. Larimer's. This assault does not sit well with me, and I should prefer that you are both somewhere safe."

"Oh, no!" the woman exclaimed. "Please, I beg you. Not yet." She looked at Lucy with pleading eyes. "Despite the mishap that just transpired, I should very much like to stay outside where I can breathe fresh air. I cannot bear to be locked up again."

"Locked up?" Duncan looked puzzled. He glanced at Lucy.

"Miss, I can assure you," Lucy said, trying her best to keep from scowling at the woman, "we have not locked you up." Changing the subject, she asked, "Shall we go to the market? It will do you good. The constable can accompany us."

Lucy gave Duncan a meaningful look. This might be the opportunity they were looking for to bring the woman back to where Lucy had first discovered her.

"Surely Constable Duncan has more important duties?" the woman asked. "You may attend me at the market."

"What if that man is still about?" Lucy asked. "What if he tries to attack you again?"

Seeing the woman frown, Duncan bowed slightly. "I, like any of the king's men, am entitled to an occasional break from duty," he said. His tone was decisive. "I shall go inform Hank." He headed into one of the back rooms to speak with his bellman.

Lucy and the woman stepped back onto Fleet Street. "I do not quite think it proper for me to be seen in the company of a constable," the woman said, her tone once again sounding haughty. "I see, though, that I seem to have little choice in the matter."

When Duncan approached, the woman did not accept his proffered arm. "No, thank you. I shall manage on my own. Which way?"

Lucy pointed in the general northerly direction of Holborn Market, and the woman began to walk quickly along the street, without looking back at either of them. Her gait was purposeful, and her stance was proud. All in all, she moved like a gentlewoman who waited on no one.

Duncan raised his eyebrow, and Lucy shrugged, following after the woman.

Mindful of Dr. Larimer's instructions not to let the woman grow too tired, Lucy called out to her. "Pray, slow your step. I am afeared that you will be overtaxed by this short journey, and Dr. Larimer will not be pleased. He said not to let you grow exhausted."

"Kind though Dr. Larimer may be," the woman panted, "the whole place smells like physicks and medicines and reminds me how unwell everyone thinks me. I simply cannot slow down."

Lucy found herself a few steps behind the woman, with Duncan easily matching her stride. Naturally, he had not offered Lucy his arm, nor did she take it.

"A pleasant enough day," he murmured, looking about.

Lucy agreed. The soft fog from the morning had long been dispelled, along with the chill in the air. In the distance, she heard church bells begin to toll. Once. Twice. Two o'clock.

Duncan put a hand on her arm. "Let us slow down a trifle. We can keep her in our sights." He moved closer to her as they slowed. "Have you learned anything more of her identity?" Duncan asked, speaking softly so that his question would not be overheard.

Lucy shook her head. "Mr. Sheridan is still convinced that she is Octavia Belasysse. He remembers the birthmark on her wrist. But she still claims no memory of that name."

Duncan snorted. "A recollection of a birthmark is little enough to go on."

"Dr. Larimer is hopeful that her memory will be restored in time," Lucy offered. "He is loath to cast her out, though, in case she indeed is the daughter of a baron."

"And if she is Erica Nabur, wife of Gunther?" Duncan asked. "What then?"

Lucy shrugged. "She shall be released from the physician's charge, and I shall return to Master Aubrey's." She gave a half smile. "I suppose, as Erica Nabur, she will have to give back Mistress Larimer's dresses, too. Oh, how disappointed Mistress Larimer will be, if this woman does not turn out to be the daughter of a baron!"

They both laughed. Then Lucy turned back to something Duncan had said earlier. "You know, Mr. Sheridan also said she had always had fits. That is why he is convinced this woman is Miss Belasysse. I got the feeling they might have been closer once. He knew her brother, and her family, back at university."

"I see," Duncan said, guiding Lucy around a still-steaming pile of horse manure.

"And what's more, she said his name in her sleep. 'Leave me alone, James,'" Lucy said. "I just know she was referring to Mr. Sheridan. But naturally she claimed not to know him when I asked her about him later."

Duncan repeated her words. "How curious," he said. After a short pause, he asked, "Didn't Dr. Larimer say that the wounds on her neck indicated that someone had been letting her blood? Someone with great knowledge and skill? A surgeon, or even a physician?"

"Yes," Lucy said slowly. "What are you getting at?"

Duncan scratched his forehead. "Is it a coincidence that this woman was found traipsing about near Dr. Larimer's residence?"

"Well . . ."

Duncan did not wait for her to reply. He seemed to have seized on a new idea. "Mr. Sheridan has been acting familiarly toward this woman, which belies his usual manner toward his patients, does it not? He is certainly familiar with her treatments."

"If he knew her before—" Lucy paused, realizing the direction of his thoughts. "You think that Mr. Sheridan had something to do with her condition?"

Duncan shrugged. "It is something we must keep in mind," he whispered. "Let us catch up now with this woman. Perhaps she will say something that gives us more clues to her identity, so we can find out once and for all who treated her in such a terrible and strange way."

·9·

When they reached Holborn Market, Lucy watched the woman's expression to see if she recalled anything. But she seemed distant and uninterested in the market, if anything a bit disdainful of some of the cheaper wares. At one point she did whisper to Lucy as they looked at silk wraps. "They are trying to say that these silks come from China. But it is clear that they are from a weaver in Lyon, and should not command the price that merchant asks."

Lucy was not sure if that was true or not, but the woman clearly spoke with an unexpected knowledge of the quality of the silks and clothes being sold at the market.

When the woman was sniffing some early flowers, Lucy tugged on the constable's red sleeve. "I think we should lead her over to Holborn Bridge. Before she grows too weary. We might not get this chance again."

To the woman she said, "Miss, let us begin our journey back

before you get too tired. We should not like for Dr. Larimer to refuse you such a stroll again."

"I *am* growing weary," she murmured, grasping Lucy's arm. Once again she had dropped her imperious manner.

They left the market, and casually Lucy led them toward Holborn Bridge. She mounted the three steps. "Do you know," she said, her voice even, "this is where I first encountered you."

Lucy pointed. "Just there, beyond the bridge. About thirty steps away. You appeared out of the fog." She glanced at the woman, keeping her tone light. "You looked to me a most unnatural specter." She smiled. "Then you sneezed, and I knew you to be flesh and blood."

The woman did not smile. Instead, she began to look about, a wondering expression on her face. Moving over to the stone bridge, she mounted the three steps before gazing into the muck and ill-flowing water below. Just then the wind picked up, and they all grimaced.

"Oh, that smell!" She looked at Lucy. "I remember, I think, crossing this bridge with you?"

"That is right," Lucy said. She desperately wanted to ask more questions, but she remained silent, allowing the woman to capture what she could of her memory.

The woman looked down at her bandaged hands. "You washed my hands," the woman replied. "There was bl-blood on them?"

"Yes," Lucy nodded. "Not here. At a well outside of Holborn Market. Past the crowd."

The woman nodded, still seemingly lost in thought. "There was another woman, though? Someone who was with me?" she asked Lucy.

Lucy shook her head. "I saw no one else."

The woman walked quickly across the bridge and down the three stone steps on the other side, carefully moving into the burnt-out expanse.

Lucy exchanged a puzzled glance with Duncan, and then they both followed the woman over the bridge. "I wonder who was with her," Lucy said.

"People have been living out here, amid the rubble," the constable replied, in a low tone. "Illegal, of course, but such activity is hard to contain."

He looked about, at the foggy gray expanse in front of him. "Not a day goes by that I do not remember the terror that the Great Fire brought. And when I first came out here to patrol the grounds, the destruction was so immense, I could scarcely take it in."

Lucy nodded. "I remember, too," she said softly. A few days after the Fire had subsided, she—along with hundreds of other glazed-over Londoners—had been part of the brigade of laborers tasked with clearing away the rubble. For days, they had toiled, side by side, shoveling debris into buckets and wheelbarrows for hours on end, earning a few coins a day. A dead body had even been discovered, with a puzzle upon his corpse. That story had become *From the Charred Remains,* a tract that sold well among the Fleet Street sort.

Now, the three continued to walk, carefully picking their way through the wasteland. Here and there they came across small stone circles, full of ash, soot, and charred lumber likely pulled from the remnants of shops and homes that had once lined the narrow streets. In a few places, whole stone walls remained, and by those there was usually a stamped-out campfire. Clearly, the walls provided some shelter from the cold for anyone unlawfully living in the ruins, and likely kept their campfires from being detected by any soldiers who might be patrolling the area.

So far, though, the campfires they encountered were still cold. "Who knows when they were used last," the constable commented.

As they continued to move through the rubble, the woman suddenly stopped at the stone walls of an old shop or home and began to look about, a dazed expression on her face. "Oh!" she said softly. "Oh!"

"Miss?" Lucy said, touching her elbow. "What is it?"

"I remember being here," the woman whispered, holding her hands to her head. "Recently."

Lucy came and stood beside the woman. Beyond the stone wall, she could see the remnants of a great hearth that had probably once been at the center of a kitchen. An old pot was still hanging from an iron hook at the center of the main hearth beam.

Cautiously, Lucy stepped within the stone walls and sniffed the pot, which smelled faintly of leeks and meat.

Bending down, Lucy touched the embers. They were still exuding the faintest bit of warmth. She looked around. Something about the way that the stones were arranged—two stones together, an old wooden beam balanced against half of an old three-legged stool. Clearly, they were being used as furniture. "Someone has been here recently," she said to Duncan, who nodded.

"Miss," he said, turning to the woman, "do you remember anything of your time here? Who you were with?"

Instead of answering the constable, the woman sank down in

the soft mud by the wall. Burying her face in her hands, she began to moan softly.

"Miss," Lucy said again. "Please. We would like to help you. Is there anything you can tell us about how you came to be here, or who you were with?"

At that, the woman opened her eyes and fixed her gaze on another part of the rubble, where there was a break at the location of the original front entrance.

Following her gaze uncomfortably, Lucy could see a bit of blue cloth sticking out of the ground. "What is it?" she asked, but the woman did not reply.

Lucy went over to examine the area. She could see that a pit had been made, now partially covered by a layer of blackened rocks laid in rows—possibly to keep what was buried from rising to the surface.

She glanced at the woman, who was just watching her, with the slightest furrow to her brow. With some trepidation, Lucy knelt down and dug out a medium-sized clay jar that was partially sticking out of the earth. Hoping it was not the contents of a chamber pot or an offal pit, she opened the jar. A ferocious aroma from inside assaulted her nose.

Gagging slightly, she dumped the contents on the ground. A dead bird and some dried herbs were inside, as well as a few other small bones, probably from a rodent.

"A witch's jar?" she wondered out loud. She had heard of such things, often buried at the front of a house or above something precious, with the intention of keeping the object hidden below it safe.

Removing the layer of stones, Lucy reached down and pulled

out a wadded-up blue cloth, which was quite cold and damp to her touch.

"What is that, Lucy?" Duncan asked, walking toward her. He was clearly trying not to alarm the woman, trying to keep her humors balanced and calm.

"I am not certain," Lucy replied, in an equally calm manner. She darted a quick glance over her shoulder. The woman was chewing on her thumbnail, her eyes wide as she watched Lucy.

Carefully, Lucy stood up, shaking the blue cloth in front of her. "Oh!" she exclaimed softly.

It turned out that the cloth was actually a woman's dress, partially blackened by fire and full of charred rips and tears. It seemed that someone had tried to burn the garment. From a single glance she could see that the quality was clearly fine; this was a linen dress for a gentlewoman, not the woolen dress of a servant or a tradesman's wife.

Behind her the woman gasped a single word. "No!"

When Lucy turned to look at the woman, she saw that she was staring at the gown in utter horror, tears silently streaming down her cheeks. Her cheeks were sucking in and out as she labored to breathe in short frantic huffs.

Duncan's eyes had widened when he looked at the front of the dress. Lucy turned it toward her. A long stream of something dark had cascaded down the fabric. Someone else might have mistaken the stain for mud, but Lucy knew exactly what it was. Dried blood.

"Was this gown yours?" Lucy asked the woman, holding it up closer, her own hands trembling.

At that the woman began to scream in earnest, full anguished cries that racked her entire body.

"What in Heaven's name——?" Duncan began.

Without thinking, Lucy did as she had seen Dr. Sheridan do the day before—she slapped the woman hard across her mouth.

The woman quieted down instantly, and once again began to just sob quietly into her hands.

Constable Duncan stood up. "Stay here," he said to Lucy. "Attend to her. I will look around. Maybe we can discover something of what happened here."

Lucy sat down next to the woman, her back against the low stone wall. She looked around. Had this been a house? A shop? Her knowledge of how the streets here had looked before the Fire was scant. If she had been a bookseller prior to the inferno, she might have been far more knowledgeable.

Just then the woman let out a strangled sound, and her eyes rolled back in their sockets. Immediately she began to thrash wildly about, her body convulsing uncontrollably. Lucy knew that this time a slap across the mouth would not suffice.

The devil has her, Lucy thought to herself. She could not refrain from touching a charred wooden beam. Even as she made the old superstitious gesture, she could almost hear the magistrate's stern voice. *Stuff and nonsense,* she could hear him say.

"She's having another fit," she said to Duncan, who had remained beside her when the woman's fit started. "Help me hold her down, lest she hurt herself with all this flailing about."

Together, they knelt down beside the woman, trying to still her legs and arms. Lucy tugged the bloodied dress under the woman's head, to soften the impact as her head repeatedly banged against the hard ground. Remembering what Dr. Larimer had done the day before, she reached for a small stick on the ground and forced it between the woman's teeth. "Help me roll her," she said to Duncan.

Before long, the woman's limbs stopped jerking violently. Her lips parted and, as she heaved a great sigh, her whole body relaxed.

"I think the fit has subsided," Lucy whispered to Duncan. Gingerly, they released their hold on her.

The woman's eyes opened, and, after looking about, she tried to sit up quickly. "What happened? Why are we here?" She looked back and forth between Lucy and the constable in despair. "What has happened to me?"

"Shhh," Lucy said, as soothingly as she could. Even though she knew the magistrate and Dr. Larimer would scoff, she peered deep into the woman's eyes to see if she could discern someone else in there, as William Drage had recommended in *Daimonomageia*. She saw nothing, except terror and confusion.

Without saying anything, Lucy put the remains of the dress into her sack. Standing up, she brushed off her skirts. "I think we need to return to Dr. Larimer's," she said.

It was all Lucy and the constable could do to get the woman back to the physician's home. Together they nearly carried the woman, who now seemed completely fatigued. When Mrs. Hotchkiss opened the door, Lucy bid her fetch the physician. Molly put her arm around the woman's waist and led her upstairs to her chamber.

Duncan's face was speculative as he took his leave. "I do not like any of this, Lucy. I do not like that that man Nabur came after you today. And I like that bloody dress even less. I'm going to explore that area by Holborn Bridge a bit more," he said. "Pray, send me a note, should you learn anything more about the identity of our poor lost woman." He took a step closer to her. "There's more to this, Lucy. I can just feel it."

Once upstairs, Lucy poured the woman a bit of the mulled wine that was still on the side table. It had not been warmed, but Lucy thought it would soothe her spirits. The woman sank back into the bedding, closing her eyes.

It was not long before there was a knock at the door, and the two physicians walked in. "Mrs. Hotchkiss said the poor lass was quite weary when you returned from your excursion to the market," Dr. Larimer said quietly, glancing over at the drowsing woman. "At least she is resting well enough now."

"Yes, sir," Lucy replied. "Although she had another fit by Holborn Bridge."

"At Holborn Bridge!" Mr. Sheridan exclaimed. "What possessed you to take her to that spot?" Was there a tinge of worry underlying his anger? It was hard to say.

"Sounds like she suffered another epileptic fit," Dr. Larimer said. "I can prepare another tisane for when she wakes. Unfortunately, we can only treat her symptoms. I do not yet know how to ward off the onset of her convulsions." He looked down at the woman. "Her color looks good now, at least. The best thing we can do for her is to let her sleep."

"I do not know what you were thinking, taking her on such an exhausting walk!" Mr. Sheridan said sharply, crossing his arms.

"I thought it a good idea for her to get some air," Dr. Larimer told his assistant, a bit sharply. "And I agreed that bringing her to Holborn Bridge might help her regain her memory."

"And did it?" Mr. Sheridan asked, sounding more wary than curious.

Lucy shook her head. "No, but something odd occurred before we even reached the bridge, when we first set out from this house." Quickly she described the man they had encountered on the path. "He said she was her wife, and that her name was Erica Nabur. He knew all about her bad memory, and that she was being looked after by Dr. Larimer."

Mr. Sheridan frowned. "The man called her Erica Nabur?" he asked. "I just do not believe that to be true. I know she does not recall herself as Octavia Belasysse, but I have grown more certain of her identity with every passing moment. I am going to send another message to the Belasysses' London residence. I will only be satisfied when one of her own family members looks upon her countenance and says yea or nay to her identity."

"If she is Octavia Belasysse, what did that man want with her?" Lucy asked, turning back to Dr. Larimer.

"That, I do not know," Dr. Larimer said. "But I believe that it is now our godly duty to protect her. Whether we want to or not."

"Did you learn anything else on your journey?" Mr. Sheridan asked Lucy. "Did you discover any other clue to what happened to her?" His tone was snide and dismissive.

Lucy opened her mouth to tell them about the dress and then shut it again.

"No?" Mr. Sheridan asked, rubbing his hands together. Did he look relieved? "So all this trouble to this poor woman, for a simple goose chase. I hope you do not take such liberties with her again."

"Yes, sir," Lucy replied, gazing at the physician's assistant.

There was a flash of anger in his tone, and something else. Guilt. *What are you hiding, Mr. Sheridan?* she wondered, as she shut the door behind the two men.

Crossing the room again, Lucy sat on the edge of the woman's bed. "Miss Belasysse?" she asked softly.

The woman's eyes flew open. "Yes?" Her reply was natural, although heavy with sleep.

Hoping she would not trigger another fit, Lucy carefully pulled part of the dress out of her bag. "Is this gown yours?" she asked.

With a sigh, the woman leaned over and stroked the sleeve. "Such a lovely blue," she said, her eyes fixed on the gown. "He said that he wanted me to look nice for when we traveled." She rolled over in the bed, away from Lucy.

"Who? Who said it?" Lucy asked. "Who gave you this gown? Where were you traveling?"

But the woman did not reply. A moment later, Lucy heard a soft snore from the bed.

Getting up, Lucy poked the embers in the fireplace a bit, and after throwing in a handful of twigs, managed to get a small flame flickering.

Settling back in her chair, Lucy picked up the remnants of the blue gown again and began to examine the cloth more carefully. Like the underclothes the woman had been wearing, the gown was made of a fine woven cloth. The hand-stitching around the lace-holes and the embroidered sleeves suggested an expert seamstress had created the garment.

Lucy ran her hands over the burnt parts. A goodly portion of the right side of the dress, from sleeve to the knee, had been burnt, but in patches. She glanced at the woman sleeping on the bed. If this dress belonged to this woman, she could not have been wearing it when it was on fire. Such burns would have resulted in terrible injuries, and this woman had no burn marks upon her person, as Lucy had seen for herself. No, it was more likely that the gown had been removed and set on fire, although, judging by the wetness, doused before being completely destroyed.

But then why had rocks been laid across the dress? Someone had tried to hide the dress, of that she felt certain.

Standing up, Lucy held the garment against herself. It did not quite reach the tops of her boots, suggesting it had been hemmed for a woman of smaller stature than herself. This was surprising, because the woman, asleep beside her, seemed a good inch taller. Perhaps the dress did not belong to the woman after all.

Lucy frowned. The woman had all but acknowledged the dress belonged to her. Had she borrowed it from someone shorter than herself? Or, perhaps, someone unfamiliar with her size had given it to her. Maybe she had even stolen it from someone. Who knew? Everything about the woman was a mystery. Lucy shook the dress impatiently.

Sitting back down, she examined the hem of the skirt. To her surprise, a portion of the hem looked inexpertly crafted, with many thread loops showing. She pulled a candle closer to examine the loops of knotted thread more carefully. The thread was a thicker yarn, and it had not been dyed to match.

Feeling the hemmed cloth closely, Lucy felt something hard underneath. Inserting a fingernail carefully under one of the loops to make a small hole, she withdrew a coin from the hem, which gleamed dully in the low light of the room. Out of habit, she bit the coin. Gold.

Feeling more lumps, she continued to pull at the other threads, revealing coin after coin, until finally there was a stack of fifteen coins in all. All gold. A veritable fortune.

Hearing the woman stir, Lucy swept the coins and the dress back into her pack, questions swirling in her mind. Where had the woman been going? Why did she have a fortune sewn into her dress?

Throughout the night Lucy found herself staring at the woman. Her slumbers were quite deep now, and she was not snorting and grunting as she had the night before.

Who are you? Erica Nabur? Octavia Belasysse?

And what did that man want with you?

Finally, when it became obvious to Lucy that sleep would remain elusive, she decided to write down the woman's story for Master Aubrey. She pulled out a few sheets of paper from her pack and sat at the small table, one of the few other pieces of furniture in the room.

Lucy began to write in her painstaking way, her fingers clutched inelegantly about her quill pen. The pen had been a gift from Adam, and for a moment she stared at it, thinking of the sadness she had sensed in his gaze when he had given it to her. Three years ago, when she had first begun to serve as a chambermaid in Master Hargrave's household, when she had so admired Adam from afar, she never would have dreamed that he would one day come to love her as well. He had always been too honorable to take her as his lover, as other men in his position might have done. Yet sometimes it was hard to imagine a real life with him. That world of gentry belonged to the people she served.

With a sigh, she turned her attention back to the tract. *A Tale Most Strange, of a Woman Found near Holborn Bridge,* she had be-gun to write, thinking the title might interest Master Aubrey. For a long while, she stared at the page, the candle on her table burn-ing down. She knew from the notches the candle-maker had cut into the tallow that nearly an hour had passed.

Upon rereading her words, she knew the next lines should de-scribe the woman's circumstances. *Covered with blood, witless and unsure of her surroundings.* Or even better, speak of how the woman had been *be-deviled and removed of her senses.*

Or should it be be-witched? Lucy held the *Daimonomageia* close to the candle, idly reading through the descriptions again. Such curious explanations they were.

Then she scratched out everything she had just written. Truth be told, she felt a bit ashamed writing about the woman in this way. Even if she were to sign herself as Anonymous, as she had done before, it was hard not to feel a pang, knowing the suffering and misery the woman had experienced. To call her a demon felt unjust, and she knew Dr. Larimer would not be very happy. Of course, on the other hand, if she were to write about the woman, her family might be alerted to her presence, and they might be reunited.

It was this thought she was pondering when Lucy blew out her candle and laid her head down on the table, where she finally drifted off to sleep.

·10·

A rapid knocking at her bedchamber door woke Lucy the next morning. Although it seemed only a few minutes had passed, Lucy could tell by the light coming through the partially opened shutters that it was far later in the morning than she usually arose.

Before she could even respond, Molly had flung the door open and stood staring at her, taking in her rumpled dress. "You are awake? Why did you not answer when I knocked?"

Lucy looked down at herself, still confused. During the night she must have moved over to the bed, but never bothered to remove her gown. Now she was glad that she was not in her night-dress. She would not like to have looked lazy or indolent to the servant. "What is it?" Lucy asked, smoothing some wayward hairs behind her ear.

"If you please, miss, there are visitors for *her*." She nodded at the woman's bedchamber door. "The master bid me to tell you to come at once."

"Visitors? Who?" Lucy asked.

Just then, the door between the chambers was flung open. Molly gave a short squeak of surprise and fright, crossing herself in the old way. The ancient sign against deviltry and witchcraft lived on, emerging in times of terror and anxiety, even though England was no longer a papist nation.

For the woman was standing there, her hair streaming wildly about her body, and her eyes once again with that horrible stricken look. "Who is here for me?" she asked.

"I dunno, miss," Molly said, backing out of the room.

The woman turned to Lucy, clutching at her arm. "What if it is that man again, trying to take me away with him?"

"Then Dr. Larimer will jump on him, Mr. Sheridan will sit on his legs, and Molly will run for the constable," Lucy said, far more brightly than she felt. "And you will be quite safe. I promise you."

They could hear loud voices from below. "For now, let me help you freshen up," Lucy said. With quick fingers, she redid the woman's hair so that it looked more presentable. Rather than the low loose bun that she herself wore, Lucy pinned the woman's hair a bit higher on her head, styling it more in the manner of a gentlewoman. The woman kept her eyes closed, averted from the mirror even though it was still covered.

Opening the wardrobe, Lucy brought over a taupe and green morning gown. "Mistress Larimer left you this. Pray, let us be quick."

After she had been buttoned into the simple but stylish gown, she turned to Lucy. "Am I fair?" she asked.

"Quite fair," Lucy replied, marveling at the transformation. There was nothing of the wild woman she had just seen. "Like a lady."

Indeed, with the fine dress, the woman had seemed to naturally stretch out her long swanlike neck and slim arms, taking on a finer form altogether. Something in her manner changed as well, and her prior nervousness gave way to a new haughtiness. She tucked her amulet out of sight. "Lead the way, Lucy. If you would."

When they reached the drawing room, the woman stood in front of the closed door for a moment. They could hear several voices talking at once. The woman took a deep breath and nodded to Lucy. Understanding what she wanted, Lucy opened the door with a grand flourish as she might have done back in the days when nobles would on occasion visit the magistrate's household.

The woman pushed past Lucy, and as she entered, there were several shocked cries from around the room.

"Octavia!"

"Daughter!"

Three strangers—one older man and two women—were standing there in the middle of the room, varying expressions of shock on their faces. The two physicians and Mrs. Larimer were off to one side, looking similarly bemused. Another woman, dressed in the subdued tones of a lady's maid, was standing beside them.

For a moment, after the initial flurry, everyone stood silent, staring at each other. The older of the two women—elegantly turned out, with graying blond hair—finally regained her senses.

"Daughter," she said at last, swallowing. "You are alive. How can this be?"

"Yes, Octavia, how can this be?" the younger woman echoed. "We had a *funeral* for you!"

"I knew it!" Mr. Sheridan exclaimed from the side of the room, thumping on the table in triumph. "I was convinced it was you, Octavia! Octavia Belasysse, that is who you are. I knew it all along!"

Dr. Larimer put up his hand. "Let us proceed in a more thoughtful fashion." He turned to the older woman. "Can you confirm then, Lady Belasysse, that this woman is Octavia Belasysse? Your daughter?"

Lady Belasysse nodded tightly but did not speak. The man, with a great shake of his white hair, began to talk. "Yes, without a doubt, this woman is Octavia Belasysse. My name is Harlan Boteler, and this woman you have been tending to is my niece—the younger child of my only sister, Jane." He gestured to Lady Belasysse, before pointing to the younger woman. "This is Susan Belasysse, Octavia's sister-in-law."

Lucy looked at Susan Belasysse more closely. This was the wife of Henry Belasysse. Her features were not refined in the way of the aristocrats, but rather more bulbous and fleshy. The young woman had pasted two small black patches on her cheek, one by her lip and the other below her right eye, coy bits of spotting that noblewomen had adopted from the French. Lucy remembered what the tract had said of this woman: *Though of a very small proportion of beauty, she is said to have much life and vivacity and will soon do her duty by producing an heir.* Right now, she looked more anxious than lively.

Dr. Larimer nodded, turning back to his patient. "Can you confirm this?"

"Yes, it is I. Octavia Belasysse," the woman whispered. Her voice was full of wonder and something else. Fear?

Lucy frowned. Up until this moment the woman had claimed she had no memory of her identity. She crossed her arms.

Catching Lucy's impatient gesture, the woman—Miss Belasysse—gulped. "It all just came back to me now. Upon seeing my mother." She looked at the younger woman, who was still gaping at her, as if seeing a specter. "Susan. My brother Henry's wife," Miss Belasysse whispered. To Lucy's surprise, she added, "I can recall your wedding. You had flowers in your hair." Tears began to slip down her cheeks. "Like a child, you were."

"Yes, I had flowers in my hair," Susan Belasysse replied, sounding a bit stilted. She seemed about to say something else, but after Harlan Boteler laid a warning hand on her arm, she fell silent.

Miss Belasysse's eyes fell on the more drably dressed woman in the corner. "Hetty, I remember you. My mother's lady's maid."

The woman identified as Hetty bobbed her head but did not speak.

"Well, is this not pleasant?" Mrs. Larimer said, with a nervous little titter. "So wonderful to be reunited again." Her voice trailed off as everyone ignored her.

At last, after an uncomfortable silence, Harlan Boteler stepped forward and kissed Octavia on the cheek. "Niece. I am glad to see that you are well."

"Thank you, Uncle," Miss Belasysse replied. Though she allowed him to embrace her, she remained stiff and unyielding.

"Let us get to the heart of the matter," Lady Belasysse said, folding her arms. "Your uncle Harlan told us you had passed, but clearly that is not so." She gave her brother a baleful look. "I was certain that the woman we would meet here would be an impostor. And yet here you are, alive. How can you explain this most outrageous fact?"

"I do not know!" Miss Belasysse replied, pressing her hand to her head.

Seeing Octavia Belasysse was starting to sway, Lucy went over to her. Taking her elbow, she murmured, "Let us sit down."

"Let us *all* sit down and have a restorative," Dr. Larimer said.

Mrs. Larimer nodded at Lucy, clearly trying to regain her role as hostess in this odd scene. "If you would, Lucy."

Lucy began to pass out pewter cups and pour out some red wine that the physician kept inside a small cabinet. An uncomfortable silence again fell over them. Lady Belasysse's eyes had narrowed as she stared at her daughter, in what looked to be more anger than joy. She clutched the cup tightly in her hand, but she did not take a sip.

"Daughter," she said again, through clenched teeth. "I demand that you cease this tomfoolery at once and tell us where you have been these last ten months." Her tone grew harder. "Do not tell me again that you do not remember."

Octavia Belasysse looked stricken, and her eyes filled with tears. "Mother," she said. "Oh, Mother!" Then she buried her face in her hands.

"Daughter!" Lady Belasysse said again, in an even colder tone. "Desist with that unseemly caterwauling. Tell us at once where you have been."

"Mother, I am not lying. Pray, do not ask me to remember! I know something terrible happened to me!" Miss Belasysse gestured at her bandaged wrists and then toward Dr. Larimer in despair. "I can remember you and things from long ago, but I do not remember where I have been this last year. I swear that to be true."

Fortunately, Dr. Larimer intervened with a bit of an explanation. "As I believe my fellow physician warned you in the letter he sent, your daughter has not been well. She has been afflicted with a condition—"

"The falling sickness," her mother interrupted, a bit impatiently. "Certainly we are well aware of her affliction. The spells she suffered made her forgetful as a child, that is true. But never did she lose her memory to such a great extent as you described in your letters." Here she glared at Mr. Sheridan. "Do not ask me to believe that the last ten months have been wiped clean?"

"It is quite true, I can assure you," Mr. Sheridan said. He seemed outraged by the insinuation. "Why would she have withheld the truth from me? I am, after all, a longtime friend of her brother's."

"Yes, I remember *you*, Mr. Sheridan," Lady Belasysse said. "Do not suppose that *I* have suffered from loss of memory myself."

Mr. Sheridan opened his mouth but then closed it again, as if thinking better of what he was about to say.

Taking advantage of the silence, Lucy spoke quickly. "I do beg your pardon," she said. "Lady Belasysse, if I may. You asked where your daughter was these past ten months. Could you tell us where you saw her last? Help us to understand why you believed her to be dead?"

Lady Belasysse coldly surveyed Lucy, taking in her cap that was likely askew, her rumpled dress, and her shoes, still caked with mud and ashes from yesterday's trek through the ruins. "Who might you be?" she asked. *And why do you presume to speak to me?* Lucy could almost hear her add.

"I have been tending to your daughter these last few days," Lucy replied evenly.

"And a marvelous job she has been doing, too," Dr. Larimer said.

Lady Belasysse inclined her head. "I thank you."

"Let us return, then, to the matter at hand. Lucy's question is a good one," Dr. Larimer said. "I must understand the fallacy concerning this woman's death. You held a funeral for her, for God's sake. Pray, do explain how this strange miscommunication came about."

Here, Lady Belasysse gave her brother an affronted look. "Harlan," she said, "I imagine you could explain this 'strange miscommunication.' I am quite hard-pressed to understand it myself." Her voice rose slightly. "You informed me that my daughter had died in the last bit of sickness that had come from the plague! That you had looked upon her body before she was buried. You seemed so assured of her death, I should like to know how such an odd thing came about."

They all turned expectantly to Harlan Boteler, who coughed. "About ten months ago, at the request of her father, Sir John Belasysse, I chaperoned Octavia to London from the family home in Lincolnshire. He wanted to see his daughter before he returned to his post in Tangier."

"I did not wish her to travel to London," Lady Belasysse

explained, with an appealing look to Mrs. Larimer, who nodded in motherly understanding. "I was concerned that her health was worsening and that she might injure herself during one of her fits."

Lucy nodded, too, having seen Miss Belasysse's fits for herself. The way she thrashed and flailed about, and became so confused after every fit, it was no wonder that a mother might be worried.

"Yet you allowed me to travel to London anyway," Octavia said pointedly.

Lady Belasysse pursed her lips but did not speak.

Her uncle shrugged. "It was important to your father that he see you before he left for Tangier."

Octavia crossed her arms. "And where is my father now? Why did he not join you?"

"He returned to his post a short while ago," Lady Belasysse replied, frowning slightly at her daughter. "Naturally, we will send him word. I did not like to raise his hopes until I had laid eyes on you myself." She turned back to her brother. "Harlan, if you would continue? I still do not understand the source of this confusion."

Harlan glanced at his nephew's wife. "Susan accompanied us as well, with the thought that she would join up with her husband, Henry, at the family's London residence. Hetty here came along, too, to look after the ladies' needs." He rubbed his hand over his eyes. "We did not realize then that Octavia's condition had progressed so rapidly. She frequently wandered off, in one of her confused states."

He touched his sister's arm. "My dear, I am rather afraid to say that your concern was foremost in my thoughts. When she disappeared, I thought you had foretold the worst."

"How did her disappearance come about?" Mr. Sheridan demanded. "We still have yet to hear a clear explanation."

"Yes, do tell," Miss Belasysse added, with a funny twist of her lips that wasn't quite a smile. Lucy gave her a quick glance. Did she remember something more than she was letting on?

Susan Belasysse jumped in then. "We three had been invited to dine at the Lord Mayor's house. However, an hour before a carriage was to pick us up, my dearest sister-in-law informed Hetty that she was planning to take a short walk, just down the street. Naturally, we thought nothing of it, for Hetty was still attending to me. When she did not return, we grew worried." She glanced at Mr. Boteler.

Harlan Boteler picked up the story. "Susan, Hetty, and I searched everywhere, trying to find some clue to what might have happened to her. For hours we searched, and into the night we waited."

His eyes flicked back to Susan, who gave him a slight nod. "The next morning," he continued, "I received word that a body matching my lovely niece's description had been found. Drowned. I accompanied the parish priest—of St. Giles—to the pond where they had found the poor woman's body. I went and looked at the body—"

Here, he covered his eyes. "But I did not study the poor soul's face, as I ought to have done, may the good Lord forgive me. So distraught was I by the stillness of the form before me that I closed my eyes when they pulled back the sheet." He paused. "I told the priest that the dead woman was indeed my niece. God forgive me for the lie that I told. I truly believed, in that moment, that she was dead, and that her death was upon my head."

"What?" Dr. Larimer exclaimed. "You did not look upon her countenance?"

Mr. Boteler stood up and began pacing about the room. "I was so devastated by guilt and anguish—how can I make you understand? I rushed away from the pond, leaving the priest along the swollen banks with that fair corpse." He glanced at Susan Belasysse, who made a funny sound, before continuing. "By the time I returned, the priest had already disposed of the body, sending it to a pauper's grave."

"After the plague, bodies were no longer left untended for long," Dr. Larimer commented.

Mr. Boteler looked at his sister. "I lied about the nature of her death because I was ashamed of the truth—that I had not looked after her as I had been expected to do."

Lady Belasysse's face grew pinched. "I received your letter, saying that she had been buried in a common field. The daughter of Lord Belasysse! That could not be borne. We had a private funeral where we lived, at the family seat in Worlaby, in Lincolnshire. Suffice it to say, the casket was empty." Again she looked at Mrs. Larimer, who nodded.

Mr. Boteler turned back to his sister and took hold of her hand. "Forgive me, Sister. Believe me, this has been a terrible source of anguish for me these long months."

"That is all fine and good," Susan Belasysse burst out. "I am quite glad that Octavia is not dead at all. But now we must deal with a more pressing concern. Namely—where is my husband?"

"Hush, Susan," Lady Belasysse hissed at her. "Now is not the time."

Everyone turned to stare at Susan Belasysse then.

"My brother?" Octavia said, her face growing ashen. "Whatever do you mean?" she whispered. Lucy could see her hands starting to tremble in her lap.

"Your husband is missing?" Lucy asked.

Susan Belasysse sat back on the bench. "I have not heard from Henry in over a week. He left our home rather abruptly and journeyed to London. He said he had an important matter to take care of that could not wait. I thought he would be staying at the family's London home. Only when we arrived the dim-witted servants said they'd never seen him. Where is he?"

"Perhaps he was delayed, or he had another stop to make before arriving in London," Mrs. Larimer said. "When did he tell them he expected to arrive?"

"That's just it," Mr. Boteler said. "They had received no such missive from him, nor has he set foot in the house."

Lucy pondered this for a moment. Usually, if a family was away and servants were left to tend the house in their absence, word would be sent prior to their return, so that the rooms could be aired and the bedding turned. And as if answering her thoughts, Mr. Boteler added, "The message that we had sent to *him* announcing our impending arrival we found sealed on the table."

From her seat, Lady Belasysse sniffed loudly. "The servants were quite unprepared for our arrival."

Susan Belasysse stood up then and stared at her sister-in-law. "Do you not think it strange, that you appear from God-knows-where, and your brother disappears, in the same week?"

Though the question was not addressed to her, Lucy could not but nod in agreement, particularly when she thought of the bloodied state in which she had found Octavia Belasysse four days before. And to think Henry Belasysse, her brother, was now un-accounted for, was rather odd indeed.

Dr. Larimer gave her a shrewd glance, and in that look she knew he was thinking the same thing. He shook his head in silent warning. Now was not the time to speak, Lucy knew that.

"I do not know—it is strange," Octavia Belasysse said, faltering. "I have not seen my brother for these last ten months."

Lady Belasysse stiffened in her chair and gave her daughter-in-law a hard stare. "It is not for a wife to question her husband's whereabouts," she said. "I have no doubt that you mis-understood what my son told you. He is likely attending to busi-ness that was not fitting for your sensibilities." She gave the others a tight smile. "I just wish Susan had seen fit to inform the servants of our arrival."

"Such a shame," Mrs. Larimer murmured. She was clearly affronted by the idea that a baroness might be treated in such a scandalous fashion, and in her own home, no less. Then, more brightly, she turned toward Lady Belasysse. "Well, you simply *must* join us for our Easter dinner. Dear Octavia is not yet fit to travel, and I cannot *bear* the thought of you being separated from her for even a moment longer."

Lady Belasysse inclined her hand graciously. "You are very kind. Given the unfortunate state of our London home, we shall be very glad to accept your kind offer."

For the next few minutes, the two women and Susan Bela-sysse continued on in this stilted way, while everyone else sat si-lently, listening to them speak about the queen and the recent goings-on at court as if this were an ordinary social call.

Throughout the conversation, Octavia sat with her eyes tightly closed. When the women began discussing fans, Mrs. Larimer excitedly recounted how she had just received the most darling lace fan from Spain. "A *man-tee-ya,* they call it," she said. "Let me fetch it."

With that, the physician's wife scurried out of the room.

Lucy glanced over at Octavia Belasysse again. The woman had paled further, and her eyes were starting to flutter. This was a look Lucy had seen before, one that she knew foretold the onslaught of the falling sickness.

"Sir," Lucy whispered to Dr. Larimer, jerking her head toward his charge so that he could take note of his patient's state.

The physician took action at once. "Please, everyone. I must tend to Octavia. She is unwell. Lucy, would you please escort our guests to the drawing room?"

"I wish to stay with my daughter!" Lady Belasysse replied.

"No!" Miss Belasysse replied, through clenched teeth. "Mother, I beg you. Leave me." She gave Lucy a pleading look.

Gently, but firmly, Lucy began to usher the women to the drawing room before they could protest further.

Hetty, looking quite affronted, gave her a sour look. "Refreshments for my lady?"

"Most certainly," Lucy said. "I shall have one of the servants bring something in while you wait."

But the door opened then, and Dr. Larimer entered the room. "I am afraid that Octavia needs to rest," he said to Lady Belasysse. "I do not think she can withstand any more visits today. Forgive me, but I do believe it is in your daughter's best interest."

Mr. Boteler took his sister's elbow, and within a few moments they had gathered their belongings and stepped back outside the physician's home.

Their carriage was still outside. A man in livery was standing smartly beside the horses. As Lady Belasysse and Susan Belasysse were being handed into the carriage by Hetty and the driver, Mr. Boteler turned to Lucy. "We will be at the Belasysse home, awaiting Henry's return. Summon us at once, if you will, when Octavia's health has improved." At Lucy's nod, he swung himself into the carriage after the women.

As the driver moved a limb of a tree branch out of the horses' path, Lucy heard angry voices starting to rise from the carriage. With a quick look about, she sidled alongside the rear wheel of the carriage so that she could hear what they were saying. She had learned a long time ago that having a quick ear and a guarded tongue was to the advantage of every servant. There was something odd about the way the Belasysses were behaving that made her especially curious. She sidled closer, silently so that no one would notice her.

Lady Belasysse hissed something that Lucy did not catch, although she did hear Mr. Boteler's peevish reply. "I believed it was for the best," he snapped. "Let us not discuss it further."

"I want to know what happened to my husband!" Susan cried out. "Do you know where he went? Is that why you won't help me find him?"

"My son has likely left you!" Lady Belasysse snarled. The venom in her tone caused a chill to run up and down Lucy's back. "You may be young enough to bear him an heir, but with too little of grace and charm that he should want you at his side."

At that, the coachman snapped the reins, and the horses jerked forward and began to trot down the cobbled street.

Lucy stared after the disappearing coach until it turned a corner at the end of the road. What had that exchange meant? She shook her head. Something was clearly amiss in their family.

· I I ·

When Lucy stepped back into the physician's household, Mr. Sheridan was carefully guiding Miss Belasysse up the long set of stairs to her bedchamber above. She had evidently recovered enough to walk, but her face still looked pale. Lucy could see that the young physician was holding her firmly, as if afraid she would break away from him. The sense of possession was once again there, and it made Lucy uneasy.

Mrs. Larimer descended then, a black Spanish mantilla in one hand. "Whatever has happened?" she asked, looking about. "Where is Lady Belasysse? Mr. Boteler?"

Dr. Larimer was watching their slow ascent, a rueful look on his face. "Yet another fit," he said. "Our *guests* have departed."

"Oh!" Mrs. Larimer said, looking disappointed. "They will still join us for Easter dinner?" When her husband shrugged, she frowned. "I will send around a note to them, inviting them properly. I am certain they will come." She turned around then, disappearing back toward her chamber, presumably to write the letter of invitation.

"Poor Miss Belasysse. I am starting to wonder if we will be able to help her at all." Dr. Larimer sounded sad. "That is the part of my profession that I do not like so well." He turned and walked into his study, although he did not shut the door behind him.

Although Lucy wanted to rush up the stairs after Mr. Sheridan and Miss Belasysse, she did not wish to irk the physician's assistant further. Instead, she impulsively followed Dr. Larimer into his study, having taken the open door as an invitation to continue the conversation.

Standing in the doorway, she very nearly told him about the exchange she had just heard out by the carriage, but then hesitated. She did not wish to be thought a gossip.

Instead, she asked him about Miss Belasysse's condition. "Is there no hope, then, sir?" she asked, feeling a flash of pity for the creature upstairs. "Is she truly too ill to cure? Is there no solace to be found for her condition?"

"I am rather afraid not, Lucy," Dr. Larimer said, seating himself at his table, pushing aside some sheaves of papers that lay scattered about the surface. "All these scholars"—he waved at a row of leather-bound books on the shelf beside the table—"and even these less learned sorts"—he shoved at the loose stack of papers—"and I can find nothing that will truly cure the lass. It is a puzzle indeed."

"But you can solve it, surely?"

Dr. Larimer sighed. "I have made every *tinctura cephalica*— tincture for the head—I can think of." He gestured to his rows of leather-clad books. "I have examined any medicine that makes claim to cure the distempers of the head and brain. Headaches, vertigo, palsies, lethargies, frenzies, coma, dullness of the senses, thickness of hearing, noises in the head, convulsions, weakness of the neck, drowsiness, glimmering of sight, and apoplexies. And I have found no help in dealing with the falling sickness."

Here he pointed to a stack of printed papers, much like the type that Lucy would sell on a street corner. "Those tell me what astrologers say I should do—tie an astral talisman about her neck." He pulled out another. "This one says I should tie bits of the Latin liturgy into a small bundle, and place it within a leaf of St. John's wort or a leaf of mugwort. All tied with taffeta! Tell me! How will tying something with a bit of taffeta—not wool, mind you—keep that poor woman from falling into convulsions every bloody hour?"

"I could not say, sir," Lucy replied. "Do you know anything about what brings them on?"

"We know so little," he said. "A stressful moment, a harsh smell, a flickering light, a loud noise. Any or all of those things."

Stretching out his hand, the physician plucked one of the books from the shelf and opened it to where a piece of paper had been laid inside. "Listen to what Bruel has to say of the falling sickness," he said to Lucy, before proceeding to read. "*'When he is deprived of his senses he falls to the ground with a violent shaking of his body, his face is wrested, his eyes turned upwards, his chin is sometimes driven to his shoulders, and oftentimes he voideth seed, odor, urine against his will. . . . They do often snort and cry out in their sleep.'*"

Lucy nodded. "I have witnessed Miss Belasysse do as he describes."

Turning the page, Dr. Larimer continued to read. "*'They often-times thrust out their tongues and it is to be feared, that sometimes they bite them with their teeth. There is likewise a gentler kind of falling sickness which doth not differ much from giddiness.'*"

"I have seen that as well," Lucy said. "He is most apt, from my limited view."

"There are some new treatments for *epilepsis* that some Dutch physicians have encountered," he said, tapping his fingers on the table. "Truth be told, I am at my wit's end. I will even look to what the Persians have to say on the subject. A few pieces have been translated by scholars at Cambridge, and they offer some interesting remedies, even if they are of a heathen sort."

Taking a deep breath, Lucy asked the question that had been plaguing her. "Where *do* you suppose Miss Belasysse has been these last ten months? She could not have been stumbling about the rubble this whole time. Indeed, she managed to stay safe from the Fire."

"Indeed. She seems to have been eating regularly and, while a bit jaundiced, does not have the abysmal health of one who has lived without shelter or nourishment. I believe that someone has taken care of her." He frowned, falling silent. "And not a Gypsy either. Someone familiar with bloodletting."

Like Mr. Sheridan? Duncan's comment popped into her head. "A physician such as yourself, sir?"

Dr. Larimer gave a short laugh. "Unlikely, Lucy. We physicians are too civilized. We deal with the internal ailments; we leave the more barbaric practices of cutting and purging to the surgeons." He began to line up his medical instruments so that they lay neatly across his table, continuing to speak of the woman's condition as he did so. "Moreover, I believe this woman's frenzy and memory loss to be a more recent phenomenon, explained by whatever trauma she experienced before you found her by Holborn Bridge. Although these holes in her memory may be connected to her illness as well."

"Her mother did say that her daughter had always had these fits, even as a child," Lucy said.

"Yes," Dr. Larimer said. "It seems clear that Miss Belasysse has no awareness of what is happening to her—or around her, for that matter—while a fit is upon her. Nor does she seem able to recall events that immediately precede a fit."

Lucy thought back to the odd conversation she had heard just now among the Belasysses out by the carriage. "Do you think that Mr. Boteler's account of her disappearance was a bit strange? Do you think it as he described?"

He frowned. "His account seemed plausible enough to me." Dr. Larimer might have said more had his wife not sailed in then. "If you will excuse me, Lucy," he said. "I should like you to stay with Miss Belasysse now. And if you would, please send Mr. Sheridan back to me."

When Lucy entered Miss Belasysse's bedchamber a few moments later, Mr. Sheridan stepped hastily away from the bed where Octavia was reclining. Lucy thought he might have been holding the woman's hand again, but he released it when she came in.

"Checking the movement of blood in her veins," Mr. Sheridan said. "She is improving." Without looking at Lucy he said, "No need for your ministrations."

"Dr. Larimer has sent me to keep watch over Miss Belasysse, and he wishes you to rejoin him downstairs," she said.

"Pray tell the good doctor that I shall look after her, should she suffer another fit. Having suffered a seizure of the sort we just witnessed, we must assume that she might suffer another in short order."

Lucy nodded. "Let me help her rest more comfortably." Quickly she took out the pins she had only just put in the woman's hair a short time before, so that her long tresses came unbound and fell about her shoulders. She thought she heard Mr. Sheridan sigh.

"Mr. Sheridan," Octavia Belasysse murmured, "you may leave. Lucy can tend to me well enough. I am certain she will call for you, should she require your assistance. Is that not so, Lucy?"

It was clear from her tone that she did not wish to be with Mr. Sheridan any longer. Lucy opened the door wider. "If you would, sir," she said firmly.

Reluctantly, Mr. Sheridan left the room, but not before giving Lucy a warning look. "I expect you to watch over her. Do not let her leave, or grow overexcited. I shall be quite unhappy if you take her on another *excursion.*"

"Yes, sir," she said stiffly. "I shall look after her as I would my own family members."

To her surprise, his arrogant expression relaxed, and for a moment something like gratitude appeared in his eyes. "Thank you, Lucy," he said, before stepping out into the corridor.

Slowly, Lucy closed the door behind him. His response was not as she had expected.

When she turned back, she found that Miss Belasysse had curled herself into a ball on the straw pallet, blankets pulled to her chest, staring straight in front of her. Alarmed, Lucy could see that tears were once again flowing from her eyes.

"Miss Belasysse," Lucy asked gently, "are you in pain? What can I do to help you?"

"No, Lucy," she replied, with a heavy sigh. "I do not think that there is anything that can be done. Every breath I draw is a torture for me, and I cannot but wonder why the good Lord has sought to trouble and afflict me in this manner."

"Would you like me to bring a clergyman here?" Lucy asked. "Surely if you are in need of spiritual solace and comfort—"

"No more clergy! There are many who have sought to relieve me of the demons who anguish me. Since my childhood, I have had people pray over me, run their hands over my body, ply me with terrible treatments, fill me with the most dreadful concoctions. Quacks all!"

Lucy could not help but take a step back. For a moment, the woman seemed as Lucy had first met her—strange, tormented, possessed. She shuddered despite herself. "Is there no one who can bring you a bit of cheer?"

The woman's voice grew stony and flat. "I have no one in this world who cares for me in the manner you suggest."

"Surely your family? Your mother, or your uncle? Or even your sister-in-law? They came here because they are worried about you—"

"No!" Miss Belasysse interrupted, sitting bolt upright in the bed. "I do not know why they have come, but it is not because they are concerned for my health or my well-being."

"Why ever not?" Lucy asked. "They should like to nurse you, and who better but your own mother?"

"Oh, Lucy, how little you know!" The woman's words were not haughty, Lucy could see, but rather sprang from a place of deep melancholy.

Lucy knelt down on her knees beside the woman. To her surprise she leaned over and put her head on Lucy's shoulder. "I must admit to you that some of my memory has returned," she whispered. "There is much of my youth I can now recall. Winters in London, summers in our family seat." Her voice, though muffled, was bitter. "I can tell you that my mother kept me hidden away from others for much of my childhood, for fear that my illness would be discovered."

"Mr. Sheridan said he recalled meeting you in Cambridge a few times," Lucy said.

"Ah, yes. I think my memory had begun to stir when I met James, er, Mr. Sheridan." She smiled to herself. "Henry had insisted to my parents that I be allowed to join them when they came to visit him at university. Mr. Sheridan was on hand once when I had one of my spells at Cambridge. It was a crowded tavern, and the noise and the sounds just began to overwhelm me."

"Did Mr. Sheridan help you?" Lucy asked.

"Well, he was still a student then. I remember great shouting when I came to—he thought they should have been tending to me with more care. Poor Mr. Sheridan, he did not know then what my parents and other doctors have long known—there is no real cure for the falling sickness."

"Then you must remember where you have been these last ten months!" Lucy said eagerly.

"Alas, that I do not. I cannot explain how strange it is that such a hole remains in my memory."

"Well, what is the last thing that you *do* remember?" Lucy asked.

"I remember journeying to London with my uncle and Susan, and our maid, Hetty. I remember that people were just returning to London after the sickness had subsided. Uncle Harlan told me that my father wished to see me before he left for his post at Tangier. Susan came as my companion, I recall, with the hopes she would be reunited with Henry. I was hoping we would see Henry in London as well."

A shadow crossed her face. "She was so very young when they married, you know. She is not even Henry's first wife. He only married her for her fortune, which is considerable. She has very little wits or charm." That was what the tract had said of Susan Belasysse, and for the first time Lucy wondered how the author of the piece had come by that description.

But she did not state what she was thinking. Instead, she asked Miss Belasysse, "Do you remember what London was like then, after the plague? Perhaps you can remember the Great Fire?" she asked. "Maybe that will prompt a memory."

Miss Belasysse looked up at the ceiling. "I do not remember the Fire. Or do I? Watching the smoke from the distance—did I do that?" She shook her head. "I do not know. Pray, let us remove ourselves from this cumbersome talk." She gestured to the great Bible on the table beside the bed. "I know that you can read, Lucy," she said. "Read some passages from the Bible. That will distract me from my ills."

Lucy complied, but was little able to focus on the words. It did not help when Miss Belasysse said, "Lucy, I may seem addled to you, but even I know that you have just read the same passage twice now."

"What you said just now puzzles me," Lucy said, setting the Bible aside. "When I served in the magistrate's household, we only returned to London after the plague because Master Hargrave believed it was right and proper for us to do so. As a magistrate, he thought it was his duty to help restore London to order. Those who could stay away most certainly did."

"I see," Miss Belasysse said. "That was most sensible."

Lucy's next words flew out before she could keep them reined inside her wayward mouth. "Forgive me, but I find it so strange that your father would have requested that you return to London at such a perilous time. Or that your brother would wish that of his wife."

Even though she could see that Miss Belasysse had begun to breathe faster, Lucy continued on. "How is that your father felt no such compunction? Why was it so important for you to see him before he left for his post? Why, in the name of heaven, would your uncle have thought it proper to bring two gentlewomen such as yourselves into the city at such a time, when anyone who could kept away?"

"I do not know!" Miss Belasysse replied, moving her hand to the Bible. "I remember seeing the sick and dying," she whispered. "When we four arrived in London, gathered by the churches, they were. I was fearful, I remember now. Uncle Harlan said it was not the plague that was making them sick, but another sickness that followed. So long as we stayed away from them, he said, we would be fine."

"Do you remember seeing your father then?" Lucy asked.

"I do not remember anything more!" Miss Belasysse said through clenched teeth. Then, without warning, she pitched the heavy Bible as hard as she could across the room, so that it struck the wall and crashed loudly to the wood floor.

For a moment, both women stared at the leather-bound

volume lying facedown, its pages terribly crumpled. Lucy could almost hear the minister intone from the Book of Isaiah: *Thus saith Hezekiah, This day is a day of trouble, and of rebuke and of blasphemy.* Without saying a word, Lucy knelt down to pick up the Bible.

Miss Belassyse sank to the floor. "Good Lord, I am accursed. I know it now to be true." And she began to sob.

After smoothing out the yellowed pages the best she could, Lucy placed the Bible gently back on the table and then helped the woman back into her bed. She then poured the last of the tisane into the woman's cup.

"Drink this," Lucy said. When the woman's sobs had subsided, she said, "I shall ask Dr. Larimer to mix you up another batch. Please just lie down now while I fetch it."

As she was about to walk out the door, Miss Belasysse weakly called her name. "Lucy," she said. "Please, I beg you. Do not tell anyone that some of my memories have returned. Promise me."

Against her better judgment, Lucy nodded and hurried out of the room, shutting the door quietly behind her.

When Lucy entered Dr. Larimer's study a few moments later, she found the physician and Mr. Sheridan in quiet conversation. They looked up expectantly when she came in. The woman's sad plea in her thoughts, she simply told them that another tisane was likely needed. "She is quite agitated, sir. I have been unable to calm her."

"I will look after her," Mr. Sheridan said, picking up a recently made elixir. "Clearly, Lucy is not up to the task." With that, he stalked out of the room.

"I am sorry, sir! I have done my best with her——" Lucy began to say, but stopped when Dr. Larimer held up his hand.

"Do not mind Mr. Sheridan," the physician said. "This woman affects him deeply, and I do not know why." He stared at the door through which his assistant had just left. Clearly, he was puzzled by Mr. Sheridan's behavior. In a lower tone, to himself, he added, "There is a guilt there."

"A guilt, sir?" Lucy asked.

"Ah, Lucy. I was just musing to myself." He sat down at his desk and dipped his quill into a small jar of ink. "We have another task at hand. I should like to send a note to the constable. The disappearance of Henry Belasysse is no small matter, and the Lord Mayor should also be informed."

Lucy waited while Dr. Larimer scribbled out a note and handed it to her. "Please take this to Constable Duncan. Since Sheridan is with our patient, I give you short leave from your duties."

·12·

Shortly after, as Lucy approached the makeshift jail on Fleet Street, she encountered Duncan and Hank just as they were leaving. Hank was pushing a large wheelbarrow.

"Good day," she called, looking at the wheelbarrow curiously. "I have much news."

"Lucy, we have an important matter to attend to," Duncan replied. "Might you tell me your news later? Indeed, I will need to stop by Dr. Larimer's soon, and you can tell me then."

"This cannot wait," she said. "Which direction are you traveling? I can walk with you for a short spell, before I must return."

"Very well, then," Duncan said, firmly shutting the jail door. "We are venturing back to Holborn Bridge. Now tell me your news."

Quickly, Lucy recounted everything that had occurred since she had seen him the day before. About the Belasysses' visit to the physician's home. About the circumstances surrounding Octavia's "death." About Miss Belasysse regaining her sense of identity. "Though she still could not recall where she has been this past year, and I think there is rather something odd about that," Lucy added, before letting on what she had heard Lady Belasysse say to her brother by the carriage.

Hank gave a sharp whistle.

"That is not the last of it, either," she added, handing Duncan the note from Dr. Larimer. "Her brother seems to be missing as well. Henry Belasysse. He's an MP," she added for Hank's benefit. "Dr. Larimer wishes you to inform the Lord Mayor as well."

"Indeed?" Duncan frowned, exchanging a glance with the bellman. "That is unfortunate. I asked Hank here to search the ruins by Holborn Bridge more thoroughly, after what you and I had discovered there yesterday." He paused.

Hank jumped in. "Found a body, I did. Stabbed through and through."

"Oh, no!" Lucy cried. "A man's body?"

Hank nodded in grim satisfaction. "Covered over with bricks and stones from the rubble, he was. Been dead for a few days, at least. Maybe a week."

"Well, Dr. Larimer will have to say for sure. I was going to fetch him later so that he could examine the corpse, but given your news, I think it would be best if I alert him now," Duncan replied. "I will hold off informing the Lord Mayor, until we know for certain the identity of the dead man." He looked meaningfully at Lucy. "I think we must be prepared for this man to be Henry Belasysse."

"Who would have killed him, do you think? The tanner's

wife? Or perhaps another member of his family?" Lucy asked. "I think there were many who were angry that he was pardoned and did not face punishment for his crime."

Duncan raised his eyebrow. "That would not surprise me either. I shall look into them, should this indeed prove to be Susan Belasysse's missing husband."

When they reached the street that veered off toward Dr. Larimer's, Hank continued on to Holborn Bridge, where the man's corpse lay, while Constable Duncan accompanied Lucy back to the physician's residence.

Hearing of the grim discovery, Dr. Larimer sighed. "You were right to bring this to my attention, Constable. Mr. Sheridan and I should like to see the corpse ourselves. If he has indeed been murdered, we shall bring him back here to examine him more thoroughly." He looked at Lucy. "I ask that you do not allow our patient to be on hand when we bring the body in."

"Yes, sir," Lucy replied.

"And Lucy," he said, his eyes now looking upward at the ceiling, "let us pray that this body is not the brother of that poor woman upstairs."

When Lucy entered Miss Belasysse's bedchamber, she expected to find the woman had grown calm. Instead, Lucy was taken aback by the renewed fury in her eyes. All of their earlier intimacy seemed forgotten.

"Get out!" the woman cried. "To think that I trusted you!"

"What is the matter?" Lucy asked. Could she already have heard of the corpse that was being brought to Dr. Larimer's?

But Miss Belasysse's next words proved she was referring to something else entirely. Miss Belaysse held up Lucy's copy of William Drage's *Daimonomageia* and waved it about in the air. "I found this! You think I am accursed! You think I am possessed by demons. You have been plying me with elixirs because you believe me beset with a devil's curse."

"No, miss," Lucy said, speaking lightly although she was annoyed that the woman had looked through her belongings in her absence. "I do not believe you to be accursed. That is just a tract I had in my possession. Indeed, the real devil of this story is Lach, my master's apprentice. He is the one who slipped it into my satchel before I came here. Only a jest, to be sure."

"Why would he do that?" The woman, she was glad to see, was starting to lose the terrifying look in her eyes, as a more natural curiosity overcame her.

Lucy shrugged. " 'Tis his way, I suppose. He is rather mad himself, I now suspect." Seeing that Miss Belasysse was starting to calm down, she began to tell her stories about Lach, as much to distract herself from the body as anything. "One time, as I recall, we were setting a new piece called *Strange News from Kent: The True Story of a Monstrous Dog Born with Two Heads.* Lach and I had been arguing about whether a dog with two heads would need to eat twice as much. I said not, but Lach said—" and she continued the story, which ended with Lucy being sent out to sell, because Master Aubrey could not bear their bickering.

Finally, Miss Belasysse smiled reluctantly, her earlier anger overcome. "Tell me more," she said, sipping her mead.

Glad that she seemed calm, Lucy began to tell her some of the stories that she would sell on the street corners. Ordinarily she would point to the woodcuts as she talked, but Miss Belasysse did not seem to care, asking her questions both about the penny pieces and her trade.

Even as she spoke, though, Lucy could not stop thinking about what the constable and the physicians were doing. Was the murdered man Henry Belasysse? Finally, after an hour had passed, she heard the distant sound of men's voices from the corridor below. She suspected that Dr. Larimer and Duncan had returned.

"Let me take these dishes back to the kitchen," Lucy said to Miss Belasysse. "There might be a bit of pie or some cheese to round out your supper."

"Oh, heavens above, Lucy. Is that not what Molly is employed to do?" Miss Belasysse said, rinsing her hands at the basin. Her voice sounded a bit petulant. "I should like to hear a few more of your little stories."

"I am supposed to check in with Dr. Larimer," Lucy said quickly. "To see if he would like you to take any tonic or a tisane before your nightly slumbers."

"It is hardly time for my slumbers," Miss Belasysse grumbled. "Still, you might ask if he can add a little sugar to the tonic. The last was so very bitter."

Lucy hid a little smile as she bobbed her head before leaving the bedchamber. Sugar indeed! Even for Dr. Larimer, sugar was a costly good that was not just added willy-nilly to a drink. A bit of honey was possible.

As she descended the stairs, she was just in time to see Duncan and the physician talking in the corridor. Dr. Larimer said something to the constable before disappearing into his study.

Lucy moved quickly toward the constable. "Was it Henry Belasysse?" she whispered, darting a quick look down the corridor to make sure she had not been heard.

The constable shrugged. "I do not know. He could be the right age, and his hair is the right color. Dark brown. But the man looks rather unkempt, and is not of slender build, as I have heard tell Henry Belasysse is." He looked around. "Hank will be bringing him along in the wheelbarrow any moment. We came ahead so as to have the room prepared for the body's arrival."

Still whispering, Lucy asked, "And the manner of his death? Stabbed, as Hank said?"

The constable frowned. "Yes, several blows." He pulled out a knife. "With this, I presume. Found it nearby, near an offal pit. Like someone tossed it that way."

Gingerly, Lucy took the knife the constable held out to her. The knife was the kind with a spring that could be folded over and kept in a coat pocket, common among tradesmen and laborers. It was simple but sturdy, probably intended for the everyday cutting needs a man might encounter in his day's work. Her own brother, Will, had a serviceable knife just like this one.

This one had been well handled and used with some regularity. Opening it, she frowned as she took in the brownish stain along the metal surface. "The tip is broken," she commented, running her finger along the blade's edge. It was dull. "Not been sharpened for some time."

Lucy was about to hand it back to him when something about the wrought metal handle caught her eye. An insignia had been cut inexpertly into it, near the hilt. "A. B.," she read. "The initials of the blacksmith who made the knife?" she asked, looking up at the constable.

"More likely the initials of the owner," he replied. "The blade smith would have added the symbol of the guild, I would think, not a personal insignia."

Lucy handed the gruesome object back to the constable. "Perhaps they are the initials of the murderer," she said.

He shrugged. "If I could be so lucky. I will keep a lookout for a man named A. B., I suppose." He consulted his pocket-watch. "Hank should be here shortly with the body."

"Constable," Lucy said, hesitating, "do you think—?"

"That Miss Belasysse may have had something to do with the man's death? Lucy, I do not know. Given the state in which you found the woman, I think we cannot rule out that possibility."

Lucy thought of the woman upstairs. Could she be responsible for such a hideous deed? It was hard not to remember the blood on her dress. The cuts on her hands that Dr. Larimer thought might have been self-inflicted. The fit that Miss Belasysse had fallen into when she saw the bloodstained dress.

"Not to mention the coins," she murmured, half to herself.

"What?" the constable asked. "What coins?"

Quickly, Lucy explained about the coins that had been inexpertly sewn into the gown. Seeing him frown, she added, "But I can assure you, the woman's fear is true. She does not sleep well, and her melancholy strikes me as quite a real and terrible burden."

Duncan took a step closer. Lowering his voice, he stated the very thought she dared not speak. "That woman upstairs—Miss Belasysse—could be a murderess. You realize that, do you not?"

"She could be, I see that," Lucy admitted. "However, she might be wholly unconnected with that man's death."

"That may be true. Still, you must be vigilant."

"I will be," she said, touched by his concern. "No need to worry about me."

Duncan laughed. "Worry about you? Why ever would I do such a thing? I have seen you face down murderers before. I just meant that you should keep your ears open and mouth shut. She might tell you something important, which you can convey back to me."

"Oh," Lucy said, feeling a bit abashed. "I will do that."

Then he grinned at her suddenly and touched her shoulder. "But do take care. We know nothing of this woman, or of what she might be capable."

Hearing the physician's heavy tread in the corridor, the constable stepped away from Lucy. "We will be bringing in the body now."

Lucy nodded and went back up the stairs. But instead of returning to Miss Belasysse's chamber, she lingered at the top of the stairs, just out of view. Crouching down, she could hear Hank and Duncan as they wheeled the corpse into another room whose door had been closed until then.

"Watch it!" she heard Duncan growl.

"Pardon, sir," Hank replied.

Lucy moved quickly back down the steps and into the shadowy doorway of the drawing room so that she was not noticed. Mrs. Hotchkiss had been holding the door open. From her resigned expression, Lucy sensed that she had seen bodies carried in before. As she passed, Lucy heard her uttering a small prayer.

Softly, Lucy stole down the corridor until she stood by the half-open door of the room with the corpse. She wondered whether

Dr. Larimer would cut open the body. Though he and Sheridan did not perform surgery—such carnage was the work of tooth-pullers and barber-surgeons—she knew that Dr. Larimer at least possessed a keen interest in understanding the humors and other forces that worked on a body. She did not know if Mr. Sheridan shared that same interest.

Without making a sound, Lucy slipped in after the men to hear their conversation. Both physicians, Hank, and Duncan were all standing around the body, which had been laid atop a long table that seemed to have been designed for such an examination.

From what she could see, the man had rather greasy black hair. He looked to be in his thirties or even forties. He was wearing a common whitish-gray shirt with a brown wool vest over it, a black cord keeping the vest closed. His brown pants were loose fitting and dirty, and his leather boots looked well-worn. All the clothes of a tradesman, but of what trade she could not determine. If he had had a coat it was gone now. Maybe someone had stolen it.

For a few minutes, no one noticed her. Hank was the first to see her, and she raised her finger to her lips so he would not say anything. With a quick grin, he just shook his head at her.

Catching the bellman's motion, Mr. Sheridan turned around and, upon seeing her, frowned. "Miss Campion!" he exclaimed. "This is not for a young lady to see. Even one of your sort."

She rolled her eyes at his insinuation. Biting her lip, she looked at Dr. Larimer, who chuckled.

"I should send you out," he said. "But there might be something you can explain to Mr. Sheridan."

Lucy looked at the ceiling, trying to keep from smirking, lest she truly anger Mr. Sheridan. There had been another time, during a different examination of a corpse, that she had pointed out something the physician's assistant had missed. Indeed, he had never truly forgiven her for this bit of surprising knowledge.

Lucy sat quietly on a low bench while the men quietly conferred among themselves. Mr. Sheridan had uncapped a small jar of ink and picked up a long quill, preparing to take notes about what they discovered.

"Where was the body found?" she asked Duncan, who had come to stand beside her.

"About a half mile east of Holborn Bridge, where you encountered Miss Belasysse. Looked like someone had pushed a stack of bricks on top of him. Hank only found him after his third pass through that part of the debris."

"Looks like his nose was broken," Mr. Sheridan commented, studying the man's face. "See how the bridge is uneven. That was a fracture."

"Did the break occur recently?" Constable Duncan asked.

Dr. Larimer moved a lantern closer to the man's face. "I do not think the break was recent. I see no bruising around his nose or on his cheekbones, or any other swelling."

Nodding, Mr. Sheridan wrote something on the paper.

Dr. Larimer continued looking at the torso of the body. "He was definitely struck multiple times with a knife, including once in his left shoulder blade," he said. "However, the wounds appear to have been rendered unevenly, for they are not all equally deep." He looked up at Mr. Sheridan. "Remove his vest and shirt," he said.

Carefully, Mr. Sheridan cut the man's shirt open so that several long bloody gouges were revealed. Together the two physicians studied the wounds.

"The deepest blow, I believe the one that killed him, was

struck here, under his heart," Dr. Larimer said to the constable, who had come closer. He pointed to a deep gash on the man's chest. "But I do not think that was the first blow. Note these other wounds," he said, pointing to two other gashes. "I believe that he was struck from behind first. A downward movement of the knife, like so." He made a swishing gesture with his hand.

"Is this the knife?" the constable asked, producing the knife he had found near the body.

Mr. Sheridan picked up a measuring stick and compared it to the broken end of the knife. "Possibly," he said. "The measurement is very close, but we cannot say with certainty."

"Ah, but I think we can," Dr. Larimer replied. Very carefully he took up a pair of tongs and, opening one of the knife wounds with his fingers, managed to pull out a bit of broken blade. Wiping off the blood, he fit the knife and the broken part of the blade together. They fit together neatly.

He looked at the constable. "I suspect you have found your murder weapon," he said.

"Can we discover anything about the person who knifed him?" Duncan asked. "Can you tell the height of this man's attacker? Perhaps from the angle of the wound?"

"The man had to have been very tall," Mr. Sheridan said. "Given the downward trajectory of the initial wound."

Dr. Larimer clucked his teeth. "Not necessarily, my good man." He raised his hand very high, gripping one of his own instruments to demonstrate. "The blow could have been driven by fury or passion, not true strength. A woman could have delivered such a blow." He looked at the other men. "Help me stand him up."

Grimacing, Hank and the constable hauled the corpse to a standing position, so that the man's feet were on the floor. He appeared to be about the constable's height, maybe an inch shorter. "Body has begun to lose its rigor," the physician said.

"Let us see if a woman could have done this. Lucy, come here," the constable said. He handed her the knife. "Take this."

Lucy held the knife in her fist, with the blade pointing up, and gingerly waved the knife around.

"No, no," Dr. Larimer said. "The angle is all wrong. Turn the knife upside down, so that the blade is pointing down."

Lucy did as she was told, repositioning the knife in her hands.

"Come closer, Lucy," the constable commanded.

Trying not to breathe in the malodorous stench of the corpse, Lucy neared the dead man. Raising the knife as high as she could, she swung her arm down gently in an arc so that she very nearly touched the dead man's shoulder blade with the knife's jagged point. *This is what it feels like to kill,* she thought. A wave of nausea passed over her, and she dropped the knife.

"All right, Lucy, thank you," Duncan said, looking at her with concern.

Dr. Larimer nodded. "Yes. That was helpful. If we assume that this man was standing when he was struck, his assailant had to have been a bit taller than Lucy, at least by a few inches. Otherwise the angle of the wound would not match."

"So he was struck from behind. Then what?" the constable asked, picking up the knife from the floor.

The two physicians studied the man's body. "He has wounds on his hands, and then the wounds here and there on his chest," Dr. Larimer said.

Lucy tried to envision the scene. "He was struck from behind and turned around to face his attacker."

"And his assailant continued to slash at him," Duncan said.

"That explains the cuts on his hands. He was trying to ward off the blows."

"Two of the blows just glanced off his chest, as if he had managed to keep his assailant at bay," Mr. Sheridan said, and Dr. Larimer grunted his agreement.

From her corner, Lucy commented, "He has mud on his knees. Perhaps he was kneeling when he was struck."

"Lay the man back down, if you would," the physician instructed the men. "It was the last deep blow to his chest, a straightforward downward blow, that killed him. That was the last blow, too, because at that point the knife even broke off in his chest."

"So he fell backward and his assailant drove the knife in?" the constable asked. "A nasty business."

For a moment they all regarded the corpse. "Thus, we are unable to rule out a woman from having committed this vicious attack," the constable said, exchanging a quick glance with Lucy. "I need to speak to Miss Belasysse," he continued. "I need her to tell us if she knows who this man is. Please bring her here, Lucy. Do not say why I have summoned her. I would like to observe her reaction."

"Sir?" Lucy asked, turning to Dr. Larimer. "I have seen her thrown into a nervous fit over less."

The physician nodded. "Yes, we shall have her take her restorative first. That will keep her convulsions at bay, but still keep her lucid enough to answer your questions."

·13·

Her heart beating quickly, Lucy went upstairs and entered the chamber occupied by Miss Belasysse. The woman was tracing a long crack in the wall. She glanced at Lucy. "I thought you were planning to bring me a piece of pie or some cheese."

"Miss Belasysse," Lucy said, "Constable Duncan has returned, and he should like to speak with you."

A muscle twitched in the woman's cheek. "I do not think I should like to see him again. Send him away." Though her tone was haughty, Lucy caught the slightest undercurrent of fear.

Lucy sighed. "I do not think he will go away, miss. He is here because he—" She hesitated. "There is something he should like to show you. Something about which he desires your opinion."

Miss Belasysse swung her limbs over the edge of her bed and stood up, straightening her dress. "Very well, then," she replied. "Take me to him."

As they descended the stairs, Lucy wished she could warn the woman about what she was about to see. But Duncan had not given her leave to do so.

Miss Belasysse gripped her arm as they approached the room next to the physician's study. The constable was standing there, as if guarding the door, a grim set to his jaw.

"Lucy," she whispered, "I am frightened."

"I will stay with you," Lucy whispered back.

"Miss Belasysse," Duncan said. "Thank you for speaking with me again. I will get to the point."

The woman clenched her hand tighter around Lucy's arm. "Yes?"

"I regret to say that a man has been found dead, near Holborn Bridge where Lucy found you."

Miss Belasysse paled. "Dead?" she asked. "Who is h-he?" Then she began to sway. "Is it my brother?" She looked anxiously up at Lucy. "Is it Henry?"

"We do not know," the constable said, with a great gentleness. "We thought you might know him." He gestured to the door. "We have brought him here for examination."

"I hardly think I should be called upon to perform such a disgraceful undertaking," Miss Belasysse whispered, taking a step back.

"You must—!" the constable began, but fell silent when Lucy took the woman by both shoulders and looked into her eyes.

"Miss Belasysse," Lucy said, "I know what the constable has asked you to do seems a terrible thing."

The woman looked as if she were about to topple over. "I cannot go in there," she whispered.

"I do understand. If it were my brother, Will, in there—" Here, Lucy looked upward and sent a silent prayer of thanks that it was not.

Miss Belasysse stared into Lucy's eyes for a moment, and seemed reassured by what she saw there.

"I promise," Lucy continued. "It will be so quick. You need only look at his face for the most fleeting of moments. Is that not so, Constable Duncan?"

Duncan nodded and opened the door. It was clear he would brook no more dissent from the woman. He handed them both posies to hold before their noses.

They walked in, the stench of death assaulting their nostrils. Miss Belasysse nearly sagged. "I cannot—" she began, but Lucy caught her by the arm.

"You can," Lucy whispered, and half pulled the woman forward to the body lying on the table in the middle of the room. Thankfully the man's body, even his face, was completely covered by a white sheet.

Dr. Larimer looked at Miss Belasysse kindly. "I regret that we must ask you to do this," he said. "But I am afraid it is quite necessary. Are you ready, my dear?"

Miss Belasysse shrank back. "Can you not ask my uncle Harlan?"

"We sent word to your uncle, but we have not heard from him," Duncan said easily. Lucy glanced at him, wondering at his lie.

"If you would," Dr. Larimer said to Miss Belasysse. "It will just take one moment."

Mr. Sheridan glanced at Miss Belasysse and then drew back

the sheet, just enough that the man's head and shoulders were exposed. There was no evidence of his knife wounds or any of the blood they had noted before on his clothes. The doctors had evidently cleaned the body to make the viewing less distressing for Miss Belasysse.

Miss Belasysse started to tremble. "It is not my brother. Praise the Lord. I do not know this man." She turned away.

Lucy saw the constable exchange a glance with Mr. Sheridan. *Of course,* she realized then. Mr. Sheridan had already known that it was not Henry Belasysse, having known the man as a friend of the family. She did not think they would have compelled Miss Belasysse to look at the dead man otherwise.

"Please," Lucy said, touching the woman's arm. "Look more carefully this time. Are you certain that you do not recognize him?"

Miss Belasysse stood up and looked down at the man. "I tell you, I do not recognize this man." The faintest look of revulsion crossed her features. "How did he die?"

"Stabbed," Constable Duncan said, studying the woman's face. "Once in his back. And several times on his chest. The fatal blow was through his heart."

"How shocking," Miss Belasysse said, her eyes widening. Lucy saw her glance down at her bandaged hands before she clasped them together. Duncan also noticed the gesture.

Miss Belasysse turned back to Dr. Larimer. "Please, I feel rather unwell. I should like to return to my chamber now."

"Allow me," Mr. Sheridan said, extending his arm to her, then leading her out of the room.

"A bad business, to be sure," Dr. Larimer said to the constable. "What do you make of it?"

Duncan glanced at Lucy. "I do not believe her to be innocent in this man's death," he said. "There is something about her manner that suggests guilt."

"But she denied knowing him," Lucy said.

"Such denial means little, I should say," the constable replied. "She most certainly would not be the first person to lie about a crime she committed. Moreover, even if in truth she does not recognize him, that certainly does not prove her innocence in this man's death."

Lucy frowned but did not say anything more.

"I think many would feel affronted by the idea that the daughter of a baron would have committed murder," Dr. Larimer stated. Then he added, "I myself have come to believe that the murderer's ilk defies categorization by wealth or standing."

"What do you think, Lucy?" the constable asked. "Do you believe in your charge's innocence? I know you saw her rub the cuts on her hands when we discussed this dead man's knife wounds."

"I do not know," she admitted. "Could it be that the man attacked her, and she sought to defend herself?"

"By wresting the man's knife from his hands?" Duncan asked. "Could that be so?"

"Or she did this without knowing what she did?" Lucy said. Even to her own ears, her suggestion sounded weak.

Dr. Larimer shook his head. "You have seen her in a fit, Lucy. She is not sensible, which I can say with certainty. But she could not even walk of her own volition or drink a cup of water when a fit is on her." He sighed. "No, if she did brandish a knife in the manner we are purporting, then I think she would have been in possession of her senses."

The constable nodded. "The Lord Mayor is pressing me for action. I think he would be happy enough, with the evidence that is suggested by Miss Belasysse's demeanor, to place her under arrest."

"Oh, no!" Lucy protested. Even though Newgate had burnt down in the Great Fire, she could not bear the thought of Miss Belasysse being cast into jail. Her own brother had stood trial for murder a few years back, and the whole experience had been quite terrifying.

Constable Duncan shifted uncomfortably back and forth on his feet. "Her actions are questionable, surely you must agree."

"Please," Lucy said. "She is not well. You saw it yourself. Her fits."

The physician nodded. "I am rather afraid that if left unattended, the poor woman would die of the falling sickness in that terrible place. You would be condemning her to death, just by placing her under arrest, even before she came to trial."

"She is the daughter of a baron," Mr. Sheridan said, walking back into the room. Evidently he had caught the end of their conversation. "That has been confirmed. As such, we must treat her with the respect due her station."

Duncan clenched his jaw. Lucy could tell he was not happy with the direction the conversation had taken. "If she did commit this crime, she should stand trial, not be pardoned like her brother was. Yes," he added, seeing Lucy's surprised look. "I remember her brother's case well. Henry Belasysse was pardoned for the murder of a tanner, without even standing trial. It is not my inclination to protect criminals."

Lucy swallowed. He was well within his rights to arrest the

poor creature upstairs. The law was most certainly in agreement that it was up to the accused to plead their innocence, and right now things looked quite bleak for the woman.

But before Lucy could say anything, Duncan spoke again. "However, I should like to speak to her uncle and mother again. Something of their explanation sorely bothers me, and I should like to discuss these matters with them further." Then he frowned. "It is unlikely that her ladyship will receive me."

That was certainly so. He could hardly knock on Lady Belasysse's door and question the noblewoman about her earlier statements. He might not even be allowed to set foot inside their residence.

"Sir, your wife did invite them to partake in your Easter dinner on Sunday," Lucy said, looking over at Dr. Larimer.

The physician rubbed his chin. "That is so," he said.

"I thought that the constable might be on hand," Lucy said to Dr. Larimer, "when the Belasysses return, sir."

Mr. Sheridan made a funny sound in his throat. "I do not think that Lady Belasysse would be all that inclined to dine with a constable." He looked back at Duncan. "No disrespect of course, Constable Duncan," he said in his snide way.

"None taken, of course," Duncan replied easily.

"Very good, Constable. I cannot have you interrogating her while we dine, naturally, but I shall tell Mrs. Hotchkiss to set you a meal in the kitchen." Dr. Larimer looked at Lucy. "Is there something else?"

Lucy wanted to be on hand when the Belasysses returned to the physician's household. In a rush she continued. "Indeed, I was going to ask you, Dr. Larimer, if my brother, Will, and I might be here for dinner? In the kitchen, of course. Master Hargrave always gave his servants the day off on Easter, but I thought since I am tending Miss Belasysse, you should not like me to be very far away."

Mrs. Larimer walked in then, apparently catching only the last bit of Lucy's comment. "My heavens! Master Hargrave releases his servants from their duties on Easter?" She clapped her hands together. "However does the poor man fare? With a bit of cold mutton, I suppose. No, we shall invite him here. Herbert, send dear Thomas a note first thing."

"I will, my dear," Dr. Larimer replied. "A splendid suggestion, to be sure. I should very much enjoy seeing Thomas for Easter dinner."

"Oh, I must speak with Mrs. Hotchkiss," Mrs. Larimer exclaimed. She was about to walk out of the room when she stopped abruptly as though an idea had struck her mid-step. "Dear Lucy," she said turning around, "certainly you may join us. Your brother, too, if you like."

"Why, thank you, mistress," Lucy said, pleased and a bit stunned by the unexpected invitation. Constable Duncan gave her a quick smile, as though he understood the honor she had been bestowed.

"Not at all," Mrs. Larimer said, waving her hand. "I was hoping that you might be on hand to help serve. I remember that Master Hargrave always thought so highly of you, and I know that you were not one to spill or make waste. Then you may enjoy your meal with your brother at your leisure, once our meal has cleared. We should not need you very much after that. You may ask Molly for an extra apron. Unless, of course, you thought to bring one of your own?"

"Oh," Lucy said, feeling her cheeks warm a bit. Of course, as Miss Belasysse's nurse, she was not being asked to join the family for Easter dinner. Indeed, she had not expected such a thing. But even less had she expected to serve the family's meals. She did not quite know what to say. The cut from the slight was keen.

Not realizing what had just transpired, Dr. Larimer rubbed his hands together. "Just so, just so. We shall have a splendid dinner, I should think."

When the men resumed talking and Mrs. Larimer left, Lucy slipped out of the house and sat down on the bench under the old tree. Unshed tears stung her eyes.

The sound of a twig breaking behind her made her look up. Duncan was looking at her, a bit ruefully. "Thank you for inviting me to Easter dinner," he said. "That was quick thinking. I agree, it will be good for me to be on hand, should the Belasysses say anything of interest."

"So you can listen at the door, and with any luck, they will say something while I lay the ham before them," she said, trying to sound more merry than she felt. But it was hard to keep the bitter tone from her voice, and it seemed Duncan heard it, for he swiveled back to look at her.

"Something like that," he said, searching her face. Though he grinned at her, she could see the puzzled look in his eyes. "Lucy—" He hesitated. "Had you expected to be invited to dine with the family? When Lady Belasysse—Lady Belasysse!—is to be the guest of honor?"

Lucy shrugged and looked away. "Sometimes Master Hargrave would dine with us," she said.

"But in the kitchen, is that not so?"

When she didn't answer, he continued. "I beg you to give them

no mind. You are worth ten of them, there is no doubt of that."
He began to walk across the courtyard, to exit through the metal
gates to the path that led back to the street.

Before he left, he said, "And no matter what, I am very glad
to take a meal with you and your brother. It is an occasion I will
look very much forward to."

For a moment she smiled, before his next words chilled her.
"After all, we may very well find the evidence we need to arrest
Miss Belasysse for murder."

·14·

"Molly, deliver this note to the Hargraves, if you would," Lucy overheard Dr. Larimer tell his servant the next morning. They were in the kitchen, and Lucy was preparing a hot drink for Miss Belasysse. She assumed this was the invitation for the Hargraves to dine with them on Easter.

"After I am done with my slops?" Molly asked. "Mrs. Hotchkiss will be after me for certain. And my chopping?" She gestured to some potatoes. "Then after that I've got my pots, and Mrs. Hotchkiss says—"

They would never know what Mrs. Hotchkiss would say, for Dr. Larimer held up his hand. "Fine. Please take care of your more pressing tasks. We should not like to disturb Mrs. Hotchkiss. Within a half hour's time, if you would."

Seizing the opportunity, Lucy scrawled a note for Adam, hoping that he would not have to report to the Fire Court on a

Saturday morning. She did not write too many other details for fear of it landing in the wrong hands, but she did explain that she needed to speak with him about an important matter. Duncan's last words before he left the night before had disturbed Lucy more than she wished to admit. She pressed the note into Molly's hand before she left for the Hargraves' home. "For Adam Hargrave, you understand?"

About an hour later, Molly came to her. "Mr. Hargrave came back with me. I settled him in the drawing room." That the servant had done so suggested a stature for Lucy that was unexpected. For a wild moment, she thought to tell the girl that she could not receive visitors in such a way. Instead, she swallowed and replied, "Thank you, Molly."

When Lucy entered the drawing room, Adam stood up. He kissed her on the cheek and drew her to two chairs embroidered in an exotic style that Molly had told her was called "Turkey work." Dr. Larimer had just bought these chairs from a furniture dealer with ties to the East.

"Lucy," Adam said, his dark blue eyes searching her face. He pulled out the note she had written that morning from a pocket inside his coat. "Tell me the meaning of this. It sounds urgent."

"It is." Taking a deep breath, she then explained that the constable wished to arrest Miss Belasysse for murder. "I am quite concerned about her, you see. As one who suffers from the falling sickness she might not survive should she be imprisoned."

"Yes, I imagine that to be so." Like Lucy, he had seen inside the Newgate prison firsthand, and other jails, too, she suspected.

He knew the atrocities and fatal indifference that would await this woman before trial. "The law presumes guilt, not innocence, Lucy." Adam stood up and began to walk around. She had seen him do this before when he was trying to puzzle through a problem. His father did the same thing. "I am afraid that, other than being the alleged daughter of a baron, this woman has very little in her favor, and everything against it. The blood on her, the cuts on her hands—all suggest that she had wielded a knife. Then a man's body, full of stab wounds, turns up in the same area where she was discovered, witless—" He sighed. "It is not surprising to me that Duncan is suspicious of her. Lucy, does she deserve your goodwill?"

"I do not know, Adam. Someone claiming to be her husband followed us the other afternoon. Said her name was Erica Nabur. He knew all about her problems with memory. Said she frequently wandered off, which I suppose she has done in the past, according to her family. He tried to get her to leave with him. I think that is rather suspicious, too."

"Someone came after you?" Adam asked, tensing. "Why did you not tell me this straightaway?"

"Well, I am telling you now," Lucy replied, pressing her hands together. "I did not think to tell you—we were quite unharmed, you see."

She thought she would leave out the part where the man grabbed Miss Belasysse's arm and Lucy laid into him, kicking and punching. Adam most certainly would not like to hear about that, and she hated to trouble him further. "Besides, we told Constable Duncan directly after it happened."

"You went to see Duncan?" Adam sat back in his chair, pulling away from her slightly.

"Well, yes." Looking down into her lap, Lucy pulled idly at a thread on her skirt. Then she continued. "Miss Belasysse—though we did not know for certain that was her name—swore she did not know the man who claimed to be her husband. Of course we know that to be true. I asked about his papers and—"

"Oh, Lucy," Adam groaned. "You challenged him?"

Hearing the worry in his voice, she touched his arm. "I am sorry, Adam. I do not mean to trouble you." Trying to divert him, she continued on more brightly. "Do you not think it was suggestive that someone came after Miss Belasysse as he did? I think now that the man may have known who she was. If so, what did he want with her?"

Once again, Adam's eyes grew speculative. "Ransom? She is quite wealthy, of course. Or perhaps he had seen her in her addled state and thought it would be easy enough to have his way with a woman he could lay claim to as a wife."

Lucy cringed. She had not thought of that. She thought back to the man's shifty demeanor, and inwardly agreed that such a disgusting thing might have been on his mind.

"Well, we cannot dwell on that man right now. We have a more pressing matter at hand." She paused. "I was thinking. If she were indeed involved with that man's death, what if Miss Belasysse were not in her right mind when the murder occurred? If she were witless at the time of the crime, as she is now?"

Adam shook his head. "Very difficult to prove insanity, without a witness."

"And if she had been defending herself?" Lucy persisted. "Would that alter anything?"

"Such an act would be considered at best accidental killing, and at worst manslaughter," Adam explained. "If the former, she would not likely be hanged. If the latter, well, I cannot say. It would depend upon the nature of the judge and jury. Even if she were not hanged, she likely would still live out her days in prison. Hardly a better sentence, as you well know."

Lucy shivered. "Her brother, Henry Belasysse, killed a man. In a tavern. He was pardoned for the crime. Perhaps she might be as well."

Adam stroked his chin. "That happened a few years ago, did it not? I recall that event. I do not mind saying that both Father and I were unhappy with that decision by His Majesty. As you and I both know, there are many others who deserved a pardon for their alleged crimes, and killing a man should not be such an easily pardoned offense."

Lucy looked around, hoping that no one was passing by. His words bordered on treason. She did not know Molly or Mrs. Hotchkiss well enough to know where their loyalties lay. Seeming to realize this, he lowered his voice. "Indeed, her brother's pardon may bode poorly for her, as I remember there was quite a cry when people learned of it."

"I see," Lucy said. She recalled her brother's anger when he heard tell of the pardon. A jury might well feel similarly, as might a judge. "Could we find a witness to the murder? Maybe someone saw what truly happened to that man."

"How do you propose we do that?" he asked, a wariness appearing in his eyes.

"I was thinking to return to where I found her, by Holborn Bridge. The constable said the body was half buried under a pile of rubble not too far away. And I know people are living out there.

Someone must have seen something, I believe that to be true. I think the people who are living there might be more likely to speak to me than to the constable. If I could just go and talk to them—Adam, what is the matter?"

Adam had tensed at her words. "Lucy!" he exclaimed. "Do you hear what you are saying? What you are proposing could get you killed!"

"Adam, I—"

"Please, Lucy. Enough," he said, putting up his hand in his characteristic way. "I cannot allow you to traipse about the ruins looking for a witness to a murder! Heaven only knows what might befall you!"

Lucy clasped her hands together in frustration but did not say anything. Instead, she moved to the window, staring blindly out into the street. A moment later, Adam came behind her and gently turned her toward him. "I did not mean that I would not help you. If you can get an hour away from your nursing duties, I will accompany you to the site myself. See what we may discover."

She smiled up at him. "Thank you."

As they were talking, Mrs. Larimer entered the room. "Why, Adam Hargrave," she said, extending her hands. "Whatever are you doing here?" She glanced at Lucy. "Are you here to speak to my husband?" She linked her arm in his. "He is working, but allow me to bring you to him. Tell me, you and your father *will* be able to dine with us tomorrow evening, do say that it is so. Ever since your dear mother passed, I feel that I do not see you nearly as often as we ought."

"Yes, we are very pleased to dine with your family," he said, throwing an apologetic look at Lucy over his shoulder.

"We have the most interesting guest staying with us," Lucy heard Mrs. Larimer say, as they moved down the hallway toward her husband's study.

Lucy watched them, feeling a faint flush rise in her cheeks. *Stupid!* She berated herself. *No one would understand Adam Hargrave with Lucy Campion, former chambermaid. Such a thing can never occur.* Even if she was no longer sure about the depth of her feelings for Adam, the slight still stung.

Nevertheless, she followed them down the hallway in time to hear Dr. Larimer greet Adam. "Ah, Mr. Hargrave, it is good to see you. I trust Lucy has filled you in about our rather surprising patient?"

Adam nodded. "She has." He glanced at Lucy. "She also informed me that the constable might feel duty-bound to arrest the poor woman. What say you?"

Dr. Larimer scratched his nose. "Oh, blasted Jupiter! I do not wish to see it happen, but the dress was all bloody, and she has cuts on her hands. Those cuts suggest to me she had been using a knife recently. I have seen them on the hands of butchers, you see. Moreover, the man was probably killed a day or two before Lucy found her wandering about in her mad fugue. By her actions and demeanor, she has as good as admitted that she killed the man."

"But why? Who is he? What do we know of the victim?" Adam asked.

"We know very little of the man. His nose was broken, and he looks to have had a number of injuries, long healed. Nothing recent, except the stab wounds." Changing the subject, he asked, "And will you be joining us for a late Easter dinner tomorrow afternoon? At three o'clock? You received my note?"

"Yes, indeed," he said. "I am sure Father will confirm on our behalf." Glancing at Lucy, he said, "I daresay, I am rather intrigued by this whole matter. I might walk over to Holborn Bridge and explore the area a bit more myself. See what might be seen." Without hesitating, he added, "I thought Lucy might accompany me."

"Oh?" Mrs. Larimer asked, her brow rising. "How odd."

"I find it a sensible notion," Dr. Larimer said. "Lucy can show you where the woman was found. Besides, she has proved to be a very observant lass. She may see something else of interest."

Mrs. Larimer gaped at her husband. She drew him away from the others, but Lucy could still hear her whisper to him, "Have we not employed Lucy to look after Miss Belasysse?"

"Molly can watch her for a spell," he assured his wife. For him, the matter was decided. "And Mr. Sheridan should be finished with his patients, should Miss Belasysse need a physick. Truly, my dear, it is in all our best interests to get this matter resolved."

"What if it turns out that we have been harboring a *murderess*?" Mrs. Larimer hissed back.

"Then the easier it will be for me to breach my compact with her, as her physician," he replied. To Lucy and Adam, he said, "Go inform Molly that she must keep an eye on our patient. I have given you a few hours' leave."

"Thank you, sir," Lucy replied, before heading off to find Molly.

She found the servant polishing silverware, in preparation for the Easter dinner. Although Molly greeted her with a smile, that smile fell away when Lucy stated her request. "It will be just a short while, I promise," Lucy said.

But Molly was unconvinced. "Devil duty," she muttered. "That is what you are asking of me! It is not natural. Accursed, she is."

Lucy, however, was prepared for this resistance. She sidled closer to Molly. "How about for a red ribbon?"

Molly's eyes lit up, but remained wary.

"Two?" Lucy asked, looking quickly around. "They will look very pretty in your hair. You could wear them to Easter service. 'Tis a day for finery, after all."

Molly held out her hand, looking triumphant. Lucy hid a smile. She had another ribbon in her pocket and a penny as well, which she had been prepared to give up had Molly held out for more.

·15·

As Adam and Lucy walked to the burnt-out area, she was glad that for once the sun was beaming down, bringing a rare brightness to the day. She commented on that, and he remarked on the relief of better weather after the long dreary winter. Then they lapsed into silence, their earlier conversation still hanging oddly between them.

"You are quiet," he finally observed. "Are you being overworked by the Larimers?"

"Oh, no!" she said. "Indeed it is nothing like when I worked for—" She broke off.

"My father," he said, finishing her thought with a sigh. "Which reminds me. I imagine that my sister is halfway to the New World by now, and preparing to scold the magistrates there." Though he chuckled, he looked serious. "To be honest, although I cannot say I agree to their methods, there is something about the Quakers that I admire."

"What is that?" Lucy asked.

"Their insistence on following their conscience, to do what is right," Adam replied. "They are not shackled by convention and social niceties. They are only shackled, well, by the stocks and irons that seek to suppress them. They do not hesitate to rot in jail, should their conscience bid them to do so. That there is no man above another, that all should show deference only to the Lord—that is something that I admire."

Lucy glanced at him in surprise. She had heard him speak favorably of the sect before, but never with such admiration. "Adam?" she asked. "Has your conscience moved you to join the Quakers?" She gulped. "To set off to the New World, like Sarah has done?"

He gave a short laugh. "Ah, my poor father. Whatever would he do if both his children were lost to the Friends?"

But Lucy noticed that he did not answer her, and she did not press him. She was grateful when they arrived at Holborn Bridge shortly afterward.

"There I first encountered Miss Belasysse," she said, pointing to the approximate spot along the old river. "Over there"—she pointed again—"Constable Duncan and I found the small camp-fire and Miss Belasysse's dress." She led the way to the site and squinted as she peered in all directions. "I think that the man's body was found just over there," she said, "from what Constable Duncan told me."

Adam climbed on top of a pile of rubble and stared around. "Let us go that way," he said, pointing in a northeasterly direction. "I see some old homes that have not been cleared. Perhaps we can discover someone in the debris there."

Moving carefully, ever wary of breaking an ankle, they climbed over the rubble. Lucy was glad she was not wearing one of her few better dresses.

Beside another stone wall, Lucy found a mound that looked like a campfire. Indeed, there was a small tin cup pointing out of the ground. "Adam, I think someone might have been living here."

Kneeling down, Lucy carefully pushed the dirt around, and a warm ember touched her skin and she drew her hand back. "Someone had a fire here, early this morning."

Suddenly the desolate nature of the ruins began to affect her. Maybe feeling the same odd sensation, Adam drew closer to her. Lucy felt grateful for his nearness. She was about to speak when a flutter by another nearby ruin caught her attention. "Adam," she whispered, "I think someone is watching us." She crooked her finger very slightly. "Just over there."

"Who is there?" Adam demanded, standing in front of Lucy. "Show yourself!"

No one moved. Lucy still felt shivers of anxiety running up and down her back. It did not help that the wind picked up then, chilling her further.

Then an old woman emerged from the ruins. She was all in black, and her clothes were tattered and worn. She looked to have been living in the ruins for quite some time, although she seemed nothing like the Gypsies who sometimes roamed along the edges of London, with their colorful weavings and strange haunting songs. She looked more like the squatters who had taken up residence outside Covent Garden, likely forced there after the Great Fire destroyed so much of the city.

She stared at them now, arms crossed, eyes dark. "What's your sort doing here?" she asked. "Trying to send me off, are you? Not hurting anyone, am I?"

"We are not trying to run you off, madam," Adam said, with a slight bow. "Rather we seek information, about an event you might have witnessed, maybe a week ago. A man was killed very near here, and we would like to know more about how the act transpired."

The woman shrugged, not mollified by the gesture of respect. "Dunno nothing of that."

As she turned away, her tattered cloak parted, revealing an object tied about her neck. "Please," Lucy said, pointing to it. "What is that?"

The woman touched the piece. "Nothing to you, that is for certain."

"I saw something just like it on the woman I am now trying to help," Lucy called after her. "She is in great danger, I fear. Perchance you know something that might help her."

The woman paused abruptly at Lucy's words. Though she did not look at Lucy, she had cocked her ear and appeared to be waiting.

Lucy touched Adam's arm. "Will you stay here? I would like to speak to her alone."

When he nodded, Lucy approached the woman, who was still looking away. "I found a woman here, distraught and upset."

"What did you do to her?" the woman asked sharply. "Have her thrown in jail? Put her in the stocks?" There was a bitterness there. "What did you do with the amulet?"

"You know about the amulet!" Lucy exclaimed. "You knew the woman of whom I spoke."

The old woman grunted. She seemed to be waiting for an answer from Lucy before she would speak.

"She still has the amulet," Lucy replied. "She is resting, in the care of a physician. No—I do not jest," she said at the woman's incredulous look. "Truly, I have been requested to nurse her to health myself."

"Hmph," the woman muttered. "There is much wrong with that lass. More than a physician can cure."

"Did you see what happened to her?" Lucy asked. "Please, it is important. You must know that."

The woman shook her head. "No." She scrabbled at the ground with her stick. "It was easy enough to guess that she had been set upon."

"So you did not see what happened. Do you think anyone did?"

The woman shook her head. "I do not know. There are a few others who live out here, but like me, they move about. Keep to themselves. I can tell you this, though. If they saw something, not a one will come forward. The Lord Mayor's not going to set them up in some fancy place to live as their reward, is he? No, they will keep their mouths shut."

"Why are you talking to me now, then?" Lucy asked.

The woman stayed silent.

"You took care of her, didn't you?" Lucy pressed. "Why?"

"I do not know why. Reminded me of my daughter, I suppose. She came to me out of nowhere. So confused. Then she had one of those fits. Like my own daughter used to have. I thought she was the angel of my daughter coming to see me." She swallowed. "She was wearing them both around her neck." She held up her own amulet. "She took this one off and gave it to me. Said I was her protector and wanted me to have it."

"How did you help her?" Lucy asked.

"Thought she should hide the shine of wealth. Covered her amulet over with the scrap of taffeta. Put a bit of rosemary in first."

"Why? To help her remember?"

"Not to remember what had happened to her. To remember her name. And to help her with the demon inside her, bringing on her fits. Thought the rosemary would help."

Lucy nodded, making a note of this piece of information. This meant Miss Belasysse had already lost her memory when she came upon this dweller in the ruins.

The woman continued. "I made her take that blue dress off, too. Did not want to attract attention with all the blood. Besides, she seemed anxious-like. I started to burn the dress, but the flames got too high too quick, and I thought it might bring the wrong sorts a-visiting. So I doused it with some water I had planned to use to make a bit of rat broth."

Lucy gagged at the idea of eating rats. Seeing this, the old woman chuckled. "Cannot choose the delicacies we eat out here, now can we?"

"Never mind that," Lucy said, swallowing down the bile that had risen in her throat. "What happened to the woman? Why did you leave her?"

The woman sighed. "I went to beg for a bite to eat for me and her. From the market. I left her sleeping in a bundle of blankets. When I returned, she was gone. I searched all over for her."

"That must be when I found her," Lucy said, trying to reconstruct the events.

The woman nodded again. Then she placed a gnarled hand on Lucy's hand. "Please, miss. You seem a decent sort. That lass is not right in the head, anyone could see that. She does not deserve to be hanged. Not when there are sorts who would take advantage of a poor addled lass like that."

"Will you give your name? Testify on her behalf?" Lucy asked, a bit helplessly.

At that the woman gave a harsh chuckle. "I have nothing to say, do I? She was worse even when I found her. Looked more guilty than innocent, that is the only thing I could swear to. Just take care of her," she said. "Lord forgive us all our sins." With that she hobbled off, and Lucy did not detain her again.

Adam approached Lucy. "Did you learn anything?"

She started to recount what the woman had told her. However, before she had gotten very far, Adam held up his hand. "Do not tell me any more. Such hearsay can be read into evidence and will damn the woman for sure."

After that, they continued to search the ruins for anyone who might have known something about what happened to the woman, to no avail. Not another soul stepped forward, although Lucy sometimes felt that there were others hiding and watching.

Finally, after an hour, Lucy said, "I must get back."

As they walked, Adam said, "From what I can determine, there remain several great questions." Ticking off his fingers, he said, "One, what is the identity of the man who was killed?"

"And who murdered him," Lucy interrupted.

He nodded. "Yes, two. Who murdered him? Three—"

"Did Miss Belasysse know the murdered man or not? Has she forgotten him? Was she lying?" Lucy interrupted again.

"Yes. And four . . ." He looked at her expectantly, a slight smile on his face.

Lucy thought about it. "Four. Well, the question we've had since we first realized that she lost her memory. Where has Miss Belasysse been this last year?"

"Precisely. We do not yet know how to answer the first three questions. I think we should focus on the one we might be able to answer. At least we have access to the source."

"She cannot remember anything," Lucy reminded him doubtfully.

"Well, then we need to pay attention to what she says. She may reveal more than she intends to." He began to walk more purposefully. "Tomorrow, when we speak to the Belassyses, we must find out what else they know. Someone is hiding something about her disappearance, that much is certain. And at least *they* cannot claim to have lost their memory."

·16·

The Easter-morning church bells had been ringing, calling sinners to their fold with each chime. Lucy, however, was to stay home from the service and tend to Miss Belasysse. Dr. Larimer did not believe that the frail woman could handle the press of people, or, as Lucy suspected, the interminable length of one of the minister's sermons. "All we need is for Miss Belasysse to have one of her fits while praying in the presence of the Lord," she had overheard the physician say grimly to Mr. Sheridan, "and she'll be strung up, to be sure."

Lucy had shivered, but inwardly agreed. Even though it was unlikely that the congregation would actually hurt a patient who was under the protection of Dr. Larimer, certainly their goodwill would not last should they witness one of the frenzies in which the devil himself seemed to have taken hold of her wits and body.

As the bells continued to chime, Lucy felt a qualm pass over her. It was strange to stay home from church, particularly on Easter Sunday. Even a few years ago, when the flush and chills of a distempering fever had been heavy upon her, she had been present to hear the minister's words. Only in the most dismal days during the plague had she not attended church, and she prayed now that the Lord would forgive her this absence from his house. Hopefully, he would also forgive her the secret joy she had felt when informed she had been excused from sitting on the numbingly hard pews for the entirety of the morning service.

As was the custom every Sunday, everyone in Dr. Larimer's household would walk to church together, and all but Mrs. Larimer and Miss Belasysse had already assembled. Being Easter, everyone looked noticeably cleaner, having all bathed in lilac water last night, each one having his or her turn in the tub. Now all were wearing their best church-going clothes. Molly was wearing the red ribbons that Lucy had just given her. As Lucy had suspected, the Larimers had overlooked this girlish indulgence. Mr. Sheridan looked a bit tidier than usual, although he had not discarded his common dour expression. He was tapping his foot now as if eager to be off.

Finally, the two women arrived. Dr. Larimer called out to Miss Belasysse as she approached them. "Ah, Miss Belaysse," he said. "Your family will be joining us this afternoon for a late Easter dinner."

Lucy watched her warily, to see whether that announcement would provoke any distress. But the woman just nodded and asked, "Has there been any news of my brother?"

"None, I am afraid."

"I am very much looking forward to resuming my acquaintance

with your mother and uncle tonight, my dear," Mrs. Larimer said to Miss Belasysse. "Dear me, your sister-in-law is so very young, is she not?"

"My brother married her when she was but thirteen," Miss Belasysse said. "At the urging of her parents, he complied." She turned to Lucy. "I hope you will be on hand for Easter dinner this afternoon?"

"Oh, yes, Lucy has kindly agreed to help serve," Mrs. Larimer said.

"Help serve?" Miss Belasysse asked, looking at Lucy in great surprise. "I am very much hoping that Lucy will be seated with us for Easter dinner."

"Oh," the physician's wife said, looking embarrassed. "I do not know that"—she lowered her voice as if doing so would keep Lucy from overhearing her words—"it would be quite proper if Lucy joined us at our table. Your *mother* will be there. As a baroness, I hardly think, dear, that Lucy is quite the right company—"

"I need Lucy at my side," Miss Belassyse interrupted. "I do not want her to serve me. I want her seated alongside me."

"Oh, dear," Mrs. Larimer said. She looked at her husband, who just shrugged. He was clearly not going to get involved. "Very well. Lucy," she said in a loud voice, "I should very much like you to join us for dinner." Her voice was strangled. "Will your brother be dining with us as well?"

Lucy hid a smile. It was clear that the thought of being joined by another person in trade was not particularly palatable to Mrs. Larimer. "I did receive a note from my brother that he planned to spend Easter with Master Aubrey and Lach. They are heading to the Swan. But"—she hesitated—"I had hoped that he would be able to keep Constable Duncan company."

"Constable Duncan?" Mrs. Larimer repeated, looking at her husband.

"Yes, I consented to this yesterday," Dr. Larimer said, starting to tap his feet. "Let us go now before we are late for the service."

"The constable? Oh!" Lucy could hear Mrs. Larimer say as they began to walk down the street. "What ever will Lady Belasysse think?"

Once everyone else had left, Miss Belasysse tugged at the embroidery that Mrs. Larimer had left for her. When Lucy set a cup of hot mead down beside her, she was surprised to see how quickly knots had formed in the delicate material.

"Miss, may I be of service?" Lucy asked, gently taking the wooden hoop from her. "The threads ought to go thusly." She began to show her the proper method.

Miss Belasysse pushed it away. "Just take it, Lucy!" she said irritably. "Never have I had much skill with a needle. My nurse-maids, you see, always thought I would fall into a fit and prick myself." She grimaced. "I suppose dear Mother was concerned that I would bleed all over her precious cloth, and that it would be ruined. I am sorely lacking in all of the feminine arts, you see."

She began to laugh then, an odd shrill noise that sounded like she was close to tears. "Shall I prick myself? Shall I bleed? Have I not bled enough?"

"M-Miss Belasysse?" Lucy asked, hesitantly. "Perhaps you should have a bit more of your tisane? I think that would calm you—"

"Am I a hysteric? Are you afraid of me now, Lucy?" She

began to laugh harder, even more uncontrollably. "Perhaps you should be!"

"I am not afraid of you," Lucy said, trying to keep her feelings of misgiving out of her voice.

Miss Belasysse stopped laughing abruptly then and instead heaved a great sigh. She slumped back in her chair. "I fear I have used up my few spirits this morning. If I am to have strength for this afternoon, I must rest." Seemingly with great effort, she removed herself from the room. Lucy heard her clomp inelegantly up the stairs as if the weight of the world had once again descended upon her.

That is the melancholy speaking, Lucy thought, trying not to feel irritated. Dr. Larimer had warned her that there would be little they could do once her melancholic mood began to descend more fully. Still, Lucy never had the luxury of lying about in her bed, even on the few occasions when she had been quite ill. None of her masters, as just as they were, would have brooked such slovenly and lazy ways.

Even as those thoughts ran over her, Lucy felt a pang of remorse at her annoyance. Living with the falling sickness was certainly a bane upon Miss Belasysse's being that would never be lifted in her lifetime.

Lucy began to wander about the physician's empty house then, wondering what she should do. She could not let herself be idle, even on the Lord's Day. She ran her hand across the closed door of Dr. Larimer's study, wishing she could go inside to look at his books. What it would be like to take one of his books and sit in the garden to read, or even, more shockingly, stretch out on her bed and throw herself wholeheartedly into the words as she had never been allowed to do. But such an act was nearly akin to treachery, for she had no good reason to be in his study when the family was out of the house or to take his belongings without his knowledge.

Instead, Lucy did things here and there that might reasonably fall under her duties as Miss Belasysse's nurse. She started a stew for the family to eat when they returned home from service, to tide them over until they sat down for dinner at three. She checked that Mrs. Hotchkiss had properly laid out the forest green gown Miss Belasysse was to wear that evening, another frock loaned to her by Mrs. Larimer. As she moved about the room, she was careful not to disturb the woman, who seemed to have fallen back into a restless and unforgiving sleep.

After that, to pass the time, Lucy pulled out the tract she had begun to write the other day. "*A Tale Most Strange, of a Woman Found near Holborn Bridge,*" she said out loud, then crossed the words out heavily with several swipes of her pen. Turning the paper over, she started again. "*A Death Along the River Fleet, or—*"

She paused. What would be the second part of the title? She ran the quill back and forth across her cheeks, until she straightened up with a smile. She began to write again. "*Or, The True Account of a Most Strange Murder That Did Occur at Holborn Bridge.*"

With the title in place, she began to write in her laborious uneducated script, a tract about the murder that she hoped would please Master Aubrey.

Hearing the church bells chime two hours later, she decided to go outside to collect a few of the flowers she'd seen beginning to grow along the grassy stretch in front of the house.

Leaning against the stone wall of the house, Lucy stared up at the clouds, enjoying the slight warmth of the sun on her cheeks. Above, two birds flitted by, chirping at each other, and a third followed with a twig in its beak. Readying for a nest, no doubt, she thought. Taking a great breath, she inhaled the fresh April air with a sense of deep enjoyment.

These last few hours had been rather precious; indeed, she could not remember the last time she had done such little labor. With a guilty pang she thought of the unopened Bible upstairs, and she said a little prayer to God, asking him to forgive her for indulging in what was truly a merry pastime. However, she could not wait to finish the tract and give it to Master Aubrey. Would he think it fine enough to print?

"If he does not like it, I will change it until he does," she whispered to herself. "And won't Lach be mad when Master Aubrey prints another of my pieces?" She giggled, thinking of how annoyed the redheaded printer's devil would be if he had to sell another of her pieces on the streets. "I should turn it into a ballad, and hear him sing my words."

The sun went behind the cloud then, and a brief darkness overcame Lucy's thoughts as well. *How lucky I have been, to be apprenticed to Master Aubrey,* she thought. *Whatever shall I do if he should choose not to keep me on?*

Get married, she supposed. As always, her thoughts drifted then to Adam, and to Duncan, too. In particular, she remembered the exchange she had had with Adam the other day. These last few weeks, since the day they had all saved Sarah from the clutches of a murderer, he had still been kind and courteous, but she'd sensed a new reserve there. He had not otherwise sought to renew his addresses and indeed, seemed to be in a waiting, watchful state. Only when they had spoken in Dr. Larimer's courtyard had she seen the reserve fall away. "Have you left Master Aubrey's employment?" he had asked, his tone so wistful. And then so disappointed when she said she never wanted to leave the printer's shop.

Was she daft? Some people would say so, she knew that for certain. But others would say she was the practical one, and he the fool. Had Mrs. Larimer not been wholly astonished by the notion that she might sup with Lady Belasysse? Lucy could scarcely imagine a day when she would ever be truly welcome in the circles in which the Hargraves traveled. And then there was Duncan—

Her thoughts were interrupted when someone coughed. "Pardon me, miss."

Lucy's eyes flew open. A tall, thin man dressed completely in black was standing before her, a large black satchel gripped in his hand. He wore a somewhat worried expression on his face. "This is the residence of Dr. Larimer, is it not?"

"The doctor is not here. He is at Easter service," Lucy replied. *As so should you be,* she added to herself. She looked at him more closely. "Why do you ask? Are you in need of a physician?"

He opened his bag. Lucy could see it was full of bottles and vials. "I am an apothecary," he said. "I thought he might have interest in my wares."

Lucy looked at him doubtfully. "I do not know how Dr. Larimer obtains his medicines. I am sure you should take it up with him directly." She started to go, when he put his hand on her arm.

Growing alarmed, Lucy jerked her arm away, even as the man apologized. "Miss, I am sorry, I did not mean to offend you. I just wanted to speak with you. The patient you are looking after, is she a young woman? Maybe a little older than yourself? I thought I saw you with her yesterday."

"Who is she to you?" Lucy asked, with a quick glance up and down the street. She could see the first few people returning home after their church service had concluded. Their presence soothed her somewhat. Surely they would pay heed if the man attacked her. "Do you know her?"

The man was starting to look visibly nervous now, sweating. He held out a large vial toward her. "Please. For her fits. It will help her. I promise what I say is true."

"Why in heaven's name should I trust you?" Lucy asked, making no move to take the bottle. "This could be poison!"

"Please, I would never hurt her. You must believe that to be so." Then, to her surprise, he unstoppered the bottle and took a great sip. "See? It is harmless. Why would I wish to poison myself?" Before she could reply, he continued. "Please, if this were a deadly bane, I'd be turning blue, gasping for breath, or going into spasms right now. Am I doing any of those things?"

When Lucy only stared at him, he replied. "Nor, I promise, will I succumb to a long-lasting poison in three days' time. Can you please just believe that I am trying to help her? Have your physician test it first. He will know what it is, I can assure you."

"Who are you?" Lucy asked. "Tell me why you have brought this medicine to her. Who is she to you?"

"I do not wish to say," he said, his words coming out in a rush. "Please, believe me. I do not wish to bring her any harm. In God's name, on this holiest of holy days, I ask that you please just give her the tincture—sixty, eighty, or a hundred drops, more or less, as her distemper requires—and when in extremity, thrice or four times a day." He spoke even faster. "Well mixed in a glass of sack or other wine. Have her take it first thing in the morning, and the last at night. Do you understand?" He peered at her intently.

"Yes, no—who are you? How did you know about her?" Lucy persisted.

"Please, repeat it to me. I must know that you understand the dose."

Seeing that he would not be dissuaded, Lucy dutifully repeated the instructions he had just told her. Years of remembering ingredients and recipes with Master Hargrave's cook had made such a skill come naturally. This recipe seemed particularly easy to recall.

"I must go," the man said, looking more nervous when the lanky figure of a young man could be seen walking directly toward them and even more nervous still when the man called out a greeting. "Good Easter, Lucy!"

It was Sid, a pickpocket Lucy had met on streets of London, before the Great Fire. An orphan, Sid had long survived the streets by stealing a bit of this here and a bit of that there, but for the last few months, he had been doing odd jobs for Master Hargrave and seemed to be mending his ways. They were friends, although he could be a scamp and a bit of a rogue.

"That is all I may do for now." The man in black turned and began to walk quickly away. "I must go. Godspeed."

"Wait, stop!" Lucy called.

"What was that all about?" Sid asked, a mischievous look on his face. "Stepping out on young Master Hargrave?" Giving her a mocking bow, he held a note toward her. "A note from his father, for Dr. Larimer."

After taking the note, Lucy gripped his arm. "Sid," she whispered. "Please, I need you to follow that man. Find out where he is going. Do not let him out of your sight."

Sid looked down at her. "Desperate, are we not?" His tone was still teasing.

"Please, Sid. I must know." When he didn't move, she tried to explain. "He told me that he is an apothecary, and he seems to have some knowledge of a woman in my charge. I need to know more about him. Please, follow him quick. He is almost out of sight!"

In a most infuriating way, Sid yawned. "Depends. What is it in for me?"

"Half a crown," she said desperately, regretting the huge sum the moment it came out of her mouth. She batted away his hand. "Not now. Early tomorrow morning. Whistle near the kitchen, and I will meet you there." She pointed to the large oak tree still mostly bereft of leaves. "Be quick now, or you will lose sight of your prey."

"Right-o!" Sid replied, finally taking off.

Lucy stared after the young thief for a moment. She knew she did not have to warn him to take care. In his years of being orphaned on the streets, Sid had long ago learned how to look out for himself, and become adept at the art of thievery, even if he was not always as subtle as he assumed. He had, however, proved himself quite helpful and resourceful in the past, when she had needed his assistance. She could only hope that he proved so useful today.

Before long, Dr. Larimer's family and servants returned from Easter service and began to settle in for the afternoon. Lucy waited anxiously for a time to speak to Dr. Larimer privately.

This moment finally occurred when Mr. Sheridan went to check on Miss Belasysse, Mrs. Larimer followed the servants into the kitchen to confer about Easter dinner, and Lucy was able to follow Dr. Larimer into his study. In her pocket, she had both the letter and the vial.

She handed him the note first. "From Master Hargrave."

"Ah, wonderful!" Dr. Larimer said, reading the note. "Thomas has confirmed the presence of himself and his son for our Easter meal. Lucy, would you be so good as to inform my wife?"

"Certainly, sir," she said. More hesitant now, she held out the vial. "There was another delivery as well."

"Oh? On Easter Sunday?" he asked, still glancing at his letters on his table. "From whom?"

"From a man who promised that this substance would help Miss Belasysse control her fits." Lucy found herself plucking at the folds in her skirt, but forced herself to stop. *Young ladies do not fidget,* she could remember Mrs. Hargrave reminding her daughter, Sarah, on many an occasion. Lucy strove to remember such lessons even if, strictly speaking, they had not been intended for her.

Dr. Larimer put down his quill and stared at her. "Whatever do you mean? Who was this man?"

Lucy told him about the man who had stopped at the house. "He knew all about her condition," she explained. "Unlike the other man who tried to trick us into thinking she was his wife, this man seemed genuinely concerned about her."

Frowning, Dr. Larimer took the bottle. "I do not like this," he said. "It could be poison."

"I thought so, too," Lucy agreed. The man had seemed so eager to help, though, and there was such a sadness there, that deep in her heart, she believed that the stranger's intentions were good. "He did drink a bit of the liquid to prove that he was not seeking to poison her."

"He did, did he?" Dr. Larimer asked, still regarding the vial with distrust. Carefully, he unstoppered the container and poured a bit of liquid into a small marble bowl, holding it close to his eyes so he could see the color.

"He said he was an apothecary?" the physician said over his shoulder. "What did he look like?"

Lucy described the man. Though she did not say this to Dr. Larimer, she had been struck by the man's soulful nature as well as the dark circles that ringed his eyes. He had been a man who did not sleep well, of that she was certain.

"All in black, you say?" he asked. "That sounds about right. Apothecaries always wear black, to show how seriously they take their practice. They are a solemn lot."

Dr. Larimer rolled the drops about in the bowl, before he held it to his nose and sniffed. "He certainly knew how to mix the potion properly. Strange, I thought I knew most of the apothecaries in London," the physician mused. "Even before the Fire, when their hall at Blackfriars was destroyed, there were only but a few plying their trade in the City. All members of the Society of Apothecaries. Any would know to speak to me directly. Or Mr. Sheridan." He looked at Lucy. "Why would he approach *you* in such a manner?"

"Maybe he is lying about being an apothecary, and could not run the risk of you questioning him. He could have pilfered the vial from someone else," Lucy replied, watching him work. "Still, he knew that she would be in need of this medicine."

Finally, Dr. Larimer put the tiniest bit of the liquid on his littlest finger and gingerly touched it to his tongue. With a grimace he said, "St. John's wort and perhaps a few other ingredients. Yes, it could work. No, it is not poison. I should like to confer with Mr. Sheridan first, who I believe is with Miss Belasysse right now. Come along, Lucy."

A few moments later, they entered the bedchamber. "We have a medicine that may help your fits," Dr. Larimer said to Miss Belasysse, passing the vial to Mr. Sheridan. "An apothecary stopped by with it earlier, and gave it to Lucy."

Miss Belasysse had been lying in the bed, but sat up abruptly at Dr. Sheridan's words. "An apothecary?" she asked.

"Wherever did that come from?" Mr. Sheridan said, uncorking the bottle. Setting the bottle down on the table beside the bed, he gingerly sniffed the cork. "What apothecary is selling on the Lord's Day?"

"Someone brought it for Miss Belasysse," Lucy said, watching the woman's face. She'd seen a flash of recognition there. "Moreover, I think she knows who it was."

"No," Miss Belasysse said, starting to tremble. "I do not know who brought it, but somehow I can remember that this is no poisonous bane."

Before anyone could stop her, she picked the vial off the table and took a deep swallow.

"Miss!" Dr. Larimer said, scandalized.

They all watched her carefully.

"I am fine," Miss Belasysse said, wiping her lips. She put the vial back on the table and lay back. "I cannot tell you how I knew, but I am certain that it was not a poison. I-I remember this taste.

You will see, I soon shall be resting more comfortably than I have in days."

"But how can you be so certain?" Mr. Sheridan said angrily.

She smiled slightly. "I remember someone telling me something as I would drink it. *This will soothe those wild beasts inside you,*" she said softly, her eyes glazing over a bit as she tried to grasp the memory. "I knew it would be all right. I can almost just remember."

They all watched her.

"What do you remember?" Lucy asked her.

The woman opened her eyes and shook her head. "No, the thought has fled. I almost remembered something, though."

Is this a trick? Lucy wondered. The woman had already admitted to regaining some of her memories. Miss Belasysse, she noticed, did not meet her eye.

The elixir, whatever it contained, seemed to be having a powerful effect on the woman. She looked up at Mr. Sheridan. "James, am I to be arrested?" she asked, terror creeping into her voice. "I know you all think I have something to do with the murder of that man. That corpse you brought here the other day. I know you do!"

He sighed. "The constable has his suspicions. I do not know what will happen. I will try to keep such a travesty from occurring, I promise you that." He touched her shoulder before he left.

"I expected as much," she said hazily. "I wonder what my family will say." Tears began to slip down her cheeks. "Please, I cannot go to prison. I will not survive the shame of it."

"Now, now," Dr. Larimer said. "Let the elixer lead you to sleep." He left as well.

Lucy sat beside her. "The man who brought this medicine to you," she said, watching Miss Belasysse's face. "He said he was an apothecary. And he knew what you needed. Do you know who he might be?"

But the medicine was already taking effect, and she sank back against her pillow. As she drifted off, Lucy heard her whisper, "Please help me. Please. I must escape this place. Help me fly, fly away."

·17·

Just after two o'clock, Lucy put the final touches on Miss Belasysse's hair, in preparation for the family's Easter dinner. The woman had slept heavily since drinking from the vial, seemingly without dreaming, for she had not moved or uttered even the smallest of grunts during her slumbers. Now Lucy had successfully managed to sweep her hair into several ringlets, dangling at the side of her neck in the French fashion. She straightened Miss Belasysse's dark green gown so that the pointed bodice no longer bunched up and the long pleats of her skirts fell evenly from her waist. This was not such an easy task, for Miss Belasysse kept pacing about, wringing her hands, peeking out the window.

"What shall I say to them?" she kept asking. "What can I say?" She put her hand to the base of her head. "Oh, my head pains me so."

"Shall I send your excuses to Mrs. Larimer?" Lucy asked. "Tell them your headache has overcome you?"

"No, I must see them," Miss Belasysse said, grimacing. "There is still much I need to know." She touched her bare neck.

The amulet was missing. "I thought the chain was pleasing to you, and"—Lucy hesitated—"the amulet seems to bring you such comfort."

Miss Belasysse touched her neck and throat again. She seemed to be considering something before she spoke. "Truth be told, I had forgotten about it," she said lightly. "I removed it for my bath. But yes, it is lovely. Let us restore it to its proper place. It is in the drawer."

How odd, Lucy thought. To have forgotten her amulet, when she reached for it so frequently, seemed strange. But Lucy's long years as a servant kept her from pointing out the oddity of the woman's claim. Instead, she silently retrieved the amulet from the drawer.

Miss Belasysse sat back on the low embroidered bench so that Lucy could affix the amulet around her neck. Reaching up, the woman gently rubbed the bloodstone between her forefingers so that it gleamed against her skin. "I must say, Lucy, I feel better already with it around my neck. The protection it provides warms me." She then said something to herself that Lucy did not quite catch. She thought, though, that the woman said, "They need to know what they have done."

"Miss? I did not hear what you said."

But Miss Belasysse only laughed. Her mood seemed to be changing, as the excitement of the evening ahead overcame her. "Oh, nothing of consequence, I can assure you. Why do you not go on downstairs, Lucy? I will join you shortly. My head still aches a bit, so I would like to spend a little time by myself, to gather myself together."

She laughed again, as if another merriment had been told her.

Silently, Lucy poured a few drops of the apothecary's elixir into a small cup and handed it to her. She did not like this new airiness about Miss Belasysse; her gaiety seemed forced. Even the moroseness seemed preferable to this jittery excitement.

Having nearly half an hour before the Larimers' guests would arrive, Lucy headed toward the kitchen, wondering if Constable Duncan had come yet.

Lucy smoothed her skirts before entering the kitchen. She was wearing her best Sunday dress, but it was nothing compared to the Easter finery that the other women would surely be wearing. Mrs. Larimer could be generous to the daughter of a baron who had arrived on their doorstep without a frock to her name, but it would never have occurred to her to lend a former servant a nicer gown for the occasion. Sometimes Lucy wished that she had accepted the dresses that Master Hargrave had offered her after his wife passed away, but she felt by all rights that they should go to his daughter. The problem with dear Sarah, though, was that she had given up her worldly goods when she became a Quaker, and had sold off several of the gowns to fund her return voyage to the Massachusetts Bay Colony.

Passing into the kitchen, she found Constable Duncan sitting at the kitchen table, a cup of tea in front of him. He was not wearing his characteristic red coat, but rather a suit that might have once belonged to a slightly larger man. He stood up when he saw her.

"Lucy!" he said, his eyes regarding her with warm appraisal. "How wonderful you look!"

She pushed a stray hair behind her ear. "Do you mind?" she said hurriedly to the constable without any greeting. "Dr. Larimer asked me to join the family for dinner this afternoon. Well, truly it was Miss Belasysse who asked me to join them. As you know, Mrs. Larimer intended that I would serve them——" Here she dropped off, looking guiltily at Mrs. Hotchkiss and Molly. "I do beg your pardon."

Molly tossed her head. "You are not one of them, you know." She smiled coyly at Duncan. "But we are fine without you here."

Lucy turned back to Duncan, trying to ignore Molly. "With any luck, you will be able to loosen Hetty's tongue."

"He could loosen mine," Molly said, winking at him.

Mrs. Hotchkiss pinched Molly's arm. "Enough of that." She pointed to a great jug of red wine on the table. "Dr. Larimer is quite kind to us *servants* on Easter," she said. "We will be merry enough, I am certain. Tongues will be loosened, never you fear." She practically pushed Lucy out of the door. "Go now. There is no place for you here."

Finding the drawing room empty, Lucy wandered about, straightening the pewter. She was slightly bothered by the way Mrs. Hotchkiss and Molly had spoken to her just now, and for a moment, she wished she could just be dining and drinking wine in the kitchen with the others.

Still waiting, Lucy began to arrange the jars of bluebells so that the delicate petals did not look wilted. She did not otherwise know what to do with herself, and was quite glad when the Hargraves arrived a bit early.

With a shy smile, Lucy greeted Master Hargrave and Adam.

"You look lovely, my dear," Master Hargrave said to her, and to her delight gave her a little bow. She giggled, and her shyness fled. Adam pressed her hand as well. "I like seeing you here," he whispered to her.

Dr. Larimer and his wife entered then as well, the men greeting each other with handshakes and much clapping of arms.

"Is Miss Belasysse all right?" Dr. Larimer asked Lucy in a low tone.

"She said her head pains her," Lucy replied, "but she is planning to join us in a few minutes' time." Mr. Sheridan frowned, having caught her words as he entered the room.

"I will look in on her," Mrs. Larimer said to her husband. "I should not like her family to think we have not tended to her properly."

Lucy flushed, not sure if the words of the physician's wife had been a rebuke. Miss Belasysse had asked to be alone, after all.

To her surprise, Dr. Larimer leaned forward and whispered, "Do not worry, Lucy. You have done a fine job tending to our guest. My wife just has visions of dining at the baron's home one day, and she should not like the opportunity to pass her by."

"I am looking forward to meeting this mysterious guest of yours, Herbert," Master Hargrave said to Dr. Larimer, an amused look in his eye. "Octavia Belasysse, believed to be dead for ten months, but instead discovered by our Lucy, near Holborn Bridge. Adam has told me something about this odd tale."

"Thomas, indeed, it is rather a strange affair. I must admit, I invited you and Adam here today with the hopes of discovering a bit more about her whereabouts," Dr. Larimer said.

"Was she well tended these last ten months?" Master Hargrave asked.

Dr. Larimer exchanged a glance with Mr. Sheridan. "It is difficult to say. She arrived at my doorstep with a variety of recently sustained injuries. She bore the marks of being bound in ropes. Yet it was clear that she has been eating; the flesh on her bones was not loose and pulling, and her color has been mainly good. She has had some bloodletting done on her neck, carried out—I presume—to lessen the regularity of her fits or perhaps to treat her memory. She has not been living in the rubble—that much I can say with certainty."

"Dashed odd," the magistrate said.

At a knock at the door, Dr. Larimer arose from his chair to greet Lady Belasysse, Susan Belasysse, and Harlan Boteler. Hetty, it seemed, had already been led by Mrs. Hotchkiss back to the servants' dining area by the kitchen.

After making introductions, he turned to Susan Belasysse. "I take it there has been no word from your husband?"

The younger woman nodded. "No, he has not yet returned." She glanced at Lady Belasysse, who sniffed.

"I daresay my son will rejoin us soon," Lady Belasysse said. "I imagine that my daughter-in-law simply misunderstood when my son informed her of where he was going." She turned to look down the long bridge of her nose at Susan Belasysse. "I wonder if you were too busy with your new frocks, my dear, and did not attend to what he told you." Ignoring her daughter-in-law's offended expression, she continued. "My son sometimes will journey to visit friends, or attend to political matters. Sometimes life in the country can be a bit *dreary* for his taste, I am afraid."

Lady Belasysse looked around the room then, her eyes landing on Lucy, taking in her best Easter frock and, without a doubt, her lack of apron. Her eyebrow rose. "My daughter's nurse is to dine with us, I see." She paused. "How good of you. *My* maid, Hetty, will be joining your other servants in the kitchen for her Easter dinner."

Dr. Larimer was spared having to reply, for Octavia Belasysse swept into the room then, importantly escorted by Mrs. Larimer.

"Mother, Susan," Miss Belasysse murmured, kissing each woman on the cheek in turn, before extending her hand to her uncle.

After a few more pleasantries, Dr. Larimer turned to the Hargraves and Mr. Boteler. "I have an excellent fine-flavored claret in my study. Let us partake before we sit down for our dinner."

After the men assented, Mr. Sheridan followed the others out with a pinched and miserable look on his face.

Lucy watched as the other four women closed together then in a tight circle, naturally formed as they began to admire each other's dresses and hair. With a pang, she felt their combined beauty keenly. Although she wished to flee the room, she forced herself to stay.

Seeing that the sherry had been decanted on the sideboard, she thought she might make herself useful. "Shall I pour the sack, mistress?" she murmured to Mrs. Larimer.

The physician's wife gave her a quick appreciative smile. "Ah yes, Lucy. That would be lovely."

Lucy lined up several small goblets and began to pour out the sherry—*el vino de Xeres*, as she had once heard a bottler call it. After she handed everyone a goblet, she hesitated. Should she pour one for herself? Then, without looking at anyone, she quickly poured herself a glass and stepped away from the sideboard, taking a sip of the sweet white wine.

No one was paying attention to her anyway for, at that moment, Lady Belasysse turned to her daughter, eying the amulet that lay against her bare skin. "Octavia, wherever did you get that exquisite necklace?" she asked. "Borrowed it from our most generous hostess, I presume?"

The physician's wife smiled, acknowledging the compliment. "Ah! I wish I could claim such a lovely object as my own. No, I offered her silver pendants for her ears, but she only wanted to wear her amulet, her only possession. Well, at least the only possession she had upon her when she arrived at our doorstep."

Lady Belasysse pursed her lips. "That amulet is *yours,* Octavia? Pray tell, who gave it to you?" She stepped forward to examine the piece.

"I cannot tell you, Mother," Octavia Belasysse said, tapping the side of her head. "I am afraid it is all muckety-muck in here, as you know."

A few steps away, Susan Belasysse was staring at the amulet. Lucy, sipping her sherry, watched her. "Do you know something of the amulet, Mrs. Belasysse?" she asked her softly.

"Whatever do you mean?" Susan Belasysse replied, crossing her arms. "Why would I know anything about Octavia's amulet?"

The others turned to stare at them. "Oh!" Lucy replied, trying to sound nonchalant. "I thought Miss Belasysse might have acquired it at a London market—Covent Garden, perchance?—before she disappeared. There are some tradesmen in London who sell this sort of piece."

Susan Belasysse gulped. "No, I remember no such thing."

"I wonder what else you may not be remembering about my

disappearance, Sister," Octavia Belasysse replied, her smile not quite reaching her eyes.

"I am sure I do not know what you mean," Susan replied.

Again Octavia smiled. "The amulet was filled with rosemary. I imagine that someone hoped to protect me from something, but I know not what. Perhaps I was kidnapped by fortune-tellers, and you have forgotten about that sad tale." Her smile grew wider. "Or perchance a group of Catholics, lost on their pilgrimage, took me on their grand quest."

"Octavia," her mother said, a warning note in her voice. "Such untruths should not be said, even in jest."

"Still, this amulet proves that *someone* cared for me," Octavia replied, now holding her fingers before her, idly regarding her nails. She must have borrowed Mrs. Larimer's little nail scissors to make them less jagged. She looked back at Lady Belasysse. "Is that not so, Mother?"

Lady Belasysse did not respond.

Feeling the odd undercurrents in the room, Mrs. Larimer clapped her hands. "I shall summon the men now. It is high time we have our dinner."

"I shall let Mrs. Hotchkiss know," Lucy murmured to Mrs. Larimer, taking the opportunity to slip off to the kitchen. When she entered, she found everyone sitting around the table, with their tankards in front of them, the jug of wine opened. Duncan was evidently just finishing a humorous story, for Molly and Mrs. Hotchkiss were giggling. Hetty still looked dour, her hands wrapped defensively around her tankard as if fearful someone would take it from her.

Lucy leaned against the doorframe, watching them. She liked it when Duncan dropped his watchful reserve. Without his uniform, too, he seemed lighter in spirit than she had usually seen him. He looked up then, the smile still on his lips.

Molly and Mrs. Hotchkiss both stopped laughing when they saw her. Lucy felt a sudden chill come over the room.

"Yes, *miss?*" Mrs. Hotchkiss asked. "Is there something you need?"

Molly looked at her with an insolent lift of the brows.

"I am sorry to break up this merry scene," Lucy said uncomfortably. Turning to the housekeeper, she added, "Mrs. Larimer is ready for you to start serving dinner now."

Mrs. Hotchkiss nodded. "All right, Molly, let us start with the soup, then."

The servants began to ladle soup into bowls, banging everything about far more than was necessary. Duncan caught Lucy's eye, then nodded his head meaningfully toward Hetty, who looked a bit sullen.

Sliding onto the bench next to Duncan so that she could face Hetty, Lucy said to the others brightly, "The ladies have been enjoying their sherry, and the men their claret."

"Fa dee da!" Hetty said, taking a gulp of her wine. "Chase you out, did they?"

Mrs. Hotchkiss and Molly both tittered a bit, and Duncan shifted in his chair.

"Why, no," Lucy said, fully sensing the unfriendly feeling in the room.

"Don't know why they gave *you* a place at the table," Hetty said, her words already slurring a bit. "I have been tending to the Belasysse family for twenty years, and I have never been invited to dine with them. Not once!" Her obvious bitterness subdued the room. Then she snorted. "Spreading your legs for the master, are you?"

Lucy flushed deeply, but was gratified with the roar of outrage from both Duncan and Mrs. Hotchkiss at once.

The housekeeper batted the back of the woman's head. "No call for that kind of filth in here. No one will say a word against my master, especially not when dining at his table!"

Duncan stood up. "Nor shall you say such a thing about Lucy, whom I know to be of the most good and virtuous sort!" He was about to continue, but Lucy cut him off.

"No, Duncan," Lucy said. She decided to ignore Hetty's ugly insinuation and respond with the truth. "It was Miss Belasysse who asked me to join the family at the dinner. Quite honestly, Mrs. Larimer was against it, but she went along with Miss Belasysse's request." Hoping to smooth out the bad feelings in the room, she added, "Truth be told, I do not fit in there."

Duncan still looked annoyed, but her honesty seemed to mollify the others.

"Do not worry, dear," Mrs. Hotchkiss said. "You shall not be in that position much longer."

"Octavia always was a bit willful," Hetty conceded. Though she did not smile, the explanation seemed to help somewhat.

"What are they talking about?" Molly asked, a bit breathless to hear more of the gossip coming from the drawing room.

Her question gave Lucy the opening she needed. "They were quite intrigued with Miss Belasysse's beautiful amulet," she explained, trying to sound as friendly and casual as she could. "They were wondering at what market she might have bought it." Turning to Hetty, she asked, "Do you remember where Miss Belasysse got the amulet? It would have been before she disappeared, of course."

The lady's maid, her cheeks a bit flushed from the wine, wiped her mouth. "She did not go to any markets," she said. "Miss Octavia wanted to, but her uncle would not let her."

"Why not?"

"I do not know. He was afraid of her wandering off, I think. Having a fit in public, with no one to help her. He would not let her out of his sight."

"Do you think she was trying to get away, then?" Lucy asked.

"No, I never saw her go off alone. He was with her all the time." She burped loudly. "Never saw the amulet either."

Lucy and Duncan exchanged puzzled glances. "Maybe she kept it hidden," Duncan said to Hetty.

At that, all the servants in the room, including Lucy, smiled. A noblewoman of Miss Octavia's sort could no more easily hide a trinket from her maid than she could hide a bear from its tamer. A lady's maid knows everything. This meant that Miss Belasysse must have gotten the amulet at a later point.

"You should return to your meal," Duncan said. "Lest they wonder where you are." Before she left, he leaned over and whispered in her ear, so that the others could not hear. "And remember, not a single one of *them* can measure up to you."

·18·

When Lucy returned to the dining room, she was directed by Mrs. Larimer to her seat along with the others. To her credit, Mrs. Larimer was quite gracious, and gave no sense of discomfort over having a former chambermaid turned printer's apprentice at her dining table.

As Molly and Mrs. Hotchkiss began to bring out the first course, Dr. Larimer and his wife positioned themselves on either side of the long table. Two men and two women sat on either side, so that Lucy was between Master Hargrave and Mr. Boteler, with Mr. Sheridan in front of her.

To Lucy's disappointment, Adam was seated to Mrs. Larimer's right, and beside Octavia, with Susan Belasysse across from him. Master Hargrave and Lady Belasysse were seated on either side of Dr. Larimer.

Not sure what she should do or say, Lucy took a sip of the Rhenish wine that Molly had just poured, still thinking about the amulet. If what Hetty said was true, and it likely was, then Miss Belasysse had not acquired the amulet before her so-called death and disappearance. But judging by Miss Belasysse's lack of response to her family's questions about the amulet, she must have already figured this out for herself.

Lucy nearly choked on her sherry as realization flooded over her. Octavia Belasysse must have some awareness of how she had come by the piece. Had she remembered? If she remembered *that,* then what else did she remember? Although Lucy wished more than anything she could question Miss Belasysse about her newly formed suspicions, she remained silent, carefully listening to the conversations going on around her.

"What a miracle it is that your daughter has been returned safely to you," she heard the magistrate say across the table to Lady Belasysse.

"Indeed," Lady Belasysse said, glancing across the table at her brother. He was speaking rather animatedly to Mrs. Larimer and Susan Belasysse. "We are rather at a loss to explain where she has been these last ten months. My dear child is a bit muddled, you see. Always has been, ever since she was a child."

Overhearing her comment, Mrs. Larimer clucked her teeth. "Such a shame, and a worry for you, too. So hard to have some-one so afflicted in one's own family, I should think."

"Indeed," Lady Belasysse murmured. "I do not deny that it has been a trial, one which my husband and I have borne these many years. Although naturally we are quite relieved to discover that she is safe and well."

"I see," the magistrate replied. "And to think you even believed her to have died. How did such a strange thing transpire?"

"You are well informed, I see," Lady Belasysse said, draining her goblet, while Harlan Boteler gave much of the same account they had heard a few days before.

As the magistrate listened in his thoughtful way, he picked up the decanter and poured generous amounts of wine into the goblets around him, adding only a few drops to his own. The side conversations stopped as they all listened to Mr. Boteler.

"It is quite a strange thing," Miss Belasysse said. "To think others believed me to have passed on." She smiled at Mr. Sheridan. "James, am I not flesh and blood?" She touched the physician's hand, a gesture as forward and intimate as her use of his first name at the dining table.

Lucy was amused to see Mr. Sheridan flush and stammer. "Yes, Miss Belasysse, yes, most certainly you are."

"Octavia! Daughter!" Lady Belasysse hissed, her smile stretching across her teeth. "Such nonsense you speak." She began to cut her beef vigorously

"Is it nonsense, Mother?" Octavia asked, her voice overly sweet. "Something strange certainly occurred, and I am hoping you can help me determine the cause."

Susan Belasysse downed her goblet of wine then. Glancing at her, Lucy could see the young woman's cheeks were growing quite flushed. She began to speak loudly across the table. "Dr. Larimer, I am of the mind you should call in, call in, who should he call in?" She thumped her hand on the table. "Oh, yes, Valentine Greatrakes. Have you heard of him?"

"Greatrakes?" Dr. Larimer asked, his jaw tight. "That Irish quacksalver?"

"Yes," she replied, not heeding the physician's words. "I am certain he could heal her. He has been known to cure people just by laying his hands upon them. Since my dear sister-in-law has not yet been relieved of her affliction, despite being in your care, it might be helpful to bring him in." She hiccupped.

"Madam," the physician replied, his expression blackening, "I can assure you, that fraud's work is not recognized by the College of Physicians."

"He passed himself off as a healer," Mr. Sheridan explained to the others, sounding a bit nervous. "I think it is best if we do not discuss—"

"But is he not at the court of King Charles himself?" Susan Belasysse interrupted. "Surely, being under the protection of the king must say much of his legitimacy?"

Dr. Larimer's face was growing an uncomfortable shade of purple. He turned to Master Hargrave. "Thomas, if you would."

Master Hargrave replied, "I am familiar with the fantastical words of this individual. The tract is called *A Brief Account of Mr. Valentine Greatrakes and Divers of the Strange Cures by Him Lately Performed.*"

"See?" Susan hiccupped again. " 'The strange cures performed.' "

"I am also aware," Master Hargrave continued, "that the tract in question contained fifty-one pages of testimonials—all written by himself!"

Everyone laughed, except Susan, who picked up her glass again sullenly. "I was just trying to help my dear sister," she said. "Someone needs to!"

"Who would like some lamb?" Mrs. Larimer said quickly. "Dear, it is time to carve." Still scowling, Dr. Larimer accepted the carving knives from Molly.

Mrs. Larimer, still trying to smooth over the tension, turned toward Adam. "Mister Hargrave, I have heard tell that you work in the Fire Court. How interesting that must be."

Adam began to talk about his work, explaining how he would take the testimony of those who had lost their property in the Great Fire, as well as detail the quibbling that had ensued between landlords and their tenants.

"I see that the lines of the new streets are starting to be laid out," Mr. Boteler commented. "Should be rather grand when it is complete."

"Yes, it is my understanding that Christopher Wren's plan was of an even grander scale, but the king did not wish to fund such a masterful and expensive project," Master Hargrave commented.

The men proceeded to speak for a few more minutes about the rebuilding efforts in the city. Lucy was quite fascinated, listening to the plans, and forgot temporarily about what they were supposed to discover.

Susan Belasysse, evidently bored by the conversation about the Great Fire and its aftermath, downed another goblet of red wine. Lady Belasysse was watching her daughter-in-law, too, a tight smile on her face, even as she listened politely to what Dr. Larimer was saying beside her.

Adam picked up the jug of wine and poured more into the goblets of others near him. Like his father, he did not add anything to either his own cup or that of Octavia Belasysse, who was speaking now to Mr. Sheridan.

Lucy heard Susan Belasysse giggle as she thanked Adam for the wine.

"Not at all," he said courteously. Catching Lucy's eye across the table, he smiled at her.

Susan Belasysse giggled again, speaking again to Adam. "Mr. Hargrave, you are not yet married, are you?" The flirtatious quality of her question was hard to miss, and Lucy found herself clenching her napkin under the table.

"No, I am not," he replied, putting a forkful of meat into his mouth.

"That astonishes me. Does that astonish you?" Susan Belasysse asked Mrs. Larimer, who murmured something that Lucy could not catch. Such personal comments were not appropriate in mixed company, and certainly not while dining together.

But Susan Belasysse would not be deterred. "A man with political aspirations such as yourself must have a wife that will bring the right people to you. That is how it is with me and my husband, Henry. He is an MP, you know."

"How fortunate for you," Adam said.

"Susan is my brother Henry's *second* wife," Octavia said then, turning away from Mr. Sheridan. Lucy did not even know she had been paying attention to the conversation. "She supplied him a pretty fortune."

"That is the nature of politics," Susan said, speaking more loudly. "I heard tell, *Adam*"—here Lucy saw Mrs. Larimer flinch at the young woman's use of Adam's first name—"that you have been wooing a chambermaid. And that she was too busy cleaning other people's dung to pay you any mind."

She laughed loudly, not heeding the shocked faces around her, as the other small conversations stopped. "I cannot imagine how such an odd rumor started, but is that not diverting? To think that Adam Hargrave might marry a scullery maid? Such a thing is laughable indeed." Now she was outright simpering. "Perhaps my husband has run off for good. I can annul my marriage, as we have not yet had children." The look she gave Adam was suggestive.

"Susan!" Lady Belasysse hissed at her daughter-in-law. "Cease your immodest words!"

"I was just asking a question," Susan Belasysse said. She took another swallow of her wine. "It's all so ridiculous, surely you can see that. How could someone like *him* choose to be with such a lowly sort?"

Lucy swallowed hard, not meeting anyone's eyes, the sound of buzzing bees filling her head.

Master Hargrave coughed. "I am certain that whomever my son chooses to marry will suit him well, in disposition, modesty, and spirit."

"Hear, hear!" Octavia Belasysse cried. "It is my fervent hope for the scullery maid—whoever she may be—that she marries a man worthy of *her,* whether he be gentry or common."

"Pffft," Lady Belasysse said. "Such nonsense you speak, Daughter."

Octavia Belasysse laughed. Standing up, she raised her goblet. "I should very much like to make a toast," she said.

Puzzled, they all raised their goblets, except for Susan Belasysse, who had petulantly slumped back in her chair.

"To my family," Miss Belasysse said, "who loved me enough to bury me in an empty casket."

Everyone set down their goblets abruptly.

"Dearest niece," Mr. Boteler said, trying to sound jovial, "we have explained to you how that odd travesty occurred. We are grateful that you have returned to us."

Octavia Belasysse would not be put off. Still standing, she said, "Mother, Uncle—did you know that when Lucy discovered me, I was covered in blood? And that the blood was not mine?"

When heads turned toward her, Lucy nodded. The Hargraves, she noticed, were alert, paying attention to the responses of everyone at the table.

"Wh-whose blood was it?" Susan Belasysse whispered.

Miss Belasysse shrugged. "Who knows? Although the constable has some idea, I'm afraid. It seems that a man was found dead—stabbed—very near where Lucy discovered me."

"A man? Killed?" Susan Belasysse faltered, looking about desperately. "Who was he? Was he—?"

"Oh, do not worry, my dear sister-in-law," Miss Belasysse replied. "He was not your husband. I know because I actually looked at the dead man's face, and I knew that to be so," she said pointedly, looking at her uncle. She turned back to her sister-in-law. "I hope that does not disappoint you, Susan. I have seen you cavorting with my uncle, and now throwing yourself at Adam Hargrave, so I imagine it would be easier for you if you were no longer tied to my brother."

"Octavia!" Lady Belasysse cried out. "Apologize and retire at once. You are clearly not well."

"Oh, Mother, I am very well. I believe I have been well taken care of. It is a strange thing, though, to think I killed a man. Or did I?" She began to laugh. "I can only hope that His Majesty would be good enough to pardon me as he did my brother."

"Miss Belasysse," the magistrate said sternly, drawing on his full weight of the authority of the court. "Are you admitting, in the presence of nine witnesses, including a magistrate and a member of the Fire Court, that you murdered the man who was found by the River Fleet, this Friday past?"

"I am admitting no such thing!" she replied. "I just thought my family would like to know that I shall likely be arrested for murder." Lucy could see her hands were trembling; she was not nearly as composed as she was pretending to be.

Adam set down his napkin. "Now, Miss Belasysse," he said. "I do not think there has been enough evidence to arrest you. Constable Duncan would not—"

"Constable Duncan?" Lady Belasysse interrupted. "He would not dare arrest a Belasysse. I shall set that doddering fool straight."

"Constable Duncan is a good man! And no fool either!" Lucy burst out. Everyone turned toward her. Feeling uncomfortable, she continued. "As Mr. Hargrave has said, he is willing to wait until there is more direct proof that Miss Belasysse was involved in the crime."

Lady Belasysse wiped her mouth with a linen napkin and set it down on the table. "It is time for us to say our farewells," she said. She looked at Mrs. Larimer, who seemed more fascinated than repelled by the exchange.

"As you please, Mother," Octavia Belasysse said, walking out of the room.

Lucy scrambled after her. She was surprised to see the woman halfway up the stairs already, bent over. To her great surprise, the woman was laughing.

"That went about as I had hoped," Octavia said, and swept on toward her bedchamber without looking back.

·19·

Lucy leaned against the wall, near the top of the stairs, her thoughts racing. It was all so puzzling. What could Miss Belasysse have meant? Why was she taunting her family by bringing up her possible arrest? What had she expected from that little scene?

It was difficult, too, to keep from thinking about what Susan Belasysse had said about her, or what Adam had thought when she spoke so warmly of the constable. For a moment, she buried her face in her hands.

Then she straightened her back. "Nothing I can do about it now," she said to herself. "Little said, soon mended." Adam would understand.

She was about to follow Miss Belasysse into her bedchamber when Susan Belasysse came stumbling up the stairs. "Lucy," she called. "I should like to speak with you."

"Is there something you need?" Lucy asked, a heated feeling coming over her. She did not know that she could hold her tongue, should the woman hurl more comments related to the lowly scullery maid and the magistrate's son. She continued to mount the stairs. "I need to tend to your sister-in-law."

Susan Belasysse followed her, putting her hand on Lucy's elbow when they had reached the top of the steps. "Wait, please," she said, stumbling against Lucy, her face so close that Lucy could smell the wine and lamb on her breath. "I did not know to whom I could speak," she said, her voice just above a whisper.

"What is it?" Lucy asked, her curiosity piqued.

"Despite what you just witnessed, I do truly care about my sister-in-law. I thought, since you have been taking care of her, you might help me make sense of something peculiar." The woman sank down on the floor, the wine evidently overcoming her again. "First, I need to sit."

Sighing, Lucy sank down beside her. The woman's furtive movements were making her uneasy. "What do you need to tell me?"

"Over the last few months, my husband has been receiving odd notes, brought to him by a messenger not clad in livery. These notes claimed to be from someone who said his sister was alive. He showed one of the notes to me. An ill-formed script, written on cheap paper. I, too, was certain that it was from a person best left ignored."

"Why did he not heed them?" Lucy asked. "If he had been receiving them for several months?"

Susan Belasysse sighed. "My husband has been set upon before. Threatened by blackmailers. He has also been beset by those angered by the king's pardon for his earlier crime—you heard Octavia's rude speech on the subject, just a few moments ago."

Lucy nodded. "Yes, I heard tell of how he mistakenly murdered a tanner and was pardoned for it." She tried to speak matter-of-factly, but she could hear the edge in her voice. It was hard when her brother was a simple tradesman, too, and moreover had not been accorded such leniency when presumed to be guilty himself of a terrible crime.

But she did not want to stop Susan Belasysse from speaking further, so she forced herself to keep her tone even. "So it was sensible that he did not pay them any heed. What changed his mind?" she asked.

"A week ago, my husband received a different letter. When he read it, he told me that someone was now impersonating his dead sister. He didn't show it to me, but he crumpled it up and threw it in the fire. 'I am going to put a stop to this!' he told me, before he packed a small valise for the journey."

"Did he tell you where he was going?" Lucy asked.

"No, he didn't say. When he wasn't looking, naturally I fished the letter out. I could see that it was like his sister's hand, but the letters formed in a more wavering way."

"What did it say?" Lucy asked, leaning forward now.

Susan Belasysse pulled out a scrap of paper from her purse and handed it to Lucy. "Make of it what you will."

Taking it, Lucy stood up and walked over to one of the candles illuminating the second-floor corridor and opened the letter. *"My dearest brother,"* she read. *"I need you to come at once. I must leave this terrible place. Your loving sister, Octavia."* She flipped it over. There was no indication of the source on the other side. "This is it? 'This terrible place'? Where is that? How did he know where to go?"

"He did not tell me. But I think he knew where in London he was going, from one of the earlier letters."

"I see," Lucy said. "But he never told you, for certain, that he would be coming to London?"

Susan Belasysse shrugged. "My husband doesn't talk to me much."

Lucy frowned. "What am I supposed to do with this knowledge?"

Susan Belasysse looked furtive again. "I am sure you can think of something." Then, with a funny whoop, she turned around and stumbled back down the stairs.

Lucy stared after her, hoping that she would not break her neck on the way down. Then she tucked the scrap of paper into her bodice and entered Miss Belasysse's bedchamber.

There she found the woman slumped on the chair, seated before the draped mirror. Her earlier gaiety seemed to have dissolved, and now she appeared listless and forlorn. Wordlessly, Lucy picked up the brush as the woman began to pull out the pins and combs holding her hair in place.

"I am so very tired and ready for my bed," Miss Belasysse said. "Do you think I will be arrested tomorrow?" She looked at Lucy with worried eyes.

"We do not know for certain that Constable Duncan will arrest you for that man's murder," Lucy said. "You said you did not even know who he was! Surely your mother and uncle will never allow it!"

Miss Belasysse gave a little sniff. "He will be here, I know it." She stepped out of her gown and raised her arms so that Lucy could place a warm woolen nightdress, borrowed from Mrs. Lar-imer, over her head. "Do not mind my sister-in-law, Lucy. She is up to no good."

"What do you mean?" Lucy asked, helping her into the bed and pulling the cover over her frail form.

The woman opened her eyes. "Did I say that?" She hesitated. "She was just jealous, I daresay, since it is obvious how young Mister Hargrave dotes on you." She looked puzzled, for the concept clearly astonished her. "His father—the magistrate—had a sur-prising manner to you as well. Treated you as he would a lady."

Lucy smiled slightly at the unexpected compliment. Then, to her surprise, Miss Belasysse touched her hand. "You have been kind to me, my dear. Better than I may deserve. Perhaps you cannot see—" She broke off.

"Cannot see what?" Lucy asked. She found herself gripping the edge of the table for support. A blow was coming, of that she was certain. *Society will never accept you as Adam Hargrave's wife.* She could almost hear the words, and she braced herself for a nega-tive response.

"How unhappy young Mister Hargrave was when the consta-ble's name was spoken. When you said that he was a good man." She gave a light laugh. "How fortunate for you to have a choice, my dear."

"Oh," Lucy said. "I do not know that I do."

"Of course you do. What is more, you can marry for love, something that women in my circle can never do." At Lucy's smile, she continued. "I am not saying that such a path would be easy. There are men and women like my mother and sister-in-law who will never welcome you to their house as an equal. Surely you are aware of that."

Lucy nodded, feeling like someone had dumped a pail of icy water on her.

"But there are just as many like the Hargraves and the Larimers, and my own brother, Henry, who can see that the world is upside down, and can adapt to what is coming. Maybe those are the people who matter." Miss Belasysse rolled over to face the wall. "I really must get some sleep."

Lucy moved over to shutter Miss Belasysse's windows and, glancing down to the garden below, saw Master Hargrave and Constable Duncan speaking together in close conversation. Seeing that Miss Belasysse had already dropped off, Lucy left the room and made her way to the back of the house and into the garden.

"Did you learn anything?" she asked Duncan, looking about. She wondered where Adam was. He seemed to notice the gesture and gave a rueful twist of his lips.

"As I was telling the magistrate," he said, "Hetty was not used to drinking wine. She fell asleep after the first course and was dead to the world after that. However, as you know, she confirmed that she had never seen the amulet before on Miss Belasysse's person."

"A lady's maid would certainly be aware of all her mistress's jewelry," Lucy said. "So then it must be as we thought, that someone gave it to her after she wandered off."

"She did tell me one interesting thing, however," Duncan added. "That Mr. Boteler is almost entirely without funds of his own. And that Susan Belasysse seems to have been paying his debts."

"Are they having an affair?" Lucy asked, thinking of Octavia Belasysse's earlier accusation. She glanced at the magistrate. "Forgive me, sir, for this gossip."

The magistrate smiled at her fondly. "Lucy, I never believe you to engage in the gross wagging of tongues. It is important to share what we know," he said. "To wit, I am not surprised to hear that he is indigent. When we were having our port, I noted several points of his conversation that suggested he was living on very stretched funds. Why Susan Belasysse is supporting him in this way is something we should discover."

"She told me something as well," she said, quickly telling them what Susan Belasysse had told her while on the stairs. She handed them the note the woman had given to her. "Shall I ask Miss Belasysse about this note? Perhaps she will remember writing it."

Duncan shook his head. "Best wait to do so, until her humors have regained their balance. Her behavior tonight . . . I suspect that her mind may be more damaged than we have assumed."

"This is very interesting," Master Hargrave said. He looked up into the sky. "It is growing dark. Adam has already left, and I should be heading home."

"S-sir?" Lucy said, faltering. "May I have a word?"

The magistrate looked at her kindly. "Of course, my dear. What is it?"

She glanced at Duncan, who clicked his heels, evidently realizing that she wished to speak to the magistrate alone. "Thank you for making sure I had a proper Easter dinner, Lucy." He glanced at Master Hargrave. "Lucy has taken pity on me, I think, more times than I deserve." After bidding them good evening, he strode out of the garden and into the street without looking back.

Lucy put her hand on the tree. She did not know how to begin. "Adam left," she said abruptly.

"Yes," he said. "He asked me to bid you good evening." He waited.

Unexpectedly, Lucy found herself with tears in her eyes. "What that woman said tonight . . ." she began.

"I am very sorry she said that, Lucy. She is young and foolish," he replied. "Do not think for a minute that people who care about you would think such utter twaddle."

"It is true that her words hurt me, sir. And they hurt Adam, too. I cannot bear such pain." She began to blink rapidly. "If I were stronger I might be able to. But I am not certain—" She broke off as her throat began to clench.

"You do not know if you still love my son," the magistrate said.

Hearing those words spoken out loud—words she had been trying to keep hidden deep within herself—was impossible to bear. Lucy began to weep in earnest.

"There, there, Lucy," the magistrate said. Putting fatherly arms around her, he let her sob onto his shoulder.

After a long while, Master Hargrave put her gently aside. "Do not berate yourself if your feelings for my son have changed. You will always have a place in our hearts, as I hope we have in yours." He patted her hand. "But if you do have feelings for Constable Duncan, who is indeed a good man as you said so fervently to-night, do not let him believe that such feelings stem from pity. A man deserves more than pity from the woman he loves."

After he took his leave, she sat outside for a long time, watching the shadows lengthen in the courtyard until at last it was time to go back inside.

Lucy grimaced as the sound of crowing roosters woke her the next morning at dawn. She had barely slept, and when she did, her dreams were restless and full of pain.

She slipped downstairs and through the kitchen, stealing past

Molly as she pulled a heavy pot off the hearth, hoping that Sid would be back that morning as promised.

Indeed, Lucy was not surprised when she heard a low whistle come from behind the oak tree in the physician's herb garden. It was a bit chilly, and she wished she had thought to throw on her cloak. She could just make out Sid's lean form in the shadows of the great sprawling tree. Darting quickly, she joined him, taking care not to be seen from the house. Her reputation would not fare well should she be seen sneaking off to see a young man in the wee hours of the morning.

Sid grinned down at her. "Good day, Lucy. Fine time for a bit of fresh morning air, is it not?"

She waved her hand at him. "Quiet, Sid! I do not want Cook or Mrs. Hotchkiss to know I have left the house. They might think I am doing something improper."

Sid raised an eyebrow. "Improper?" he asked, rubbing his hand along her arm. "Do tell."

Lucy put her hands on her hips and glared at him. "Pray, desist with these jests, Sid. Did you follow that apothecary as I asked? Tell me at once what you learned."

"All right!" In truth, he looked more serious. "All right. Yes, I followed him."

"And? Where did he go?"

Sid looked around. Bending his head down, he whispered in her ear. "Bedlam."

Lucy's breath caught. Bedlam! The asylum for madmen.

Her thoughts began to swirl. Could Octavia Belasysse have been hidden away in Bedlam these last ten months?

"She had not been starving," Lucy mused out loud, answering

her own questions. "That Dr. Larimer believed to be so." She paused, still thinking through this startling information. "It might also explain the bloodletting. And certainly how that apothecary knew about which preparation she needed. Thank you, Sid, for your trouble. I am in your debt." She turned to go.

But he moved in front of her. "Not so fast, little miss," Sid said. "I believe you owe me something?" He held out his hand. "I believe you promised me some coins? 'Twas no easy task to follow that man. The way he dodged about! Almost as if he did not want anyone to see him."

Rolling her eyes, she handed him the coins. "Be off with you now," she said. "Do not let yourself be seen."

When she reentered the kitchen, Molly was kneading dough for the day's bread. She looked cross, and a bit tousled, as if she had slept in a little longer than was expected. If the Larimers ordered their household anything like the Hargraves, Lucy suspected that none of the chamber pots had been emptied and the girl was already behind in her morning chores.

Seeing that a tray had been laid out, with a cup and saucer, a bit of yesterday's bread, and some preserves, Lucy made a quick decision. She needed to speak to Dr. Larimer straightaway, and this was her chance.

"I could take that in to Dr. Larimer if you like," Lucy said brightly, glancing meaningfully at Molly's dough-covered hands. "Miss Belasysse is still deep in sleep, and I am glad enough to lend a hand."

Molly pursed her lips. She was clearly torn between letting

Lucy help her and being annoyed at Lucy's position in the household. Thankfully, good sense won out.

"Mind you don't spill nothing," she grumbled.

"I shall be very careful," Lucy replied, hiding a smile as she picked up the tray.

A few minutes later, she entered the physician's study. Dr. Larimer looked at her in surprise. "Have you taken on Molly's duties now?" he asked. "I thought your serving days ended when you left the Hargraves."

Smiling at him, she carefully poured a bit of the steaming liquid into his cup. "Sir," she said, "have you ever had patients with a condition like that which has taken hold of Miss Belasysse?"

"To which condition do you refer?" he replied, taking a long sip. "*Epilepsis*? Melancholia? Delirium? Yes, I am afraid I have witnessed all three. The prolonged memory loss, though, that is another matter. Far less common."

"What happens to them?" She swallowed. "Those stricken with these conditions?"

He sighed. "So many of these troubled souls were displaced by the Fire. It used to be that the mad could look to their families to take care of them, or the local parish. But now——" He broke off.

Lucy nodded. She had noticed a lot more lunatics than usual, although truth be told, many were ranting and trembling like the Quakers, and she found it hard to tell the difference between those filled with the Inner Light of Christ and those beset by demons. "What about Bedlam?"

"Bedlam?" The physician set down his cup. "I have never sent a patient to that dreadful place. They are better off being taken care of by their own kin than sent there to rot." He looked back at the papers on his desk, clearly distracted by his work. "If you will excuse me, Lucy. I should like to look over the notes that Mr. Sheridan prepared on today's patients. I have one stopping by in a quarter hour's time."

"As you wish, sir," she said, backing out of the room. As she shut the door behind her, she asked herself aloud, "Could Miss Belasysse have been at Bedlam?"

"What? What did you say? Why do you think that Miss Belasysse was kept at Bedlam?"

Lucy jumped. James Sheridan was standing there. She had not heard him, having been so deep in thought.

"Oh, sir! I was just talking to myself. I did not see you standing there."

"Why did you think Octavia was at Bedlam? Tell me at once!" he demanded.

Seeing that he would not be deterred, Lucy explained how she had asked Sid to follow the apothecary on the spur of the moment, and how they had ended up at Bedlam. "We should find out more, sir," Lucy said. "Discover if Octavia Belasysse was an inmate there."

"Yes, that is my intention. As an assistant to a licensed Fellow of the College of Physicians, I can assure you that it falls under my right to inspect any apothecary that I please, and that includes anything that may be occurring at Bedlam," Mr. Sheridan replied, stiffly. "I will see who this practitioner is and whether he is irregular or regular in his trade. I will tell the keeper that I am thinking of putting another patient with him. It will give me a chance to look around."

"I should come with you," Lucy declared. "I will be able to tell you for certain if the apothecary was indeed the man who gave me the concoction for Miss Belasysse."

"It makes no sense for you to be in my presence," he said. "What physician travels with a maid? Now, out of my way!" Mr. Sheridan began to push past Lucy, who did not yield.

"Perhaps I can find my own way in. There are others who might have seen Miss Belasysse, who might know something of her circumstances."

"You will get caught," he said. "What good will that do us then?"

She frowned at him. "I won't get caught," she said. "Do not worry."

"Heavens above, you are indeed stubborn, are you not?" He looked up at the ceiling. "I am not *worried* about you. Except that for some inexplicable reason, you are a favorite of Dr. Larimer, and I should not like your disappearance on my conscience." He sighed. "We are wasting time discussing this. Get your cloak."

"Now?" Lucy asked. "What of Miss Belasysse?"

"Molly can look after Octavia. Dr. Larimer will be with a patient." Impatiently he pushed her arm. "Stop looking so witless, Lucy," he said. "You have started us on this feckless path; I do not expect you to turn back now."

·20·

Within fifteen minutes, Lucy and Mr. Sheridan set out toward Bedlam, the physician's assistant two lanky strides ahead of her. Lucy had only known Bedlam was in the northeasterly direction, above the line of the Great Fire's devastation. But Mr. Sheridan seemed to know exactly where he was going.

"It is a mile and a half from here," he said. "Try to keep up. I do not have much time to waste." She heard him mutter, "I should have hired a sedan."

Lucy shook her head. She had never hired a sedan chair, a common enough transport about the city for men and women of means. She had seen them regularly enough, certainly: two large men bearing a chair on two poles between them. A wealthier inhabitant of the finer sort of sedan might remain hidden behind velvet curtains, but others were in the open, so that all could see. She had rarely even taken a cart, let alone a fancier carriage for hire. But clearly, Mr. Sheridan came from a very different sort of people, a sort that did not take readily to such rough walking conditions.

Nevertheless, he walked quickly, and Lucy had to trot along, keeping up with his lanky stride. Despite fuming a bit over the younger physician's high-handed ways, she could not resist seeking a little more information from the sour-faced man.

"Sir, I know you mentioned before that you knew Henry Belasysse from university," Lucy said, kicking an old pail out of her way. "He was an acquaintance of your older brother's, you said?"

"Hmmm, yes," Mr. Sheridan replied. "Their family was among our acquaintances. Indeed, he was still at university when I began my studies." With a sniff, he added, "He spent a lot more time at the local taverns than either my brother or I ever did."

Lucy thought about the tract that she had read about Henry Belasysse. "And did you also know Lord Buckhurst?"

"A bit. He spent even less time at his studies." Mr. Sheridan glanced at Lucy then. "From your questions, it sounds as if you are seeking some gossip about that sad tale."

"It was just something Susan Belasysse said. That her husband—Henry Belasysse—had received a number of threatening letters from people angered by the king's pardon of his involvement in the tanner's murder."

"Such letters are treasonous," Mr. Sheridan commented. "I suggest that you not bring them up again."

Lucy was about to reply indignantly, forgetting all St. Paul's admonitions for a woman to be chaste, silent, and obedient, when she happened to look at the physician's face. He was clearly lost in thought, his mind intent on something else. "That event was bothersome to the whole family, I can assure you. Miss Octavia was quite distraught by the whole affair, and only worsened her condition."

"You knew Miss Octavia fairly well, then."

"I could see from the first time I met her that she was terribly unwell. But oh, so fragile and lovely," Mr. Sheridan said, seeming to forget with whom he was speaking. "A local family in Cambridge had put together a ball, and I had seen her dancing. As she passed me, I knew then, even with the scant knowledge of anatomy that I possessed, that her mind was not as it ought to be. I remember heading into the gardens, with only the glow of a great moon to guide our way."

"You followed her," Lucy said softly when he paused, not wishing to break the spell.

"I did. And she collapsed, and she had a fit as you have seen her, right there in my arms. I wanted to protect her, to help her, but there is so little that could be done."

"And how did her family treat her?" Lucy asked, thinking about the way Miss Belasysse had spoken about her mother.

"As well as could be expected, I suppose. Her condition left her unmarriageable, of course." There was a longing in his voice then, a long-held wistfulness. For the first time, his sharp, angular features softened a bit, and he no longer seemed his cold and dismissive self.

They fell silent after that.

"We are almost there," he said.

For the first time, their pace slackened a little. They had reached Bishopsgate and what Lucy took to be the east wall of the old hospital. Lucy stared at the great building that loomed before them, her heart beginning to pound painfully in her chest. Suddenly she wondered about the folly they were about to undertake.

Unaware of Lucy's sudden nervousness, Mr. Sheridan surveyed the vast stone building in a detached way. "Once a hospital for pilgrims, it was. For those collecting money and solace prior to setting out on the Crusades," he commented. "Bethlehem hospital, it was called, ere it became called Bedlam. Before our good King Henry dissolved all the Catholic strongholds, it was still run by the papists. A place for London's mad it has been for several hundred years."

As they approached the open gate, Lucy could feel herself sweating more as she wondered what it would be like to walk among the mad. To calm herself down, she began to sing a little of "Mad Tom of Bedlam," a ditty that Lach liked to sing while he set the type in the press. *The man in the moon drinks claret, with powder-beef, turnip, and carrot—*"

Mr. Sheridan stopped and looked down at her, pushing his glasses back on his nose. "Miss Campion. Do you mind?"

"Pardon, sir," Lucy said, stifling a giggle. "It is a rather merry song, you see, and—" Seeing his face, she stopped. "I am sorry, sir."

As they approached the front entrance, he said pointedly, "May I remind you that I am going in alone?"

"Oh, yes, of course," Lucy replied. "Try to leave the door behind you open if you can. If not, I will try to find another way inside. Let us plan to meet in three-quarters of an hour, by that tree there." She pointed to a tree on the road, outside the hospital gates.

"I am not going back in after you, if you are not there," he warned her, as he pulled sharply on the bell at the front door.

Deep within the building they could hear it clanging.

Mr. Sheridan looked about. "Step back!" he hissed. "I hear someone coming. Move over there. In the shadows!"

Lucy darted behind a tree, and not a moment too soon, for a moment later, a stout man with a bald head opened the door. "What is it?"

Did a flash of fright cross the physician's face? "I should very much like to speak to the keeper, if I may," Mr. Sheridan said blandly.

"He is busy," the man snarled, looking to shut the door.

"I am a physician. I would like to converse with him about a patient I am attending. I may wish to place him here, but I would like to know more about the treatments that are offered."

The man stared down at him. "Wait here."

Mr. Sheridan glanced back at Lucy, who was poking her head out. "Well? Did you recognize that man?"

"No!" Lucy called back softly.

A moment later, the man came back, and Lucy stepped quickly out of sight. "You may come inside," he said to Mr. Sheridan. "Follow me."

Mr. Sheridan glanced meaningfully back at Lucy. His face had paled, but she could see he had drawn up his shoulders. *He is afraid,* Lucy realized. *And yet he is braving those fears to go inside anyway.* For a moment she almost felt actual admiration for the squirrelly man.

Mr. Sheridan followed the man inside. From her vantage point he could see him pulling off his gloves, and he dropped one on the ground in the path of the door, so that it did not shut all the way. It was a sign, she thought.

Before the man could become aware of her presence, Lucy pushed through the door ever so swiftly, hoping that the interior would be dark enough so that she might be able to hide.

Once inside, Lucy had to blink a bit to help her eyes get accustomed to the darkness. She was in a main room of sorts, although one sparsely furnished. A few lit candles were placed in ancient holders along the stone walls, casting long shadows along the floor. She gagged as the pungent smell of piss and excrement assaulted her. In the distance, she could hear what sounded like a man's screams, intermittent shouts that made the hairs on the back of her neck stand up. For a moment, her mind was cast back to Newgate prison, and she could feel her heart racing in her chest.

Now, as she kept close to the mold-covered walls, a damp musty smell made her nose twitch. Before anyone could hear her, she managed to bury her nose in her cloak to let out a small sneeze.

She could see the entrance to a hallway at the end of the great room, where she assumed Mr. Sheridan and the man had gone. Moving quickly, she crossed the room and peered down the long corridor. Doors lined either side, to rooms that had likely been cells for the hospitalers of old. She could see each door had two openings—one at the height of a man's head, and the other at the floor, as a means to push in a bowl of food.

With great trepidation, Lucy moved into the hall and stood on her tiptoes to peek inside the first of these chambers. She could tell straightaway that the screaming was not coming from this room. She could see a figure lying quietly on a bed. A great stench arose from the room, and she could see that the bed was covered with filth. As she peered about the dark room, she accidentally bumped the door, causing it to creak. To her surprise, the door was not locked, and it swung fully open.

The figure on the bed tried to sit up. "Who is there?" a man weakly called, before sinking back onto the pallet. He was clad only in a simple shift, the kind a man would wear to bed. "Show yourself!"

The heavy sound of a chain could be heard, and to Lucy's disgust she could see that the man's feet and arms were shackled to the bed.

"Show yourself!" He began to scream. "Show yourself!!!"

Backing out of the room, Lucy shut the door again and then pressed herself against the wall of the corridor, breathing hard. She half expected someone to come to determine the cause of the man's shouting, but no one did. Evidently, whoever was running the place was used to the mad shrieks of the inmates.

Lucy peered into each of the next five cells. Two contained rather bedraggled-looking women. One room was uninhabited. The last in the corridor was where the great screams were coming from. Hardly able to bear it, Lucy peeked inside. There she saw a man tied to the bed, ropes around his wrists and hands. He seemed to be trying to chew his way through one of the ropes in between his mad shouts.

Seeing the ropes that bound the man sickened Lucy. She remembered the marks around Miss Belasysse's wrists and ankles. Had she been bound in a similar manner? Lucy stumbled away. Seeing a bit of daylight under the door at the end of the hall, she pushed it open and found herself in a courtyard with a wild garden of sorts.

Hoping no one would see her from the slitted windows that

lined the stone walls of the hospital, she moved toward a small stone bench that seemed to be located in the one patch of sunshine for the whole dreary place.

Within a few moments, Lucy realized that she was not actually alone.

There were a few people walking about, seemingly in their nightclothes, talking to themselves, gesturing a bit wildly. All were clearly touched in the head, but apparently harmless. At least Lucy hoped that was the case.

Taking a deep breath, Lucy approached a woman dressed in a simple day frock, sitting alone on a stone bench. Her silvery hair was tangled and looked like it had not seen a brush in many a day or night. Her face was pale. "Good day," Lucy called. "A pleasant fortune upon you."

Startled, the woman looked up, her eyes fearful. Then suddenly she smiled, a sweet angelic smile, despite several missing teeth. Her eyes were almost black, her pupils nearly completely dilated. When the sunlight hit them, she jerked back out of the sunlight with a slight whimper, as if she had been burnt.

Cautiously, Lucy said, "I am looking for a friend of mine. Octavia. Do you know her?"

"The birds will return now, will they not?" the woman asked. "The garden is too still without them. I miss them." She paused and then pulled from her bodice an object hanging about her neck. "I have this, you see. To remember the bluebird by."

"How lovely," Lucy said, taking a step closer to the woman. "May I see?"

The woman held out the pendant. It reminded Lucy of the amulet that Miss Belasysse wore about her neck, but the gemstone was smaller, and the piece seemed more ordinary. Still, like Octavia Belasysse, the woman put her fingers protectively around the piece and stepped away.

"Where did you get such a beautiful piece?" Lucy asked.

The woman giggled, an odd childlike sound. "A quail gave it to me. He also gave one to the bluebird." She cocked her head, looking at Lucy sideways. "Are you a bird, too? I have never seen you in the garden before. Sometimes the birds come and go. It is spring, and they are starting to return. At least I hope they are coming back." She began to whistle then.

"I am sorry, I do not understand," Lucy said. There was something hidden in the woman's speech, she could tell. Though her mind was clearly addled, there was something there. "What did you mean, that a quail gave it to you?"

"The bluebird knew I could not fly. So she asked the quail to give this to me. She thought it would help."

"I see." Lucy looked around, hoping no one was watching them. "And has it? Helped you fly?"

"No! They kept me clipped. I cannot fly," the woman exclaimed, the smile leaving her face. She moved over very close to Lucy's ear and whispered, "Beware the brown bird, who is cruel with sharp tendons. I have not seen him for some time, but he may still be watching from his nest on high."

"The brown bird?" Lucy asked, confused. From the serious way the woman was looking at her, it seemed she was trying to tell her something.

"He does the bidding of the falconer, who keeps us penned here."

A shiver ran up and down Lucy's spine as she started to

understand what the woman was saying. "What happened to the bluebird?"

For a moment, the woman looked confused. "The quail helped her fly away. Why will he not help me? Are there not more letters to be written?"

"Did someone write a letter for the bluebird?"

The woman smiled secretively. "Many letters, with a long curling plume."

"Where is the quail now?" Lucy asked.

She expected the woman to point to the sky or the trees, but instead she pointed to the other wing of the old hospital, where Lucy had not yet been. "There."

"Thank you," Lucy said. "I shall visit the quail." On a whim, she reached up and pulled her last ribbon from her hair and handed it to the woman. "For your nest."

The woman smiled in genuine pleasure. She looked about to flit away, then turned back to Lucy.

"But then the lion came and roared at the falconer, for letting the bluebird escape. He was quite angry indeed. The brown bird went after her, for he does the falconer's bidding. He never came back." The woman began to whistle again, and hopped away toward a tree.

Waving to Lucy, the woman reached up and grabbed a low-hanging branch. Then she swung herself into the tree, her shift pulled up so that her legs were immodestly showing. "I will fly away, too, you see. Fly away, fly away!" she called loudly.

Lucy smiled at her, a bit sadly. *I hope you do fly,* she thought. Before she left, she crooked her finger in the old way to bring a blessing down upon the woman.

· 2 1 ·

Lucy went back through the same door she had used to enter the Bedlam courtyard a few minutes ago, but this time she turned to the right, down a corridor that quickly led to another corridor with more cells for inmates. She glanced in each as she passed. A few seemed to be empty, and in others the inmate was asleep or staring up at the ceiling. In one, she saw a woman cradling a small sack in her hands as one would hold a baby. Lucy could hear her humming an old tune that she remembered her neighbors crooning to their babies as they lulled the infants to sleep.

Peering into the room at the very end of the hallway, she could see that this interior was far larger and laid out differently from the others. Unlike the cells, which contained only a bed, table, and chair, this room reminded Lucy of Dr. Sheridan's study. There were shelves full of bottles and jars, and a table covered with books, mortars and pestles, and small pots. This, she supposed, might be the workplace of an apothecary.

Seeing that the room was empty of inhabitants, Lucy went in. Immediately, she was overwhelmed with the strong scent of herbs, not unwelcome after the stench she had smelled in the corridors. She picked up one of the jars left open on the table and sniffed the sweet smell. Chickory, she thought, before setting it down and smelling another. Anise.

A collection of amulets hung from a peg on the wall. They looked similar in quality to what the woman outside was wearing. By the table, there was a shelf of heavy leather books, very much like those Dr. Larimer kept in his own study. Above the table, someone had pasted comely woodcuts of flowers and herbs on the wall. Spread out along a shelf, there were quite a few tracts and broadsides describing herbal remedies, astrological influences, and even witchcraft, including the *Daimonomageia*.

On the shelf below, someone had sorted a variety of cheap penny pieces into stacks. Atop each stack someone had written a single word on a small sheet of paper. *Infanticide. Matricide. Self-Murder. Regicide.* A last category simply read *Melancholia.*

On the table, Lucy noticed, a cup half full of a dark tisane had been left next to several open tracts. She touched the cup. It was still warm, suggesting that the inhabitant of the room might be returning soon. She kept her head cocked, so that she would be ready.

Flipping the tract to its frontispiece, she saw that it was William Gouge's treatise on self-murder. Someone had underlined the opening passage. *I suppose that scarce an age since the beginning of the world hath afforded more examples of this desperate inhumanity, than this our present age; and that of all sorts of people, clergy, laity, learned, unlearned, noble, mean, rich, poor, free, bond, male, female, young and old. It is therefore high time that the danger of this desperate, devilish and damnable practice be plainly and fully set out.*

She glanced at the tract that lay open beside it, as if someone had been reading them together. *"The Self-Murder of a Tanner's Wife,"* she read out loud. Then, with a start, she realized what she was reading: *The true and sad account of a most desperate woman, driven to madness and frenzy, after her husband, a tanner, was mistaken for a highwayman, and killed by two ignoble noblemen, Henry Belasysse and Lord Buckhurst.*

Excitedly, she continued to read, quickly finding it to be a sad tale indeed. The tract described how the tanner's wife had lost her livelihood and income because the tanners' guild would not allow her to continue her husband's trade, even though they did give her a widow's pension. *She did discover that her husband was in deep debt from a sickness with gambling. The guild would not pay off those debts, so ignobly accrued. With two young children clamoring for food, she set to begging and the meaner arts, until she had only her body left to sell.* They found her not too long after, at the base of a bridge, where all presumed she had thrown herself in a final fit of despair.

Lucy shuddered. A pathetic end indeed. And to think that these noblemen had been pardoned by King Charles. She could not help but curl her lip in disdain.

A step at the doorway and a muffled exclamation caused her to whirl around. Despite her best intentions, she had gotten lost in the tract and failed to pay attention to her surroundings.

Sure enough, the man standing there was the same one who

had given her the concoction for Miss Belasysse yesterday morning. As before, he was dressed completely in black.

"You!" he cried, looking nervously about. "What are you doing here?"

"I needed to see you. You are the Bedlam apothecary, are you not?"

"Yes," he admitted. "Jonathan Quade. I procure the herbs, mix the elixirs and tisanes, and attend to the patients. There is no resident physician, so it falls to me to keep the inmates well. Such as we can." He watched her, a question in his eyes.

"Miss Belasysse was an inmate here," she said. "Is that not the truth of the matter?"

He nodded, still watching her nervously.

The questions she had been holding in bubbled up. "Why did her family not know she was here? Or were they lying about not knowing where she was? Was she here for ten months? Who brought her here?"

After looking up and down the hallway, he shut the door behind him. "Miss Belasysse came to us at the end of June," he whispered. "In 1666, a few months before the Great Fire. I was tending to a patient when she arrived. I never saw who brought her."

"She never told you?" Lucy pressed.

He was quiet for a moment. "No. The last thing she remembered, as she told me later, was that she had been taking a walk near her family's London home. I suspect that she suffered a seizure and likely lost any memory of how she came to be here. The *epilepsia,* you see."

Lucy frowned. Before she could ask another question, he asked one of his own. "What of Miss Belasysse? Has she recovered her memory? Is she well? Or is she still—fitful?" His eyebrows furrowed. "You have not brought her back here, have you?"

Lucy regarded him closely. His concern for the woman seemed genuine. "No, she is still in the care of Dr. Larimer. I do not think she is well," Lucy admitted. "She did take the tonic you sent easily enough, and that seemed to soothe her. But she is still melancholic and very anxious. Sometimes, she is quite gay, and she alarms me."

"But she is safe." Nervously, the man began to quickly grind a few herbs together with the mortar and pestle, causing a strong aroma to arise from the basin.

"St. John's wort," he said. "For melancholy. There are many who suffer from that same complaint here, and I seek to lessen the torments of anguish when I can. Is that why you have come?" He paused, licking his chapped lips. "Or did she send you to see me?" He looked hopeful.

"Dr. Larimer needs more of the unguent you made for her. One of her physicians is here, speaking to the keeper."

"Oh, no!" he exclaimed, setting down the pestle. "I can supply him with the ingredients he needs. The keeper must not be informed of her whereabouts!"

"Why not?" Lucy asked.

"He is not a good man."

Distantly she heard a bell ringing.

"What is that?" she asked. "It did not sound like a church bell."

Mr. Quade frowned. "We use bells to help our inmates remember what they are supposed to be doing." Far off, she heard a man begin to scream. Miss Belasysse's fearful whisper echoed in her mind. *I was afraid to ring for her,* she had said. *Afraid of who might come.*

Lucy blinked. "What happened to Miss Belasysse here?" she whispered. "Was she . . . a prisoner?"

"Not a prisoner," he replied. When she waited, he threw up his hands in a helpless gesture. "Some inmates suffer from a great imbalance of the humors. Their spirits and minds are broken, and we can little understand how to help them." He rubbed his forehead. "There are things we must do to help them heal, so that they will not bring harm to themselves or others. They are often allowed to roam freely about the grounds. Most of the time we only lock them up when we feel they are dangerous. I never believed Miss Belasysse would cause harm to others, but her fits . . ."

"They tied her up," Lucy said, thinking of the marks on her wrists.

"May the good Lord show them mercy, they did. At first, I believed it was for her own good." Mr. Quade rubbed his eyes. He began to rap his knuckles on the table. "The keeper kept her locked up. I never knew why. He would not say. I asked him once, but he said that she was of 'special concern' to them."

The man's screaming grew louder. With great effort, Lucy turned her attention back to the apothecary. "I met a woman here who knew Miss Belasysse, I think," Lucy said. "She called her a bluebird."

"Ah," he said. "I daresay you were speaking to Lucinda. Mrs. Jamison, I should say. She and Miss Belasysse were fast friends, and she has been quite melancholic since she left." He sighed. "Mrs. Jamison rather thinks she is a bird. I don't know why. Harmless, though."

"She said a quail had helped the bluebird fly away. To escape."

Lucy paused, feeling a little ridiculous. "Are you the quail, Mr. Quade?" she whispered. "Did you help Miss Belasysse flee from this place?"

He nodded. "Octavia, I mean Miss Belasysse, begged me to let her leave. She asked me to write letters to her brother and her family. I began to believe that they would never reply, as every letter she wrote went unanswered. For months. Only when she sent a letter herself did her brother finally come to fetch her."

"He did come? Henry Belasysse was here?"

"Yes," Mr. Quade replied. "A little over a week ago. Miss Belasysse was delighted when he came."

"When was this?" Lucy asked.

The apothecary scratched his head. "That would have been Saturday, the thirtieth of March."

And I found her on the first of April, Lucy thought to herself. "Was she injured when she left here? Were her hands cut at all?"

Mr. Quade frowned. "Injured? Of course not. She had, of course, undergone treatment during her time here. Bloodletting and the sort, but she had not sustained any injury. Why? Is she all right?"

"She is fine," Lucy said hastily, seeing the concern in his eyes. "Could you tell me, what was she wearing when she left?"

"Her brother had brought her a blue dress so that she would not draw attention to herself when she traveled. I took the dress to her, and then led her to her brother who was waiting beyond the gate, so the keeper would not see them go."

"And did her brother say anything else about their journey? Where they planned to go?"

"I assumed to their family seat. He was nervous, naturally,

about her condition, but I gave him enough of the concoction to last them the journey home." He paused. "But his worries seem to have been for naught, as he managed to get her to the care of Dr. Larimer."

Lucy shook her head. "No, I found Miss Belasysse wandering about, senseless, near Holborn Bridge, several days after she left here. I brought her to Dr. Larimer's as I was concerned for her. Her brother has not been seen in over a week. His wife is quite worried."

He paled a bit. "I know he was afraid of someone; I do not know who. Please miss. I have told you all I know." He opened the door.

She pointed to the tract on the table. "I could not help but notice you were reading about the murder of the tanner for which Henry Belasysse was pardoned. Why is that?"

"What?" he asked, following her gaze. "Oh, yes. Mr. Browning, the assistant keeper, gave the tract to me several months ago. He knows that I am interested in better understanding melancholy and self-murder, as well as the impulses that drive a man to murder."

"So the tanner's wife killed herself? What a desperate act!" Lucy said.

"If you spent more time here, you would see the toll that melancholia and desperation take upon a person's soul." He sighed.

"But is it not an odd coincidence that Mr. Browning had this very tract in his possession?"

"No, it was no coincidence. When Miss Belasysse first came here, Mr. Browning recognized her straightaway. Said he knew for a fact that her brother was not innocent, and that even though the king had pardoned him in this temporal world, there was no pardon to be had in the hereafter."

Lucy nodded. She understood the anger over the king's pardon.

The apothecary continued. "I am ashamed to say that he taunted her with her brother's crime, from a place of deep anger. Even more so after the tanner's wife took her own life. I caught him waving this tract in front of her, tormenting her with the knowledge that her brother's thoughtless act had driven another to such a terrible end."

"Did he know the tanner's wife?" Lucy asked, wondering. "His anger toward Miss Belasysse seems so *personal*." Then a thought struck her. "Was she *here*, at Bedlam?"

He shook his head slowly. "I do not think so. Although . . ." He paused, still thinking. "Now that you mention it, I am not certain." He paused again. "I remember now there was a woman here for a short spell, shortly after the tanner's murder occurred, whom Mr. Browning had taken a particular interest in."

"Do you remember anything about the woman?" Lucy asked.

"No, she was full of melancholia. A surgeon performed some bloodletting upon her, but when she did not respond and—I suspect—when she ran out of funds, she was released." He rubbed his forehead. "Wait, yes! It must have been the tanner's wife. I never realized—"

"Why, what happened? What did you remember?"

"She had a violent outburst—just once. In full hysterics, as I recall. She screamed that her husband had been deliberately killed, by two men, and that even the king had covered the crime."

"Yes, that must have been her! What happened to her?" Lucy asked, breathless now.

Mr. Quade rubbed his eyes. "She was dragged into isolation, and that was the last I heard of it. She left shortly after that, but still well before Miss Belasysse joined us at Bedlam."

"So the two women did not know each other?"

The apothecary shook his head. "I do not believe they did."

Lucy thought about the notes that Susan Belasysse said her husband had received. "But someone believed her story, I think."

"Perhaps." He paused. "I only looked at this tract after Miss Belasysse left. This may sound pitiful, but I find I have missed her. It is the only reminder that I have of her time here."

He nodded toward the door. "I shall bring Dr. Larimer instructions for making up another batch. He could take it to another apothecary, if he does not wish to make it himself. Pray, leave here and do not come back again." He turned away then, staring at his collection of amulets, looking lost and forlorn.

Lucy left, moving quickly through the corridors, trying to keep her footsteps from echoing in the stone halls. Lost in her own thoughts, she almost moved into full view of Mr. Sheridan speaking to another man in the great hall.

Squinting into the shadowy room, she could see it was the same man who had assaulted Miss Belasysse outside the physician's house, calling himself her husband, Mr. Nabur. Ducking behind one of the great stone pillars, Lucy said a small prayer that no one would see her.

They were evidently concluding a conversation. "Well, Mr. Sheridan, I thank you for your visit today," she heard the man say to the physician. "As you can see, we do have room for a few more patients, provided they can pay their lodging and treatment fees. Any referral from you, we shall consider most closely. Good day."

After the man walked past, she was able to move through the great room and out the front door. Mr. Sheridan was outside the stone wall, looking about unpleasantly.

"Who was that man you were just speaking to?" she asked breathlessly.

"The keeper," he growled. "Not a physician at all. He just manages the building and the inmates."

She pulled on his sleeve. "The keeper. He was the man who came after Miss Belasysse, earlier this week!"

He shook his hand free of her and returned to walking at his usual brisk pace. "That does not surprise me." He kicked a stone along the path. "They think they are doing right by the inmates. Tying them up is a very common treatment for those with afflicted minds, particularly those who are not easily controlled." Mr. Sheridan continued to fume. "How could they have done such wrong to such a beautiful creature?"

"I am certain that the keeper would have little qualms in keeping Miss Belasysse tied up, as some of the others were," Lucy said. "It is shameful."

"You do not understand! They placed her there purposefully. Can you not see that?" Mr. Sheridan cried. "Where is that intelligence that Dr. Larimer and Mr. Hargrave purport you to possess?"

"Who placed her there?" Lucy asked, stopping short. "I spoke with the apothecary. He said Miss Belasysse did not know who had brought her to Bedlam."

Mr. Sheridan rolled his eyes. "It was her parents, naturally. Lord and Lady Belasysse."

"He told you that?" Lucy stared at him.

"He did not have to," Mr. Sheridan replied. "It is not mumpers and mendicants who stay at Bedlam, but those who can afford the lodging and care. Is it not obvious? The keeper was being paid quite handsomely. No wonder he tried that ridiculous guise, to pass himself off as her husband. He lost a fortune when she escaped."

"Why would they put her there? Why would they lie about it?" Lucy asked.

Mr. Sheridan was unusually forthcoming. "Her mother was ashamed of her, that was easy enough to see. Her father, too. Her brother was the only one to care a whit about her. His only redeeming quality, in my mind."

Lucy nodded. She had seen something of the mother's vitriol toward Miss Belasysse herself. However, something still did not make sense.

"Why then?" she wondered out loud. "Miss Belasysse told me that her mother had tried all kinds of healers and soothsayers and priests. Had she just reached a point of utter despair? Why would she have pretended her daughter was dead? Why have the funeral? It does not make sense."

"I do not know. And I do not wish to discuss the matter further."

They fell silent then, each caught in thought. For Lucy's part, the shrieks of the man tied to the bed haunted her for the rest of the walk back to the Larimers'.

·22·

I need to speak to the constable," Lucy told Mr. Sheridan when they reached the Larimers' home.

"As you wish," he said, without even glancing at her. He seemed distracted and tense. "No matter to me."

He went inside, and she continued on to Fleet Street, to see Duncan at his jail.

"Constable," she called when she arrived, "please do not arrest Miss Belasysse. I think there is more going on here than we realized."

"Lucy," he said, pulling over a stool. "Pray, sit down. You look quite pale indeed." He pulled over another stool so that he could sit across from her, his knees touching hers. "Tell me what happened."

In fits and starts she told him everything—everything that the apothecary had told her, even all that she had witnessed. He nodded when she described how some of the people lay tied and screaming in their beds. "But I do not think they were wholly untended," she said, thinking about the apothecary. "There were many abuses to be seen, and it was shocking to think that Miss Belasysse, the daughter of a baron, should have suffered at their hands. It was rather like a prison," she ended. "I cannot understand why her parents would have sent her there, to languish as she did."

She then described what the apothecary had told her about Henry Belasysse taking his sister away from Bedlam the week before. "We know, too, that he had made no plans to prepare the London house for their company," Lucy added. "The servants seem to have been completely unaware of their arrival."

"A bad business, indeed," Constable Duncan said. "I cannot imagine that Henry Belasysse would have sought to free his sister without a thought of where to take her. No matter how excited a state he was in when he left, surely he had time to form a plan."

"So, where?" Lucy asked.

"Let us see what we can determine." From the corner, he picked up a large roll of paper that was tied with a bit of a brown string. "Stow's survey of London," he explained as he unrolled it. "Here, hold that end down."

Lucy looked at the map, full of streets and lanes, dotted with houses and churches, cows in their pastures, and boats on the River Thames. She had seen such maps before. Master Aubrey had a rather tattered version that Lucy had consulted in the past, and Master Hargrave had a great map of London pasted to the wall of his study.

"This map does not show the destruction from the Great Fire, of course, but it should suffice." With his left forefinger, he pointed to a location on Fleet Street. "Here we are," he said. Moving his finger a bit north and east, he continued. "And here is Holborn Bridge, where you encountered Miss Belasysse. Nearby this point, I found the body of the dead man. From the amount of blood on the ground, I feel I can say with some certainty that he was killed on that spot where his corpse was discovered." With his right forefinger, he pointed to another spot. "This, here, is Bedlam." He tapped both locations at once. "The question is, what happened in the two days between the time she and her brother fled Bedlam and the time you found her, a mile and a half away, alone and covered in blood?"

Lucy continued to study the map. "Where would they have been going, though? Those pastures and lanes disappeared in the Fire. Even if they had sought hospitality with an acquaintance, all these homes were burnt up these seven months past. Surely Mr. Belasysse would have known this." She looked up at the constable. "Would Henry Belasysse truly have taken his unwell sister through the remains, on foot?"

"I do not know the man, but it hardly seems likely," Duncan agreed. He traced his finger along a faint red line that had been colored on the map. "Here, to the best of my estimation, is the line of the Great Fire, before the wind shifted and the Fire turned back on itself. This area is all burnt. I hardly think they would be walking in the ruins. Even though you did find her there." He pointed again to Holborn Bridge. "Quite a distance."

"They would have been seeking refuge," Lucy decided. "A church maybe, or even an inn." She put her hand to her head. "Or, Henry Belasysse had an acquaintance with whom he felt he could stop with his sister."

Duncan began to roll up the map. "Stow's map, as useful as it can be, is at least a hundred years out of date. I know at least five taverns and inns that are not on that map. I will take Hank and make some inquiries. Perhaps they stopped somewhere along the way. The question remains, however—what happened to her brother?" A chill ran over Lucy when he grimly added one more thing. "Even a man fleeing from a tedious wife will not keep himself invisible to others. At least, that is not the action of an honest man. And we know, from his past actions against the tanner, that Henry Belasysse is anything but an honest soul. For all we know, Henry Belasysse killed that man and is now hiding from his crime. He has killed before, that much we know to be true."

"And Miss Belasysse?" she asked.

"I am not at all convinced of her innocence either. She may very well know her brother's whereabouts." He looked at Lucy. "Can you help me find out where they may have gone? I have an idea."

When Lucy arrived at Master Aubrey's, she found Lach inside sorting letters into trays. As usual, his reddish brow furrowed more deeply when he saw her in the doorframe. "What do you want?" he asked.

"Greetings to you, too, Lach," Lucy replied. She went over to the tray and started to sort out the second typeface. "Thought I would help you a bit. Least I can do, leaving you with all the work like I did."

He shrugged. "No matter to me. Quieter when you aren't around anyway."

"I will be quiet," she said.

He just grunted in reply, and after that they worked silently for a bit.

"Lach," she said finally.

He groaned. "What? I knew you couldn't hold your tongue."

She ignored his surly tone. "Do we have tracts about Bedlam? I know *Mad Tom of Bedlam*—"

Before she could finish, Lach whooped and began to sing the popular tune, in a more raucous way than she had done earlier when walking with Mr. Sheridan.

"But I was wondering if we had any others," she continued, as if he were not jumping about, pretending to be Mad Tom escaped from Bedlam, looking for his Maudlin Maeve.

"Why ever for?" he panted, still cavorting about the room.

"To have them come and collect you, of course. You are a mad fool, Lachlin. On this point, I do not jest."

He pulled at her cap. "Tell me why you want to know about Bedlam or I shan't give you any."

"I would just like to know more about the place," she said, edging away.

He stopped then, a mocking look appearing on his face. "This is about the madwoman you are looking after, is it not?"

Lucy could tell that he would not give up asking questions until he was satisfied. "Yes, it is about Miss Belasysse. She is not mad, just confused."

"Dr. Larimer is going to tuck her away in there?" He stuck his tongue out at her. "Knew someone in that mad place once. Went in and never came out."

"What? Heavens, no." Seeing that he was not going to budge, she sighed, giving in. "We think she may have already been in there, these last ten months." She frowned, remembering what the apothecary had told her. "Someone else tucked her away in Bedlam."

"You finish putting away that type. I will be back directly." Lach disappeared into the cellar.

He returned a few moments later, blowing dust off some of the pamphlets. Clearly these were not part of Master Aubrey's regular rotation of stock.

"This one is about the keepers of Bedlam," he said, handing it to her. He looked at another and began to laugh. "This one I will keep." Another about Mad Tom, no doubt. That was all right. The one he had handed to her looked to be more useful.

"*An enquiry into the affairs of Bethlem Hospital,*" Lucy read out loud. "Oh, look, it tells the history of Bedlam. Begun in 1377, called then St. Mary of Bethlehem." She continued to skim slowly through the dense text. "*Helkiah Crooke, physician to King James, was dismissed as keeper under King Charles, after an enquiry disclosed a series of abuses and neglect.*" She paused, thinking of what she had just seen. "Abuses. Yes, I would say so."

"*The hospital is now run by resident steward Mr. Frederick Crouch, a keeper who, while not a physician himself, would sell off his own children into slavery to put a few more coins in his pocket,*" she continued, ignoring Lach as he dramatically yawned. "*In this regard, he is assisted by a second resident steward, a former jailer at Newgate, who—*"

She broke off from reading the tract when Master Aubrey walked into the shop then. "Good day, sir!" Lucy called, hopping off the stool.

The master printer's eyes brightened when he saw her. "All

done at Larimer's?" he asked. "None too soon! We have several new pieces to put together, and a few others to hawk."

"Er, well, no. I am not yet done at Dr. Larimer's," Lucy said.

Master Aubrey looked at her sternly. "I made an agreement with the physician, Lucy. I expect you to honor your obligation."

"I know, sir. I think, though, there is value in me staying a few days more."

With a quick immodest movement, she hiked up her skirts so that she could pull the piece she had been writing from her pocket. "I did write this for you, sir. Perhaps you can use it."

Master Aubrey glanced at it. *"A Death Along the River Fleet,"* he read out loud, then stopped, squinting at the next line. "Your script lacks a much needed clarity, my child. It would be best if you could improve your hand. I can barely discern your words."

She held out her hand. "Shall I take it back?" she asked.

Master Aubrey held it away, turning slightly. "No, no. Though 'tis mostly rooster scratchings, I can make it out."

Lucy hid a smile. It was clear that the master printer was a bit intrigued, as he pored over what she had written about the recently found corpse.

"It will do," Master Aubrey said, batting at Lucy when she squealed in delight. He handed it to Lach to read. "Let us get started on setting this type, you young scamp. After all—"

"Everyone loves a good murder," Lach and Lucy said together, reciting Master Aubrey's oft-repeated phrase as dutifully as children in the dame school.

"Sir," Lucy said, thinking about what she and Duncan had discussed earlier, "perhaps tomorrow I could sell a few tracts for you. I do not think Dr. Larimer would mind."

Lach glanced at her suspiciously. "What are you on about?" he whispered.

She kicked his foot. But the damage was done.

"Well, the constable and I thought we might discover where Henry Belasysse and his sister might have traveled after leaving Bedlam." She faltered as they stared at her. "By selling tracts along the way, I would not arouse suspicions, and we could more readily speak to someone who saw them on their journey. Then I could discover an end to our story." She looked hopefully at the master printer.

Lach snorted, but Master Aubrey clapped his hands together. "Excellent thinking!" He turned to his apprentice. "Lach, prepare a pack for Lucy!"

"I shall pick it up in the morning," Lucy said, as she departed. Truth be told, she was a bit sorry to go. She always enjoyed the process of setting the type, working out the quoins, composing the text. Setting the text of her own story gave her a greater thrill than could be imagined. Right now, though, other matters needed to be attended to first.

"Devil woman has her familiar now," Molly said by way of greeting when Lucy returned to Dr. Larimer's a short while later.

"What ever do you mean?" Lucy asked, starting to pull off her cloak.

"See for yourself," the servant replied, with a shrug. "The woman is out in the garden. Been there since you left, saying her spells."

"She is not a witch, Molly," Lucy said, moving down the

hallway and through the kitchen. "Nor is she accursed. She is just a bit touched, and maybe in time Dr. Larimer will make her well again."

She could hear the doubt in her own voice. Apparently Molly did, too.

"More than touched when she killed that man, wasn't she? Yes, I heard about that," Molly said. "What everyone was saying at the market, when I went to get a bit of beef for our supper." She looked about. "I tell you, my ma ain't happy that I'm living in the house with a murderess. Said I'm not to take any more ribbons or coins to look after her, either. Hope the constable comes to lock her up. What if she murders us all in our beds? Such a thing I heard tell happened in Devon, so who is to say it would not happen here. What will you say then?"

"I will not say anything because I will be dead, Molly Greenbush!" Then, surprising them both, Lucy grabbed the servant by the shoulders and gave her a hard shake. "Enough! We still do not know for certain that Miss Belasysse murdered that man! Pray, leave me be."

Leaving the startled servant to gape after her, Lucy went around to the small courtyard behind the house. There, as Molly had described, Miss Belasysse was sitting on the stone bench, stroking a small black cat who was curled up beside her. She did rather look like a witch with her familiar, Lucy thought, trying to squash the qualm of misgiving that had flooded over her. *You are a fool, Lucy Campion,* she scolded herself. Still, she did knock twice on a nearby tree, more out of habit than any abiding belief in true deviltry.

"Miss Belasysse," she said, mustering a pleasant smile. "How do you fare?"

"I am better, Lucy," she said, pulling the cat onto her lap. "Particularly since the constable has not come to arrest me, as I expected him to do." She began to tap her fingers against her leg, withdrawing them when the cat's claws captured her hand as it would a mouse.

When she put her finger to her mouth to suck the spot of blood, Lucy could see she was trembling a bit. The fear of arrest and jail clearly weighed more heavily upon her than she wished to admit.

Lucy sat down beside her and stroked the long silver whiskers along the side of the cat's face. The image of Avery, a man who so loved cats, briefly sprang to mind. She wondered for a moment how he was faring, but then turned back to the matter at hand.

"I think," Lucy said carefully, "that Constable Duncan has decided to wait until your brother turns up. Maybe he knows what happened. He might even be able to testify on your behalf, and put forth your innocence."

"Ah, yes. Until my brother appears." Miss Belasysse giggled. "Mayhap my brother committed the murder himself. Do you think Constable Duncan might believe that to be true?"

Lucy put her face close to the woman's. "*Did* your brother kill that man?" she whispered. "Please, if that is true, then you must tell the constable. Lest you be arrested for a crime you did not commit."

"He would believe that, would he not? Because everyone believes my brother to have murdered before," Miss Belasysse exclaimed, her voice sounding full of tears. "I tell you, though I remember little of the last year, I can assure you of this: My brother is no killer! He never has taken a man's life, I swear it!"

"You are speaking of the tanner's murder?" Lucy asked, still watching Miss Belasysse closely.

"It was all the fault of that drunken sot, Charles Sackville— Pardon me, *Lord Buckhurst*," Miss Belasysse explained, her tone growing more bitter. "It was he who got my brother into a terrible drunken state that evening."

"They were both pardoned by the king," Lucy said. Without thinking how her words would sound, she continued. "They were luckier than most, I can assure you of that. Had it been the poor tanner who had mistaken Lord Buckhurst for a highwayman, well, I am rather afraid that he would have been hanged within a fortnight."

The woman's face had grown pale. Seeing that, Lucy spoke quickly. "Forgive me!" she cried. "I did not heed the words that tumbled out of my mouth."

The cat looked up at her, staring with yellow eyes, obviously annoyed that Lucy's cries had disturbed its slumber.

Miss Belasysse began to stroke the cat again. "You speak the truth, Lucy. With a candor I quite admire." The cat started to purr then, deep rumbling sounds. "Had it not been for my uncle, they would certainly have been hanged," she added.

"It was he who petitioned the king on their behalf?" Lucy asked.

"No, my father petitioned the king, as did the father of Lord Buckhurst. As they were both loyal to the Crown, their petition on behalf of their sons was well received."

"I do not understand," Lucy said, trying to follow her explanation.

"Uncle Harlan was there. Tippling down with them at the tavern where the event occurred. As a matter of fact, I was there, too. We had been journeying from London together, and Uncle Harlan wanted to stop there for supper. When it began to appear that we would need to stay the night, as they were rather the worse for wear, he procured us several rooms. I waited to speak with my brother, as I was not happy with my room. Truth be told, I did not wish to stay at the inn at all, as I felt rather unsafe with so many unsavory sorts about."

"He did not heed your worries" Lucy said, trying to convey a sense of sympathy.

"No, he did not," the woman whispered. Lucy could see her hands were starting to shake. "Oh, if only we had not stayed there!" she moaned softly.

"Did you see what happened?" Lucy asked.

"No. I had heard the shot though," Miss Belasysse replied. "I knew straight away that the sound had been made from a gun, having grown up around Yorkshire with men who liked to hunt. I knew it in my heart, but oh, how I prayed in that instant that it was just a wayward clap of thunder." Taking a deep breath, she continued in her mournful way. "When I came outside, fearful that my brother had come to harm, my uncle Harlan bid me to return to my room."

She paused. "It was then that Uncle Harlan told me the terrible news. That in their overly drunken state, one of the two men, either my brother or Lord Buckhurst, had mistaken the tanner to be a highwayman set upon robbing them, and had shot him dead with Lord Buckhurst's pistol. No one could say for sure who had done it. 'Twas not so hard for the king to pardon them, either."

"I see," Lucy said slowly. This account did not fully explain what she had learned from the apothecary earlier. "How terrible this must have been for you."

"More terrible for him, I should say," Miss Belasysse said, giving a mirthless snort. Then she heaved a deep sigh. "I find myself needful of my slumbers. Let us not speak of this distasteful topic again."

There was so much Lucy wanted to ask her, about her brother, about the tanner's murder, about Bedlam, but she did not know how to bring it up. Instead, she watched Miss Belasysse walk heavily away, her shoulders slumped, as waves of melancholia seemed to crest over her.

·23·

I hope those pieces are not about the 'Confounded Constable' again," Duncan said the next day, watching Lucy pull the carefully rolled pamphlets from her bag. They were standing near the Kingfisher Inn, just before noon, one of several inns between Bedlam and Holborn Bridge where the constable thought Henry Belasysse might have taken his sister.

Carefully, Lucy unfurled one of the rolls of printed pieces and held it out for Constable Duncan to inspect. "See? *A Death Along the River Fleet—Or, The True Account of a Most Strange Murder That Did Occur at Holborn Bridge.* I can hardly believe that Lach actually set it and printed in such a timely way." Thankfully she had checked the bag this time, and taken out several tracts that regaled the reader with ridiculous tales of befuddled constables.

At Duncan's suggestion they had added a small second piece toward the end: *The Remarkable Disappearance of Henry Belasysse,*

MP, *Late of Great Grimsby.* They thought calling that piece as well might help bring out people who might have seen the man along the route they were currently searching.

"Well, let us get to it, then. Sell your wares, woman!" Duncan replied, leaning back against the stone wall of the inn a short distance away. Lucy knew he was trying not to draw attention to himself, because he was not wearing his customary red coat.

Pretending that the constable was not there smirking at her, she climbed atop one of the barrels that were stacked outside the inn. Master Aubrey had told her a long while back, when she had first started as his apprentice, not to sell inside an establishment unless she wanted to be promptly thrown out on her ear. Generally, she had heeded this warning.

The week off from selling had actually helped soothe her throat, more than any chamomile concoction, and within a few moments, she had a small crowd gathering around her. She started this time with *Strange News from Kent,* which described the odd discovery of a bag of bones that had been hidden in the cellar of an old crone. An old piece, to be sure, but one that still could summon a few listeners. She then began to tell the story of *A Death Along the River Fleet,* watching the crowd carefully. There was general interest in the story, and she sold a few tracts, but no one seemed overly attentive to the tale.

Giving Duncan a little nod, Lucy went inside to get a drink as they had previously agreed. As she entered, she found herself squinting to get accustomed to the dark interior of the inn. She sat down at a table toward the front of the establishment, near the barman, at a respectable place by the window. Even though a glance around revealed only common laborers and tradesmen coming in for a meal and a pint, she had no wish to be mistaken for a harlot.

Duncan sat down on a stool nearby. He faced a different direction and did not speak to her, so that his presence would not be off-putting to someone who might wish a private word.

As she sipped her ale, a fat man, probably in his forties, slumped down in the seat across from her.

"Here alone, miss?" he said, leering at her. "Never seen you before. Are you looking for some company?"

"I am a printer's apprentice," she said firmly, indicating her pack on the stool next to her. "I have been selling books."

"Is that right?" he asked. "Any I would be interested in?" He reached for her pack.

Instinctively, she pulled the pack a little closer to herself. She could see, from the corner of her eye, that Duncan had stiffened and turned slightly toward them.

"I have a new one, called *A Death Along the River Fleet.* It is the story of—" She stopped when she felt the man's hand groping her leg beneath the table. "What are you doing?"

"Go on." The man grinned at her. "I am quite interested in your *tale.*" He guffawed when he said the last, his heavy jowls shaking.

Before she could say anything more, Duncan had stood up and quickly pinned the man's offending arm behind his back. "Time to go, Lucy," he said to her.

When the man started to protest, Duncan pressed his arm harder. No one around them seemed even to notice, or if they did notice, they did not care. However, she could see that the barman had turned toward them, a warning look in his eye. She did not need to be told again. She hurried out of the inn. When she reached the entrance and turned back, she could see Duncan whisper something in the man's ear. The man blanched, and Duncan let him go. On the way out, Lucy saw him speak quickly to the barman, who shook his head.

When they met again in the street, Duncan said, "I think it is unlikely that Henry and Octavia Belasysse stayed there."

"Why do you say that?" Lucy asked. "How could you know?"

"That crowd all knew one another. They would have remembered a stranger, and the barman said that the beds above are rarely filled by passers-by or travelers. Regular tradesmen, mainly, passing on their way in and out of London. Come now, let us press on to the next. It is but a quarter mile from here."

Their visit to the next tavern on the list, the King's Arms, unfolded quite differently. This one was hidden in the shadows of a tight little street. Lucy looked up at the shuttered windows dubiously. "Would Henry have brought his sister here?" she wondered.

"If he had been desperate. Let us check."

As they approached the tavern, a couple came out arm in arm, clearly drunk. The man pulled the woman behind a cart. "I only have a quarter hour's time," they heard him say.

"I am going to be sick," they heard the woman reply. Then they heard a violent retching sound. Duncan and Lucy glanced at each other.

"My shoes!" they heard the man shout. Then, in a more outraged voice, "Ow, what did you hit me for!" And then, in an even more outraged shout, "My knapsack!"

The woman emerged then, glancing at Duncan and Lucy, an impudent smirk on her face. "Shhhh!" she whispered, still smirking before she darted off, disappearing within seconds.

The man came out from behind the cart then, rubbing his head. "Where did that whore go?" he demanded.

Lucy and Duncan just shrugged. Still fuming, the man walked down the street.

"You did not think to go after her?" Lucy asked, curious.

Duncan sighed. "I did not want to be diverted from our purpose." He looked at the establishment and then back at Lucy. A beautiful woman with a low-cut gown came to the door then, a drink in her hand. She looked to be waiting for someone.

"Lucy, you could just wait here," Duncan said, looking at the woman.

"I hope you will not be diverted from our purpose," Lucy teased. Or at least, she meant to say the words in a teasing way, but they fell a bit flat as she uttered them.

He glanced at her. "Of course not. Just wait here." Taking one of the tracts from her, he walked up to the woman in the doorway, who gave him a great smile. She took his arm, and they went inside together.

Shaking her head, Lucy began to look at the other shops along the street. All were a little run-down, and the people appeared weary, but no one said anything as she regarded the various wares, all the while keeping her eye on the tavern door.

"I hope that was not your sweetheart, miss," an old woman sitting in a chair said, her hands moving easily over a loom. "He might not be out for a while." She cackled a bit.

"That is beautiful," Lucy said honestly, admiring the piece on the loom. She looked up at the shop behind her. "Is this your shop?" she asked.

"Owned by my two sons," she said proudly. "One spends a bit too much time in that whorehouse," the woman said, jerking her head toward the tavern, "but the other, my Timothy, is a hard-working lad. We've been here for nigh on thirty years. My husband, God rest his soul, was a weaver with the guild. And I have long worked the loom myself."

"Do you sit here mostly, then?" Lucy asked. "A good view of the comings and goings, I would suppose."

"I see everything!" The woman laughed. "Including that Moll Cutpurse you just saw, who relieved that man of his coins. Of course, I knew her as little Lottie O'Donovan, before she took to her thieving promiscuous ways."

Taking a deep breath, Lucy asked her about the Belasysses and the man who had been murdered, describing them all in as much detail as she could muster. The old woman listened attentively. "No gentlewomen at that place, I can tell you."

"Perhaps in the evening or the night?" Lucy pressed.

The woman shook her head. "Not so likely I would have missed it. If I did, Dorothy would have told me. Right, Dorothy?"

It was only then that Lucy saw another woman perched in front of the furrier's shop. She had been so quiet and still. Like the first woman, she was seated in a chair that made her appear to be permanently fixed in the ground.

"Did you by chance see a woman with long dark hair, possibly in a blue dress?" Lucy hesitated. "Perhaps having a fit of sorts."

"The devil woman?" Dorothy commented. "Flew through the air, I heard tell."

"You saw her?" Lucy exclaimed. "Here? On this street?"

The women chuckled. "Not here. The Cattle Bell Inn. A mile or so to the east."

"Hope your man comes out soon," Dorothy commented. "If Elsie gets her hands on him, you might lose him."

"Oh, he is not—" Lucy broke off, because Duncan came out then.

"Let us go, Lucy," he said. "I am sorry that I left you on your own."

"I was not alone. I had a very nice conversation with these women here."

He noticed the women then, and touched his cap respectfully before he and Lucy continued down the street.

"And how was your conversation?" she asked. "Did you learn anything?"

"That place is a brothel."

"Yes, I learned the same thing. I cannot imagine that Henry would have brought his sister there either."

He nodded. "I am lucky to have gotten out with my money intact." He patted his jacket. "I did, did I not?" Feeling his wallet, he looked relieved.

"No matter, I have discovered where the Belasysses stayed. At the Cattle Bell Inn. Those old crones heard tell of a woman who flew through the air, before convulsing in a devil's spell. Sound familiar?"

Duncan closed his eyes, as if imagining Stow's map of London. "That is not too far. Shall we?" Unexpectedly he offered her his arm, which she took without thinking.

For a moment they walked companionably together, Lucy's hand still tucked in his arm. "Hopefully, neither of us shall have to be groped to get some information, although I imagine you did not mind it so much."

Duncan stopped then and looked down at her. "I do mind. I mind very much. Indeed, this is foolish," he said grimly. "Why am I letting you do this?"

She took a step back. "You want to find out who murdered that man, do you not? And whether the Belasysses had anything to do with his murder. And where Henry Belasysse took his sister when he left Bedlam. And what has happened to Henry Belasysse since that night."

"Of course," he sighed. "There has to be another way."

"What is the matter?" she said. "I am fine."

"Forgive me if I am a bit concerned. I let you be pawed by a ruffian—"

"Which you stopped from occurring."

"And I left you alone in a dark street outside a brothel," he continued.

"I was not alone. Those two women confirmed everything you discovered. The Belasysses were not there."

"Still, what would Adam Hargrave say if he knew I was dragging you around as I have been doing." He slapped his forehead. "Good Lord, he has grounds to murder me himself." His voice turned self-mocking. "And I think no jury would convict him, either. He would not even have to buy them off, like so many gentleman murderers will do."

Lucy was glad of the breeze that cooled her cheeks. "Stop teasing, if you would. Adam would never commit murder."

"Oh, I am not altogether teasing. Adam is too good a man to murder me outright, but surely he will be angry that I have dragged his future wife about on such an unseemly quest."

Tears rose in Lucy's eyes that she quickly blinked away. The flash of pain was real, but she was not sure of its cause. "I am not his future wife." She added, "Such a marriage will never occur." She looked toward the sun to avoid looking at Duncan. "We are heading east a bit more, are we not?"

She began to walk very quickly, with the constable keeping pace easily beside her. Neither spoke for the next few minutes.

As they neared the Cattle Bell Inn, Duncan touched her arm again. "Lucy. Forgive me. I am sorry."

"Sorry for what?" she replied, panting a bit. The fast-paced walk had been more strenuous than she realized. "Sorry that I was born into a servant's lot? Sorry that I have lived half my life serving others?"

"No, I am not sorry about you being a servant," he said, a sudden intensity to his voice. "I am only sorry if it is true that such a state has kept you from marrying the man you love."

She looked up at him then, and they both stopped. The constable's face was guarded as he looked down at her. "I do not know if that is true," she whispered. As she spoke those words, she felt the tightness in her chest loosen a bit.

For a moment, she saw the slightest flicker of hope gleam in his hazel eyes and his face very nearly relax into its more customary grin.

"Let us go inside," she said, before he could say anything else. "We could just speak to the barmaid. I know you will be quite good at that." She gave him a quick smile.

When they walked in, they took a seat at a table close to the bar. The constable ordered a small plate of cheese and meat and two ales.

Lucy looked around. The place seemed cleaner and more

respectable than most, certainly in comparison to the two inns they had visited earlier.

"Nice place," she said.

Although her voice was low, the barkeep overheard her and grinned as he set the ales down in front of them. With a mocking tip of his invisible cap, he nodded to her. "Thank you kindly, miss."

At that point, he began to tell them a few jokes. Lucy found herself laughing more than she had in a long time.

The barman eyed her appreciatively. "Nice smile, that one," he said to Duncan. "A good merry laugh."

He seemed so friendly—not surly at all. She caught Duncan's eye, and he nodded.

"You work here every day?" Duncan asked casually.

The barkeep shrugged. "Most days. Nights, too. Abe's the name."

"You must get all sorts here," Lucy said, taking a sip of her ale. "Gentry, looks like it."

"I suppose that is so," he said. "I dunno. Most do not catch my fancy like you do." He nodded again toward Lucy. Since his tone was still friendly, Lucy did not feel alarmed.

"Not too many fights, then?" Duncan said.

"No, not so much. There was a bit of a skirmish the other night. Few tables smashed." He nodded to a bunch of broken wood in the corner.

"When was that?" Duncan said. "Still not cleared it up yet?"

"Just a few nights ago it happened. No other fight that I can recall. But that was a doozy." He began to regale them with the story. "Good mates by the end, walked out singing arm in arm," he concluded, shaking his head. "Better caterwauling you'll not soon hear."

Clearly this was a different altercation that did not involve the Belasysses. Lucy decided to be more direct.

"I heard tell of a devilish woman who was here a week or so ago," Lucy said casually, hoping to draw the man out. "A fit she had? Accursed, some said."

"A devilish woman? Accursed?"

Lucy nodded. She felt a bit poorly about casting Miss Belasysse in such a way, but was pleased when a glint of recognition passed through Abe's eye. "Why yes, I do remember that woman. Genteel-looking. In a lovely blue dress. To be honest with you, she looked a bit too refined for even this place." He coughed. "At least that is what I thought before the madness struck her."

"What happened?" Lucy asked, trying to sound like one of the eager people who would gather about her when she told a story. "Did her body just begin to convulse? Did it fly through the air? I heard tell that—"

"No, no, miss. Nothing like that. I will not have you saying that witchcraft was done here. We are a godly folk, even if we do run a place where spirits flow." He looked down at Lucy's eager face and wide eyes and sighed. "Others who were here did say she was possessed. The man with her, whom she had addressed as 'brother,' told her to give them no mind."

Lucy glanced at Duncan. That seemed to confirm that the pair was indeed Octavia and Henry Belasysse. "Then what happened?" she asked.

Abe rubbed the table a little more vigorously now. "Can't rightly say. 'Twas a fit, though, of the like I have never seen." He paused then, seeming to remember something. "I have to say, it was actually quite strange."

They both waited impatiently for him to continue.

"I had been opening a new barrel of ale, you see, so I missed how the fracas started. I just know that some man came into my place without so much as asking for an ale. Went straight to their table and began speaking to the man—the woman's brother." He pointed to a table in the far back corner.

"Away from the windows, out of easy sight," Duncan murmured, studying the room. "They knew each other?"

"Can't say for sure. But I can tell you this, he made something strange happen to that woman. I don't like to say, being a good God-fearing Christian and all. But that's when—" He lowered his voice, causing Duncan and Lucy to lean in toward him. "That's when, he cursed the poor woman. Pitiful creature."

"Whatever do you mean?" Lucy asked. "How did he curse her?"

The barman shook his head. "I only know what my patrons told me. I didn't see it for myself. They said he, well, raised his hand and light flew forth."

"Light flew forth?" Lucy exclaimed.

Abe nodded. "Like an Old Testament prophet, they said. That's when I came back in, hearing the people shouting. I saw for myself. Her eyes all rolled back in her head, so we could only see the whites. I tell you, it was right strange, cursed or no cursed. When she began to convulse, truth be told, I thought maybe she was devil-owned."

"Then what happened?" Lucy asked. "Did she recover her senses?"

"Her brother knelt beside her, and that other man was standing over them, watching them. I only heard later what he had done. I just remember thinking he looked . . . satisfied."

"Satisfied?" Lucy murmured. "How odd." Seeing that Abe seemed ready to go and pick up some mugs off another table, she hurriedly asked another question, as casually as she could. "I am so curious," she said. "Did the man look like a devil? Had he a pitchfork and tail and long pointy ears?"

"Ah, miss, you have the imagination, do you not?" Abe said. "He was but a man. Black hair. His clothes were those of a tradesman. Dusty, though, as if he had been traveling."

"A devil's mark, perchance, on his face?" Lucy asked, knowing that she sounded ridiculous.

The man just smiled indulgently. "You are one for the tales, are you not? My daughter Gwen is just the same. Always tell her not to spread such tales, but she doesn't listen, does she? No marks on his face, of any sort, so far as I could tell. Except, now that you mention it, his nose looked to have been broken."

Lucy glanced at Duncan. "Recently?" she asked the barman.

"No, not recently. Not so that I could tell," he said, looking up, trying to remember. "It was all crooked, and he seemed to have trouble breathing. He made a funny rasping sound whenever he took in a breath."

"What happened to them?" Duncan asked. "The man and the woman?"

Abe shrugged. "I just know that the man—the brother—yelled at the other man to leave, and he did. After the woman had recovered, the pair of them went outside. Not surprising, really. Her brother had taken rooms above. She looked quite worn out and was probably off to her bed. To get to the rooms upstairs, you have to go outside and go in the other entrance. Thought the inn-keeper might refuse a devil woman, but their coins were gold enough."

"And did you see her the next day?" Lucy pressed. "Any more fits?" She giggled a little as if the thought were wholly amusing.

The barman shook his head. "No, I did not see either of them again. But there's a good chance my daughter Gwen brought them a bit of bread and cheese in the morning. She works in the inn, above."

"And what day was that?" Duncan asked. "Just curious, you know."

The barkeep took the question easily enough, looking up at the ceiling again, trying to recall. "Let me think," he said. "Yes, I remember it was a Saturday night. People kept talking about the accursed woman. So the next day, being a Sunday, I dipped my cloth in the church water that had been used to baptize a baby. When I got back, I wiped down the table where she had sat, and wiped down the doors, too, to keep any evil spirits from return-ing." Seeing a few men walk into the inn then, he put his cloth back over his shoulder. "Excuse me," he said, moving over to greet them.

Duncan drained his ale. "Let us walk around," he said to Lucy.

"So, it seems fairly certain that the Belasysses were here on Saturday night," Lucy said, pondering what the bartender had just told them. "Do you think that the man who 'cursed' her is the man who was found murdered?"

Duncan scratched his head. "Hard to say from the description," he said. "Dark hair, but no scratch on his face."

"The bartender said that the man's nose looked crooked, though," Lucy pointed out. "Dr. Larimer said that the nose of the corpse had been broken, but not recently."

"That could describe a great many men," Duncan replied. "Still, it could have been the same man." He looked down at Lucy. "The question is, if that is the case, what happened between Saturday night, when she and her brother were here, and Monday morning, when you found her a mile and a half away from this inn? Could they have been here the whole time?"

"We could talk to Abe's daughter. Gwen, he said her name is. Maybe she remembers seeing them."

"If Gwen works in the inn, we will have to go around to the other entrance," Duncan said. "I could inquire about a room, and you could see if she is around."

Lucy gulped, flushing slightly. She felt uncomfortable going into that part of the inn with the constable. She pointed to the door leading to the kitchen. "Maybe she is in there," she said. "I could go and see."

Duncan looked at her curiously, and she wondered if he knew what she had been thinking. "All right," he said simply. "Let us meet back here in a quarter hour's time."

·24·

Lucy slipped into the kitchen when the bartender wasn't looking. The kitchen was large, so she was able to peek inside without anyone noticing her at first. It helped that the room was a little smoky, as though someone had burnt something recently, and a few women were talking loudly to each other.

Blinking, she noticed a young girl peeling potatoes, away from everyone else, near the entrance. With a quick look around, Lucy crouched down beside the child. "Tell me," Lucy said, in as friendly a way as possible. "Is Gwen about?"

Without saying anything, the girl pointed with her knife to a cheery-looking woman with red hair who was just taking off her apron. "Got to go use the privy," she called out to no one in particular. "Be back quick."

Lucy followed the redheaded woman out a small door that led to the back of the inn. She could see a little shed out back; the privy stool was likely there. She waited while the woman took care of her necessity.

When she stepped out, Lucy called to her softly. "Gwen?" she asked. "Are you Gwen?"

"That is the name given to me by my mother," the servant replied. Though she still looked friendly, her face had grown a bit wary. "But I do ask how you have come by my name, as you are a stranger to me."

"Your father, Abe, told me," Lucy said softly. "I had a question that he thought you might be able to answer." She held her breath, feeling the lie burn a bit in her mouth.

This appeared to be the right thing to say, for the woman smoothed down her apron and smiled, her eyes bright. "What is it? I have only a few minutes to spare."

Seeing the woman's lack of guile, Lucy abandoned her earlier pretense and told a story nearer to the truth. "I am concerned about one of my friends," she said. "I am hoping that you might know something that can help her."

Quickly, without providing names, Lucy explained how she was searching for a man who had been traveling with her friend, and who might have stayed at the Cattle Bell. "The woman," she explained, "was said to be accursed, because she is thrown into frequent fits, and she may even have experienced such a frenzy in this very inn." She watched Gwen closely. "Her brother has now disappeared, and we are quite concerned about his whereabouts. Do you know anything of them? Or what might have happened to them the eve they visited?"

The woman's eyes grew wide. "I know of whom you speak. I thought it was a terrible shame that everyone spoke of that poor woman that way. I had seen her and her brother when they first arrived at the inn." She hesitated.

"What is it?" Lucy asked.

"My pa don't like when my tongue runs loose about the guests. Thinks gossip is bad for the place."

"Did you see something, then? Besides what you already said." Lucy smiled encouragingly. "Please, it's important."

"Yes, well, your friends, they were shouting something at each other. When they walked outside, to their rooms."

"Oh? They were arguing?" Lucy asked, trying to sound non-chalant. "Did you by chance hear why?" When the woman hesitated, she added, "No, I promise, I will not let on that you told me. What were they were arguing about?"

"I cannot say for sure, but she seemed to be blaming him for something. He kept saying, 'It was not my fault!'"

"'It was not my fault'?" Lucy repeated. "Did you hear anything more?"

Gwen shook her head.

"Did you see anyone with them? Another man, by chance?"

"The man who had accursed her? No, he had already left in a haste, after the woman's brother shouted at him to go away."

When another servant poked her head out of the kitchen door, Gwen said, "I need to go back in, to attend to my duties. I hope they are all right." She clucked her teeth. "Imagine, paid for two rooms, and slept in neither!"

"Neither bed was slept in?" Lucy's heart sank. That did not bode well. "Did they leave, then?"

"I suppose they must have." Gwen looked about. "Maybe they saw a rat. Sometimes that scares the guests off. Don't repeat that, mind you. Pa wouldn't like it if I told you that." She turned to go.

"Wait," Lucy cried. "What of their belongings? Their satchels? What happened to them?"

" 'Twas an odd thing, to be sure. Your friend, she had nothing of her own, which quite surprised me because she had such a grand way about her. And they had come on foot, not by carriage. She seemed quite timid, skittish, you know. Like a rabbit. But she spoke like a lady. I knew she was noble-born. He said that they would only be there one night, and that they had gotten separated from their valises. Quite odd."

A voice called out to her again. "Gwen, haven't got all day!"

"I must go. Best of luck finding your friends," she said, going back inside.

Duncan appeared then. "I should have known you would locate Gwen more quickly than I. What did you learn?"

Quickly Lucy filled him in on what the servant had told him.

"So the Belasysses did not stay the night, it would seem." He stroked his chin.

Lucy nodded. "And they were having quite a row, at least as Gwen tells us."

They began to walk around the little courtyard behind the inn.

Suddenly, there was a rustle from the bushes. "Who is there?" Duncan called. "Show yourself!"

A skinny boy, maybe ten years old, stepped out of a bush. He looked quite dirty and was clearly trying to mask a bit of fear with bravado. Lucy could see him push out his chest. He had a makeshift crutch under one arm, and his right foot and hand were wrapped in dirty bandages.

He sidled up to them. "You come to see the body?" he asked, speaking through the side of his lips.

"Body?" Duncan asked sharply. "What kind of body? Where?"

"Man's body," the boy replied. Holding out his good arm he said, "Sixpence and I'll show you."

Duncan frowned. "Three."

The boy shrugged. After Duncan dropped the coins into his hand, the boy pocketed them but did not move. Instead, he looked expectantly at the constable.

Duncan stifled a sigh. "All right, you little scamp. Another penny after you show us. No tricks, now," he warned.

They walked along into the wooded expanse that lay north of the courtyard. Lucy found herself moving closer to the constable, but she did not take his arm as she had done earlier.

"There." The boy pointed into the trees. "That is where you will find the poor stiff."

"Stay here," the constable said grimly. "Both of you."

Lucy did not wish to argue. Indeed, although she had seen many dead bodies, she was not sure she wished to see this particular one.

Instead, she knelt down next to the boy. "How long has the body been there?"

"Cannot say for sure. Found it last week. I found him when everyone else was at Sunday service, and the inn was closed. My twin sister, she works in the inn. I used to before a barrel broke my foot and hand and they said they could not keep me on." He pointed at the back door of the inn. "Sometimes they leave the door open for me, so I can get a small bite to eat. But I am not to stay inside. I usually sleep at the church, but that morning I had to go at dawn because the minister was getting the church ready for Sunday services. I came back here, to finish out my sleep," he explained. "No one pays me any mind when I am here."

"You are certain that it was not before that morning that you had seen him?"

"As certain as I know that a fox will catch a rabbit. As certain as I am that I came from my mother's belly. As certain as I am that—"

Lucy held up her hand. "Yes, I see. You are quite certain. Why did you not tell anyone?" She could not help but wrinkle her nose. "How is it that no one noticed him but you?"

The boy grinned. "The privy," he said. "That smell is enough to kill a man, I do not jest. No one will walk back this way. That is why I always found it so easy to hide." He rubbed his hands together. "That is when I thought I could make a few coins off him, you see. Him being dead, there is nothing more he can do for anybody. But he can do a bit for me, I thought. I showed my sister, and she just screamed and screamed." He looked a bit indignant. "Silly git. But I have been bringing my mates by. They pay me a penny each. Only them that I can trust. Told 'em not to tell anyone. It is my livelihood now," he said, looking eager. "You will not tell anyone, will you?"

Lucy ignored his question, for the constable had emerged from the underbrush. Even in the growing darkness, Lucy could see he looked quite disturbed.

"He is not going to take him away, is he?" the boy asked.

"I rather think he will," Lucy said. "You can understand that, can you not? He needs to be buried properly, in a churchyard. With prayers to hurry his soul on to heaven. A proper funeral. Can you see?"

The boy shook his head. "I never been to a proper funeral," he said. "Most times, when people around here die, they just get carted off to the common field. Or Houndsditch. I know that is what happened when my ma and pa died."

Lucy felt a pang of sadness for the boy, but she was watching Duncan's face. "Who is it?" she asked. "Is it——?"

For a moment the question hung in the air. Duncan nodded. "I am rather afraid that it is Henry Belasysse, given the descriptions we received from his sister and wife."

"How did he die?" Lucy asked, dreading the answer.

"Stabbed. Nay, do not look, Lucy," he said, seeing her move toward the copse of trees where the body lay. "His corpse has been stripped to his undergarments. Judging from those, and the lack of muscle in his body, he was a gentleman, to be sure, not a tradesman or laborer. I will have to send for Hank."

Lucy shivered. Another stabbing. Was it possible that he had been stabbed by the same person who killed the other man? She could not help but think of Octavia Belasysse, and the cuts on her hands.

The afternoon sun was rapidly fading. Duncan returned with the barkeep, who had lost his earlier joviality. His face was grim. "To think that boy was taking coins to show people that man's corpse," Lucy heard him say as he passed.

A moment later she heard the barman retch. "That was him. The brother of that poor woman. God rest their souls."

He was so definitive in his claim that the constable did not press him further.

Together, they watched the constable shine his glass lantern around. As he did so, Lucy caught the glint of something shining on a bit of muddy ground.

Without saying anything, Lucy picked the small object up from the ground, brushing off the dirt as she turned it this way and that. It was an elegant hand-held mirror, with an embroidered handle—a scene of birds and flowers. The glass was broken. She shivered again, thinking of what she knew about the curses that came with such mirrors. When she held it closer to her face, she caught the faintest scent of lavender.

She slipped it into her peddler's pack and headed back inside the inn. When she sat down, Abe came over and slipped a cup of hot mead into her hands. He sat down across from her, with his own cup.

"To think that poor man was lying out there this whole time," he said, shaking his head. He looked at Lucy. "I wonder what happened to the woman. His sister. I wonder if she is dead, too."

"No," she said, touching his arm. He seemed genuinely distressed by the idea that Miss Belasysse had come to harm. "She is safe."

The barkeep looked relieved. "That is a blessing at least."

She could tell he was about to ask more questions, but she was saved from further explanation when Mr. Sheridan and Dr. Larimer walked into the inn, looking perturbed. "Lucy," Dr. Larimer said, seeing her. "Will you take us to where the body was found?"

"This way," she said, leading them outside.

Other servants from the inn were starting to mill about,

curious about the body. Clearly, the boy had been selective in whom he had told about it, probably knowing he would lose the chance at a few extra coins should it be discovered.

"Just over there." She pointed, and Mr. Sheridan disappeared into the trees.

Gwen came out with an old blanket, which she handed to Dr. Larimer. "I thought the body should be covered," she said.

Dr. Larimer took the blanket from her. "Thank you. That is kind of you," he said, before joining his assistant.

They all waited then. Lucy could hear the physicians conferring together.

Mr. Sheridan came back out. "It is most definitely Henry Belasysse," he said to Duncan, looking a bit sick. "Of that I am certain."

Dr. Larimer added, "He has been dead for at least a week, which would fit with the barman's account that he had last been seen two Saturdays past." He shook his head. "We must inform his family."

Duncan nodded to Hank and another bellman who had accompanied the physicians to the inn. "Carry the body back to Dr. Larimer's residence so that he can examine it more fully," he said. "For God's sake, make sure his sister does not see him when you bring him in. We have no need for her to see him in this sorry state."

Duncan moved over to Lucy as they watched the bellman wrap the body in the sheet. "So, what do we suppose happened here?"

"Well, we know that Henry and Octavia Belasysse were inside the inn, until the other man came in and 'cursed' her," Lucy said slowly, trying to piece the events together in her mind. "When her fit began, Henry Belasysse shouted at the man to leave, and he did. Although perhaps he did not go very far."

"Right," Duncan replied. "The bartender said that the Belasysses left soon after, to retire to their rooms, he thought."

"Only Gwen said their beds had not been slept in."

Duncan began to walk about, a puzzled look on his face. "So they came out here, on their way to their rooms. Perhaps the other man surprised them then, and assaulted them. Did he then kill Henry Belasysse?" Duncan began to tap his hand against his leg. "And what of Miss Belasysse? Why did she have blood all over her dress?"

"Perhaps she tried to attend to her brother, and it is his blood on her clothes," Lucy reasoned. "If that man killed Henry, maybe that is when she fled through the ruins. When I saw her the next day, she said the devil had been chasing her. Perhaps that was he."

"But where was Miss Belasysse for the rest of the night?" Duncan asked.

"She was probably hiding from that man."

"Then how did she get those cuts on her hands?" He shook his head. "We must face facts. Once again we are brought back to Miss Belasysse—she is the link between these two men. She was overheard arguing with her brother shortly before he was killed, and in altercation with another man before he turned up dead as well. None of it bodes well for her innocence."

"Well, there were many people who were in the presence of both men before they were murdered," Lucy said. "Abe, Gwen, and everyone else in the Cattle Bell at the time! Maybe one of them murdered the two men."

Her protest was lame, and they both knew it. Given the injuries to Miss Belasysse's hands and the blood on her gown, she was clearly involved in at least one of the men's deaths, if not both.

Lucy sighed, looking at the growing shadows cast by the inn as the sun sank lower in the sky. What had happened here? How had Henry Belasysse ended up murdered?

·25·

Since it was growing dark, Lucy did not wish to cross back through the ruins alone, but instead kept pace with Hank and Duncan. The physicians rode in the cart with the body of Henry Belasysse. Thankfully, they had thought to bring lanterns to light their grim procession as they wound their way through the darkening streets.

When they arrived at Dr. Larimer's home, Molly took a frightened look at the shrouded body but gave them some welcome news. Miss Belasysse had been slumbering for the last few hours after having downed an ample dose of her sleeping draught. *At least we can hold off telling her about her brother's murder,* Lucy thought. This was followed by a second, more chilling thought. *Unless she was the one who killed him.* Lucy shivered.

"This will give you some time to see if the knife wounds match those made on the body of the other man," Constable Duncan said in a low voice to Dr. Larimer. He then dispatched Hank to bring the Belasysses to the physician's home. "Tell them we have news, but do not let on about his death. I have more questions for that family."

He turned to Lucy. "We need to make certain that Miss Belasysse does not go anywhere in the meantime."

After Hank left, and Duncan and the physicians went into the room with the corpse, Lucy went upstairs to be on hand when Miss Belasysse awoke. The woman was sleeping, her breathing light and steady. In the candlelight, she looked peaceful, with no sign of the frenzied terror that gripped her so often in her waking state. Pitiful creature, the bartender had called her, and Lucy agreed. Without thinking, she smoothed a strand of hair away from the woman's forehead.

Lucy sat down at the table and pulled the broken mirror out of her pocket. Without thinking, she began to play with it, flickering this way and that, seeing how the gleaming light moved around the room. *The devil loves a looking-glass,* she could almost hear her mother intone, and she set it down.

She looked at the great mirror in the room, which was still covered with cloth, as one would do in a house of mourning.

Why had Miss Belasysse covered the mirror, she wondered. She thought of a game that she and the other servants used to play on All Hallows' Eve. The night the spirits walked, if a woman made a wish and lit a candle before a mirror, and then blew it out, the image of her future lover would appear in the glass for an instant. She remembered trying this, giggling with her friend Bessie, feeling a pang that Bessie had never had the chance to have a husband. She could not help but wonder what would happen if she blew out the candle now. Whose face would she see in the mirror?

Idly, she pulled the cloth away and began to play with a bit of glass from the hand mirror so that it bounced off the larger mirror. Accidentally, she knocked the heavy brush off the table; it made a loud noise when it struck the wooden floor.

"What are you doing?" Octavia Belasysse cried out, having been awoken by the crash. "Why have you uncovered the mirror?"

Quickly, Lucy pulled the cloth back over the mirror, and the little dancing lights caused by the flickering candle ceased. As she did so, she remembered a conversation she had had with Dr. Larimer.

How do Miss Belasysse's fits start? she had asked. *What brings them on?*

A stressful moment, a harsh smell, a flickering light, a loud noise, he had replied.

"The mirror," Lucy said slowly. "It can trigger a fit. When it catches the light or when someone waves it about, like so—" She moved her hand in the air.

Miss Belasysse's eyes widened. She swung her legs over the side of the bed.

"What is that you have there?" she demanded. "Where did you get that mirror?"

"Is it yours?" Lucy whispered, holding it out to the woman. She could feel her heart starting to beat faster.

"Where did you get it?" Miss Belasysse asked again, shrinking back against the bed, without taking the mirror from Lucy's outstretched hand. The color had drained from her face.

"I think you know," Lucy said softly, dropping her hand back to her side. "We found it by the body of your brother. On the ground, near the Cattle Bell Inn."

The woman started to tremble. "Henry? You found him?" Her face twisted in anguish. "Oh, my dear brother. The good Lord have mercy on his soul." She began to weep. "What torture it has been."

"You already knew he was dead?" Lucy asked, staring down at her. A bit of bile rose in her throat. "You've been lying to us this whole time? Pretending to have lost your memory, for what?" She crossed her arms, her fury growing. "Because you killed your brother? And that man! And to think I defended you!"

"I did not kill my brother!" Miss Belasysse exclaimed. "No, no! You must not believe that!"

"But you knew your brother was dead! Why did you lie?"

"I did not lie! I was . . . confused." The last word came as a bit of a choked cry. Gulping, Miss Belasysse continued, tears running down her cheeks. "I know what this looks like. It is hard to explain how my wretched memory works. I promise you, Lucy, I never meant to deceive you!" She began to weep in earnest then, much as Lucy had first seen her by Holborn Bridge.

But Lucy refused to be moved by her tears. "Then explain yourself," she demanded through clenched teeth. "Explain everything! Now!"

Miss Belasysse took a deep breath, trying to regain her composure. "Somewhere deep inside me, before I came to recollect these terrible events, I always knew something was wrong. There was a grief deep inside me, a melancholia different than anything I have ever experienced." She choked back a sob. "It was not until you held up my dress in the ruins, all covered in b-b-blood, that everything came back to me at once." There was a wild look in her eyes. "I did not mean to do it!"

A chill ran over Lucy. "W-what did you do?" she whispered, though she was afraid to hear the woman's reply. "*Did* you kill your brother?"

"No! No! I already told you that!"

"Someone witnessed you arguing with your brother, the night he was killed. You were in a fury, I heard tell," Lucy said, remembering what she had learned from the tavern-keeper's daughter.

Miss Belasysse looked at her in surprise. "How did you know that?" Then she waved her hand. " 'Tis no matter. I was angry at my brother, I admit it. Even though he had finally taken me from Bedlam, I was angry that it had taken him ten months to retrieve me. Ten months! For ten months, I stewed in my own juices. For ten months, they tied me up when I fell into my fits. Priests were smuggled in to do exorcisms; astrologers would intone about Venus and Mercury. A bell would ring and I would find potions and elixirs poured down my throat. If I was not mad before, I most certainly am now."

Jumping up again, she began to pace about. Lucy stepped back.

"I was angry that he ignored my letters!" she said. "He told me that he had shown them to our uncle Harlan, who convinced him that they were not of my hand. Someone else had written them, you see."

"Mr. Quade, the apothecary," Lucy stated.

"Yes. But there were others, too, blackmailing my brother about the truth of that tanner's death. I did not know that, at the time. They came from someone else." Miss Belasysse looked up at the ceiling for a long moment before continuing. "Uncle Har-lan told Henry that someone was just trying to injure the family, by claiming I was still alive. He swore to my brother that he had looked upon my dead body." Her mood seemed to shift then. "Most of the time I thought I *was* dead." She dropped down to her knees. "But I would never have done my brother ill, to that I wholeheartedly attest."

"Can you tell me, then, what happened at the Cattle Bell Inn? If you did not murder your brother, then who did?"

Miss Belasysse began to shake. "God help me!" she gasped. "I was there when that blackheart killed him."

"Who? Who killed your brother?" Lucy asked. "Was it the man who bothered you and your brother in the inn? Did you know who he was?"

Miss Belasysse began to wring her hands. "Oh, how that devil haunts me!" She began to rock back and forth. "The brown bird!"

"The brown bird?" Lucy asked. With a flash she remembered what the Bedlam inmate had whispered. *The brown bird does the falconer's bidding.* "The dead man found by Holborn Bridge is the assistant keeper of Bedlam."

Miss Belasysse twisted her lips. "Alistair Browning. The Bas-tard of Bedlam."

"Why did he kill your brother?" Lucy asked.

"He wanted to bring me back, and I . . . I . . . well, I could not bear it. And neither could my brother. And now an evil has been done."

Miss Belasysse stood up and, with a great leap, moved to the window and threw open the shutters. The cool night breeze caught at her, stirring her unbound hair and causing her nightdress to flutter. For a moment she looked as Lucy had first seen her, full of a mad frenzy, along the River Fleet at Holborn Bridge.

Before Lucy realized her intent, Miss Belasysse had lifted one long leg over the window ledge, and then the other, so that her whole body was crouched awkwardly within the window frame. Her fingers clutched at the wooden frame above her head.

"Miss! No! What are you doing?" Lucy cried out. "Pray get down from there! You will hurt yourself." Then the woman's intent dawned on Lucy. "No, miss, please! You must not!"

Miss Belasysse looked down at Lucy. "Alas, I fear it has come to this!" she cried, her eyes dark and stormy. "I did not wish to remember! But you forced the memories back upon me. I have no place in this world."

Still a few steps away, Lucy screamed as the woman swayed. Then, still pleading, she lowered her tone in an effort to calm the woman. "Please. Do not jump." She could almost hear the local minister damning the act. "Please, you will be cast into hell. Your soul will be damned."

Miss Belasysse's face grew pinched. "Do not be sorrowful for me, my dear Lucy. I am already damned, of that I am certain. Have I not been told, nearly every day of my life, that I am a much-cursed being?" She glanced down and involuntarily shuddered. Her smile became self-mocking. "I am a madwoman, but still I fear death."

"You are neither mad nor accursed," Lucy said with urgency. "The falling sickness—"

Miss Belasysse cut her off. "I am a madwoman now, even if I was not ten months ago!" She began to weep again. "Long have I been a burden to my family. The keeper told me so. That is why I was left in Bedlam to rot."

"What do you mean?"

The woman laughed unhappily. "Do you not understand? Lunatics, such as myself, are considered to be such unreasoning creatures. Because I can never contract a marriage, I will ever be a burden to my parents, an unconscionable reminder of my un-natural state. That is why they had me locked away in Bedlam. I know in my heart that is true."

Behind her, Lucy heard the door open, but she did not turn around to see who had entered the room. She did not dare move, for fear of startling the woman, who was still more than an arm's length away.

Duncan edged in beside her. "Are you all right, Lucy?" he whispered, putting his hand on her back. His eyes were fixed on Miss Belasysse. "What is going on here?"

"Ah, Constable Duncan, welcome," Miss Belasysse said, as if greeting him in a drawing room. "How good of you to join us." She tittered, her earlier ferment seemingly dispelled. "I must say, I never thought that I should have such a close acquaintance with a man of the law."

Miss Belasysse took one hand off the window frame then, caus-ing Lucy to gasp. The woman's perch had become more precari-ous, and it made Lucy a bit queasy to watch her. She said a small prayer that the woman would keep still.

But Miss Belasysse kept talking, in that odd overly merry tone. "Shall I assume, from your presence here, that you have come to inform me that my brother has been murdered? I am afraid that Lucy has already conveyed to me this vexing news." Once again she giggled, causing a shiver to run up and down Lucy's back.

"She says that Mr. Browning was the devil who killed her brother," Lucy said to the constable. Then she thought about the initials, a sudden realization coming over her. "A. B.! The initials on the knife! Alistair Browning!"

Duncan nodded. He seemed to have already realized the same thing. "So, it is interesting, is it not?" he said conversationally. "Dr. Larimer has confirmed that the same knife killed both men. The question is, how did Mr. Browning come to be stabbed by his own knife—the same knife that killed Henry Belasysse, more than a mile away from the Cattle Bell Inn?" His voice was calm, but still watchful. "Do you know, Miss Belasysse?"

"I thought we would be free," Miss Belasysse whispered. "Mr. Quade—Jonathan—had given me money, enough to start a new life. I had suitors before, you know, but not one who stayed true after learning of my terrible illness. We thought Henry could keep me hidden until Jonathan could join me."

"That is why you had the coins sewn into your dress," Lucy said.

Unexpectedly, Miss Belasysse laughed. "Indeed. It turns out Jonathan was more of a wretch at sewing than I was. What knowledge did I have of sewing? My mother was always concerned that I would convulse while I was doing embroidery and injure myself. So I had to let him sew the coins into the dress that Henry brought me." Her laugh turned bitter. "Maybe if I had been allowed to stab myself with an embroidery needle, I might not have stabbed a man."

Duncan and Lucy looked at each other.

"You knifed him?" Duncan asked. "You admit to doing that?"

Miss Belasysse inclined her head. "That is why I deserve to die."

Lucy put her hands to her lips. "You told me, when we first met on Holborn Bridge, that a devil had been chasing you. Did he come after you, and you ended up killing him yourself? A mistake!" she declared. "A jury might be forgiving!"

Duncan narrowed his eyes. "How did you get the knife from him?"

The woman closed her eyes. As she did so, both Lucy and Duncan took a few silent steps closer to her. Lucy was so close she could almost reach the woman's knee, but she did not know if that would help should the woman pitch herself over the edge or even accidentally lose her balance.

"How did I get the knife from him?" the woman murmured. "I do not recall." Then her eyes flew open. "No! He was not chasing me. I was chasing him!"

"What?" Lucy exclaimed. "Whatever do you mean?"

The woman's expression grew distant, and she tensed again. "After he stabbed my brother, I ran over to Henry, hoping to stanch the blood. But there was so much!" Tears filled her eyes again, and for a moment, she was too overcome to speak.

"That must be how I got his blood on my blue dress. But I looked up, and Mr. Browning was coming toward me. 'You must come back,' he said to me. 'I am not going back!' I remember shouting back at him. He took a step back, and I leapt up. He took another step back, and I could see then that he was afraid of me. He dropped his knife, and I scooped it up. He turned tail and ran."

"Where did he go?" Lucy asked.

"Beyond the courtyard and into the burnt-out expanse. I saw him running, the terrible coward that he was. I picked up my skirts and took after him." She began to shake as the memory overwhelmed her. "Never in my whole life have I run so fast. I was as one possessed, and maybe I was." Her voice shook. "I wanted to kill him. I *needed* to kill him!"

Her eyes had taken on an inner fury. "On and on we ran. A devil had possessed me, and it was as if I were watching myself race across that broken plain."

She began to tremble more. "I heard a voice telling me to stop. I think it was Henry, speaking to me from the beyond. I knew he wanted me to stop, but I could not. I needed that bastard to be killed, to avenge Henry as well as myself." She took a great breath. "When the blackheart tripped over a rock, I was able to catch up with him. I knew it was my chance! I stabbed him in the back, below his shoulder." She looked down at her hand in wonder. "Truth be told, I barely knew what I had done."

"What happened next?" Duncan asked. "Did he fall over? Is that when you finished him off by slitting his throat?"

Lucy looked at him in surprise. The dead man had not sustained such an injury. Duncan shook his head ever so slightly. Ah! She realized Duncan was trying to confirm Octavia's knowledge of the crime.

Indeed, the woman looked horrified. "I did not slit his throat. I just stabbed him in the back and he fell over. I dropped the knife beside him, and I do not know what happened after that. I may have had one of my fits. I do not remember anything." She paused. "When I woke up at dawn, I was in the ruins. An old woman was cooking something over a fire. Where you found the dress."

"What did you do with the body?" Duncan asked. "And the knife?"

"I do not r-remember," the woman stammered. "That is the truth. It was at that point I stopped remembering what had happened. All of it was gone. I could not remember my name or anything about myself. I only began to remember a few days later, when you took me back there and showed me the dress."

Lucy and the constable looked at each other. "Someone else killed him," Lucy said, realizing then what Duncan had already determined.

"What do you mean?" Miss Belasysse said, squinting her eyes.

Lucy held out her hand. "Miss Belasysse, please come out of the window. I will tell you." She tried to keep her voice calm and soothing, but her heart was racing. It was all too easy to imagine the woman toppling out onto the hard ground of the courtyard below. Duncan went to the other side and held out his hand as well.

"Please," Lucy whispered.

Obediently the woman took their hands and stepped out of the window frame, as though descending from an elegant carriage. She sat down on the bed, and Lucy sat beside her, pulling a blanket around her.

"That man was struck down in a manner different to what you described. He did have other cuts, but none so deep as what would have killed him. No, he sustained a deep blow to his chest—a death blow. He was found half buried a good distance away, and the knife was found buried as well," the constable said. "I agree with Lucy. Someone else finished the act. Most likely on your behalf. Who else was there?"

"You said that you heard someone calling for you to stop," Lucy prodded her.

"Henry," Miss Belasysse said, stammering. "It was Henry who called me."

A flash of realization came over Lucy. "No, not your brother," she said. "It was Mr. Quade, was it not?"

"No!" Miss Belasysse cried out. "No, it was not Jonathan. It could not have been."

"He knew where you and your brother were going. He was the one who smuggled out the letter to your brother. He brought you the elixir that you needed. He helped you sew coins into your dress," Lucy said, touching the woman's elbow. "It seems that he would do anything to help you."

Duncan looked thoughtful. "That would mean that he had known that the assistant keeper had been sent to retrieve Miss Belasysse."

"I imagine that he simply followed Mr. Browning to the inn," Lucy said. She looked back at Miss Belasysse. "Was he there? Did he come inside the inn? Did he speak to you?"

Miss Belasysse did not answer, beginning to weep.

Duncan nodded. "I must go question Mr. Quade. Find out the truth of the matter."

·26·

"Please do not arrest Jonathan," Miss Belasysse pleaded, stumbling after Constable Duncan as he moved quickly down the stairs. "Please."

"Miss Belasysse," Lucy called, two steps behind them. "I beg you. Return to your bed. You are not well."

Duncan had just reached the front door when there came an urgent knocking from the outside. He opened it to reveal Hank standing with Susan Belasysse, Lady Belasysse, and Harlan Boteler.

Having heard the great clamor, Dr. Larimer and Mr. Sheridan had stepped out of the study.

"What in heaven's name is going on here?" Dr. Sheridan shouted.

Seeing Constable Duncan, Susan Belasysse cried out, "You have heard from my husband? Where is he? Tell me at once!"

Hank threw up his hands. "I did not tell them," he said to Duncan. "I just told them that you had news."

"Pray, come inside," Dr. Larimer said. To Molly, who was peering out from the shadows of the hallway, he added, "Wine, Molly. At once."

With a frightened look, the servant scurried off, and everyone else followed Dr. Larimer into the drawing room.

They all looked at Duncan expectantly, trepidation and fear in their faces.

"My husband is dead?" Susan Belasysse whimpered.

Duncan nodded. "I am afraid so. Stabbed, I am sorry to say."

"Oh!" Lady Belasysse said, blanching. She looked like someone had punched her in the stomach. Though she was obviously trying to maintain her composure, her voice cracked, and she swallowed hard. "Who k-killed my son?"

"The assistant keeper of Bedlam," Miss Belasysse replied. "Alistair Browning."

"Bedlam?" Lady Belasysse repeated, looking at her daughter without comprehension. Clearly, the shock of her son's death was dulling her senses. Still, she struggled to understand. "My son was killed by a madman, then?"

Before Duncan could reply, Mr. Boteler stood and held up his sister's cloak to her. "Let us leave this place," he said, glaring at Duncan and Dr. Larimer. "We have all had a terrible shock. To think we were informed of this horrific news in such a callous fashion. Unconscionable. We should return home at once, so that we may grieve privately."

"No," Miss Belasysse said, replying to her mother's question. "The keeper of Bedlam was not a madman, although it would seem that way, would it not? Given that he did strike down my brother in cold blood." Her strange gaiety seemed to be resurfacing. "Who is to say what makes a madman mad?"

"I do not understand," Lady Belasysse said. To all appearances, she seemed genuinely bewildered by what her daughter was saying.

"It is simple, Mother," Octavia replied, showing her teeth. "I have been a resident of Bedlam these last ten months. One of Old Tom's lot. Living with Maudlin Maeve. Madmen all. And my own dear friend Lucinda, who called me her bluebird, and herself a beautiful dove. Oh—and the tanner's wife, before she murdered herself. Well, truth be told, I never met her, but the others did." She giggled. "I told them to blackmail you, Uncle Harlan, for the ill you did to that poor woman, and to me. I didn't expect them to go after my brother, though."

"What madness you speak!" Harlan Boteler said, with an attempt at a hearty laugh. " 'Tis no wonder you were caught by Old Tom."

But no one else laughed. Lucy noticed that Hank stood in front of the door, as if to bar anyone from leaving.

"Well, if she ended up at the sorry place, then it is only because someone must have found her after she wandered off," Mr. Boteler continued, trying to maintain his bluster.

"That is what you wanted people to believe," Duncan said. "Why did you send your niece to Bedlam, Mr. Boteler?"

Harlan Boteler, growing slack-jawed, seemed at a loss for words.

Lady Belasysse turned toward her brother. "You left my daughter there in Bedlam? Harlan, why ever did you do such a terrible thing?"

"I d-did not," he began, but Lady Belasysse would not be deterred.

"Most certainly, you did! Where else could she have been?" she said, her voice taking on a distinct chill. "Did my husband know? Did John tell you to do this?"

Mr. Boteler had started to sweat noticeably. "I did place her in Bedlam," he conceded. "But you were at your wit's end, do you not recall? You feared her sickness would damage the family reputation, and the political careers of her father and brother! You told me that there was nothing more you could do for her. You begged me to take care of her. So I did!"

Lady Belasysse faltered. "No, that is not so." She looked at her daughter. "Octavia, do not believe him!"

"Oh, Mother!" Miss Belasysse exclaimed. "Surely you do not expect me to believe that you knew nothing of this arrangement." She sniffed. "Have I not been a source of shame to you, my whole life? Particularly when no suitor stepped forward to marry me?" Her eyes flitted toward Mr. Sheridan, who shuffled his feet and looked away.

"Nonetheless, it is so," her mother replied stiffly.

"Are you claiming, sir," the constable said to Mr. Boteler, "that Lady Belasysse believed that the family's reputation would be more besmirched by her daughter's unfortunate sickness than by her son's involvement in a murder?"

Mr. Boteler's features hardened. "Henry Belasysse was pardoned for that mishap, as you recall. It is clear, *Constable,* that you know nothing of the importance of preserving a family name, or about how marriages are contracted among your betters."

Duncan did not reply, but his jaw tightened noticeably.

Miss Belasysse's eyes narrowed. "How marriages are contracted, an interesting notion." She looked at Susan Belasysse. "Shall we talk a little bit about *your* marriage, Susan? About the vows you made to my brother? About how you broke those vows, with my dear uncle?"

Susan Belasysse cowered as everyone turned to look at her.

"What was the real reason you had Miss Belasysse locked away in Bedlam?" Lucy asked, turning back to Mr. Boteler. "She knew of your affair with your nephew's wife, did she not?"

"I did!" Miss Belasysse jumped in before her uncle could protest. "I saw them together! I did not wish to speak of it, for I did not wish my brother to be labeled a cuckold! To have his masculinity questioned by those who would work with him." She turned to Susan. "Oh, how I despised you!"

"And I despised being in my marriage!" Susan Belasysse shouted back at her. "Do you think I did not know that he only married me for my money? That everyone whispered about me? That he was breaking our marriage vows as frequently as I was?"

"Susan!" Mr. Boteler hissed at her. "For once in your life, be quiet!"

"Oh, Harlan! We can be together now, can you not see that?" she said, moving to put her arms around him. "We will have to wait until my mourning period has passed, of course, but—"

"Enough of your foolishness!" Harlan said.

"But you said . . ." Her voice trailed off, and her face crumpled.

Something clicked for Lucy then. She turned to Miss Belasysse. "Do you wonder how your brother came to be killed?" she asked.

"I know what happened." Miss Belasysse sniffed. "I saw the blackheart Browning from Bedlam slay my brother."

"Why would Mr. Browning do that?" Lucy pressed. "It is one thing to go after a man, and quite another to murder him. Was he so aggrieved by your brother, do you suppose?"

"Why, I do not think so. Although I think he tried to black-mail my brother. Perhaps when my brother did not pay?"

"No, why would he? Perhaps, though, there was someone else who wished your brother dead," Lucy said. "Maybe he had some-thing that someone else wanted." She looked meaningfully at Mr. Boteler and Susan Belasysse.

Miss Belasysse's eyes widened, and she looked toward her uncle. "Did you have my brother killed?" She swallowed. "So that you could marry your rich mistress?"

"I will not stand for such impertinence!" Mr. Boteler shouted, raising his hand to slap his niece. "Henry Belasysse got what he deserved!"

Duncan stepped in between them then, and in a neat move, knocked the man to the floor. "Shall I take that as an admission of guilt?" he asked.

Sagging against the wall, Mr. Boteler said, "I did everything for Henry! Everything! After he and Lord Buckhurst killed that tanner, it was I who told them to finish another bottle of wine each. I knew if those feckless fools were intoxicated enough when the authorities were called in, it would pave the way for a lighter sentence. The king himself pardoned them!" He waved his arms wildly.

"Oh, Brother," Lady Belasysse said, "do stop talking."

He ignored his sister and continued, his face growing redder and redder as the emotions came to a boil. "Later, I was the one who arranged for Henry to marry a wealthy heiress—this insipid girl—so that he had the means to cultivate men in power. He was appointed to Parliament, for God's sake!" He thumped his fist on the table. "I made that happen!

"All I wanted from him was a bit of money of my own to attend to my wants and needs. Was that so much to ask?" Mr. Boteler looked around at them. "But he did not want to pay me anything. 'Oh, Uncle,' he would say. 'You must mind your gambling habit. Your debts are not mine to pay.' But my debts *were* his debts, how could he not understand that? So I decided to find a way to access that lovely flow of money for myself."

"Susan began to pay your debts," Miss Belasysse said, curling her lip in disdain. "After you began an affair with her. I remember when I first saw you embracing her."

"I knew if you told anyone, you would ruin us all," Mr. Boteler replied. "I did not wish to kill you; I just needed you to be kept somewhere safe. Where you would never tell anyone what you had witnessed."

No one spoke. Everyone except Susan Belasysse stared back at him with similarly shocked expressions. Finally, Miss Belasysse regained her voice. "That day, in London. How did you get me to Bedlam? No one ever knew who brought me."

Mr. Boteler laughed without mirth. "It was easy enough. We flashed a mirror in your eyes, and you went readily into a fit. We knew from experience that you nearly always forgot everything that happened directly beforehand. We loaded you into the back of a cart, and I paid the driver to take you to Bedlam. The keeper was expecting you, along with a hefty payment."

"So there was no drowned woman?" Lady Belasysse asked. "No priest? No mistaken identity?"

"No, Sister," he admitted. "None of that story was true. I thought it would be more palatable for you if you believed that your daughter had simply succumbed to a quick end." Then, more annoyed, he added, "I did not realize that the Bedlam keepers would be so incompetent as to let her escape. When I first caught wind of her notes, I told them they had to do a better job of reining her in. Then, when I heard Henry was going after her, I told the keepers to let them go, but to follow them."

"You wanted him to be killed!" Miss Belasysse cried.

"Yes! And you as well! But you escaped, all the worse for me. When I realized you had lost your memory, I thought we still had a chance to keep you alive."

"Thank you very much," Miss Belasysse said, crossing her arms.

"That is why the keeper did not hurt you," Lucy realized. "He was trying to bring you back. Since you had no memory, he thought it would be easy enough. You were still worth a lot to them, a wealthy Belasysse as an inmate in Bedlam."

"And I assume *you* paid for it all?" Lady Belasysse said to Susan, who nodded.

"Were you truly going to marry her?" Miss Belasysse asked Mr. Boteler. "Your own nephew's wife?"

"Marry a wealthy widow, why not?" He snorted. "So long as I did not have to look at her, it seemed a pleasing enough arrangement."

Harlan sat down then and put his face heavily into his hands.

Susan Belasysse moved toward him, and he pushed her away. She sat back down, stunned.

"What a fool you were!" Miss Belasysse said, staring down at her sister-in-law.

"You never thought I was good enough for Henry," Susan Belasysse sobbed, the words coming out in short heaving bursts.

"And so you were not," Lady Belasysse said. "You are my brother's whore. Except that you were too stupid to know that whores do not pay—they *get* paid." She turned away, ignoring everyone's open jaws at her pronouncement. "I am ready to take my leave. There is nothing of interest to me here."

Constable Duncan stepped forward then, gesturing to Hank. "Mr. Harlan Boteler, I do hereby arrest you for the murder of Henry Belasysse, who was killed on the evening of March 30, the year of our Lord 1667, at the site of the Cattle Bell Inn."

Pulling out a length of twine that he kept tied to his belt, Hank began to tie up Mr. Boteler's hands, with hard strong pulls.

Constable Duncan turned to Miss Belasysse. "I am afraid, miss, that I must arrest you for the attempted murder of Alistair Browning, assistant keeper of Bedlam." Constable Duncan paused. "At the moment, I must go after Mr. Quade, to discover his involvement in the crime."

Mr. Sheridan's sallow face looked more pinched than usual. "You cannot possibly be arresting her. It was the apothecary who killed that man, I am sure of it!"

"Dear James," Miss Belasysse said, touching his cheek. "It is all right. I should be punished for the part I played."

"I will ask you to come to the jail in the morning." Duncan

gave them all a warning look. "Do not even think of leaving before then."

"We will watch over her," Dr. Larimer promised.

Miss Belasysse suddenly looked weary. Her voice cracking, the weight of the melancholy evident in every syllable, she asked, "And where would I go?" She sank into a chair. "Where would I go?"

·27·

Have a care," Dr. Larimer said to Miss Belasysse the next morning, as she stumbled in the street. He and Lucy were on either side of her as they walked toward Duncan's jail.

When they arrived, Constable Duncan nodded, relief evident in his eyes. "Thank you for escorting Miss Belasysse here." He shook his head. "If it were up to me, I would have placed her under house arrest, in your care, until her trial. But the Lord Mayor is convinced that she might attempt to leave. The Belasysses *do* have great resources at their disposal, so there is sufficient concern she could be spirited away." He looked at them apologetically. "I will not send you to the larger prison, as I did Mr. Boteler. Hank and I will look after you ourselves."

"Is Mr. Quade here?" Miss Belasysse asked eagerly, looking about. "Jonathan?" she called into the jail.

"Did he confess to the murder of the assistant keeper of Bedlam?" Lucy asked. "Did he say why he did it?"

Duncan rubbed at his chin wearily. He looked as if he had not slept all night.

"No, he has not yet admitted his guilt. In fact, he has refused to answer any of my questions."

Hearing this, Miss Belasysse pushed past them both to where the apothecary was being held, his hands on the iron gate. "Oh, Jonathan!" she exclaimed.

"Octavia, why are you here?" he asked, perturbed. "I did not want you to see me here!"

"The constable has arrested me for murder."

"What! That is preposterous!" He shook the bars. "She did not kill that man! I did!"

"But you do not have cuts on your hands, and she does!" Duncan replied.

"I was wearing gloves." He began to breathe heavily. "Please, she did nothing except be imprisoned against her will for ten months in Bedlam. I was trying to make sure that she was all right." He looked from one face to the next. "I admit it! Do you hear me? I admit to killing him!"

Duncan straightened up, and his next words were stern. "Why do you not tell us from the beginning?"

The man's face softened when he looked at Miss Belasysse. "I remember the day you were brought to us. I was worried from the start. You were so delicate, so fragile, like a gentle bird. I gave you an amulet the first time we met, with the hopes it would protect you from harm. It was a special one I had picked up, during my travels in France."

Her hands flew to her chest, grasping the amulet. "I remember when you gave it to me. So lovely, you said. You had filled it with roses, if I recall."

"Yes. Later I filled it with rosemary, when I realized how regularly you lost your memory due to the falling sickness," the apothecary replied. "I would do anything for you. That night—"

"Hush, Jonathan," she said, glancing around at the others. "Do not speak."

"I must speak. I must tell you what happened," he said, gripping her hands through the bars. "I heard the keeper telling Mr. Browning to go after you. After so many months, watching the vile way he treated you, I could not bear it if you were brought back. I knew you had to be free. I had hoped, when your brother took you away, that you would be able to live an unfettered life."

"I had hoped to live that life with you, Jonathan," she said sadly.

"I know. It was never meant to be." He paused, and then continued to explain what had happened. "I followed that vile cur that evening, to the Cattle Bell Inn—he was following you. I was there when he set upon your brother, but I was too late to stop him. When he left, I thought that would be the end of it." He searched her face. "My darling, I never would have supposed that you would chase him as you did. I ran beside you begging you to drop the knife, to come away with me. But your grief was too strong, and your anger too great." He sagged a bit. "Oh, that you had done as I had said. We should have been far away from here by now."

Miss Belasysse glanced at Lucy. "I am so sorry, Jonathan," she whispered. "I was truly possessed, by a spirit I can little explain. I drove that knife in, and he fell."

"But it was not you who killed him," he said fervently, oblivious to everyone else in the room. "When you stumbled off, there was little more for me to do, but finish what you had started. It was I who dragged the body off and knocked a few bricks on top of him so that he would not be found."

"Where did you go?" Octavia asked.

"It took me a bit to drag him away, and when I looked about for you, the heavy fog had set in. I stayed quiet so as not to draw attention to myself. When I heard voices, I thought I had best move away from the body. I went back to Bedlam, so that they would not know I was gone. No one suspected I had been missing when they began to look for him."

"How did you find out where Miss Belasysse was?" Lucy asked. "When you came by Dr. Larimer's?"

"Well, the keeper had heard tell of a wild woman—forgive me, my love—who was having fits as if possessed by an imp or spirit. A vegetable-seller informed us that she overheard what you"—here he nodded at Lucy—"had told Miss Belasysse. That you were going to take her to see Dr. Larimer. It was easy enough to find you."

He frowned and tightened his hold on Miss Belasysse's hand. With great anguish in his voice, he said to her, "The keeper told me that he came for you, my darling. When he realized that you did not remember him, he made up the story that he was your husband. He tried to take you back to Bedlam by force."

"Then you came by," Lucy said. "With the tisane she needed."

"Yes, I could not let her suffer."

Lucy nodded, but did not say anything. For a long moment, the apothecary and Miss Belasysse gazed into each other's eyes. Watching them, Lucy realized that she had written the wrong story for Master Aubrey, as a new title floated in her mind. *A*

Death Along the River Fleet; or, A True and Strange Tale of Love in Bedlam.

Three weeks later, Lucy stood at Holborn Bridge, a letter in her hand, looking down at the muddy River Fleet as it moved languidly below. The note was from Adam. He had decided to journey to the New World, where he would help further develop one of the colonial law courts. Not the Massachusetts Bay Colony, but maybe the Connecticut or even the Carolina colony.

Then there were the words that she had read so often, they were now emblazoned on her heart. *My heart will be sore without you, my dearest Lucy, but perchance, you will one day travel to this strange New World where, as Sarah has told me, the birthright of men is less fixed.*

She smiled then, as she had done every time she'd read the last few lines. *I have heard tell, too, of several petticoat authors among the colonists. Perhaps, one day soon, even a female printer may find a way to ply her trade.* And then his signature, signed with a quick elegant flourish.

A step on the bridge caused her to look up. Duncan was walking toward her. He was smiling. "I thought you might be here," he said.

"I have thought enough of this place these last few weeks," Lucy replied. At each trial, she had been called to give testimony, detailing how she had come to find Miss Belasysse, as well as everything else she had learned and discovered since that moment. "I suppose I wanted to see it again."

"I just came from the courts," Duncan said. "The verdicts were as we expected. Miss Belasysse was acquitted of manslaughter. Although she was deemed guilty of willful battery, she has already been released."

"What will happen to her, do you think?" Lucy asked.

"I cannot say for sure, but I did see Mr. Sheridan helping her out of the courtroom. I think he will look after her, at least for some time. I think it unlikely that she will return to her family."

Lucy turned so that she could sit on the stone rail of the bridge. He sat next to her. "And the others?" she asked.

"Of course, Harlan Boteler and Jonathan Quade were both found guilty. They will likely be hanged in the next few weeks, with no pardon for either." Duncan sighed. "The keeper was deemed innocent of all charges."

"He was the one who would not let her leave Bedlam," Lucy said angrily.

"I know. We can take consolation that he has been forced to resign his post. An official inquiry into Bedlam will be made as well."

For a moment, they were silent, still sitting close together.

"Adam is leaving England," Lucy said, speaking evenly. "He will be going to the New World. Carolina, maybe. To help work on the law courts there."

Duncan nodded. "Yes, he told me. I saw him at the court today. He said that he wanted to go where he could make a difference. I admire him for that, I do."

Lucy closed her eyes. She remembered another moment, as the Great Fire had begun its fearsome rampage, taking down the houses and shops of London. Adam had declared his love for her, and she for him. Sometimes it felt like the dream of her youth, even though it had only been eight months before. So much had changed, though, when she left the Hargraves' home and became a printer's apprentice. A new world had opened up, full of possibilities she would never have seen, had she remained a chambermaid.

She felt Duncan's hand cover hers, where it lay on the bridge. Opening her eyes, she found him regarding her intently. "What are you thinking about?" he asked.

"The Great Fire. The aftermath. How I became a printer's apprentice," she replied lightly. She pointed to the east. "That way, my old life and the Fire." She pointed toward Fleet Street. "And that way, my new life."

"Ah." He smiled. "I thought you might be thinking about me."

She blushed, but returned his smile. "I remember the day that I met you. Three years ago, it was."

"A terrible day that was—a woman was killed. And as I recall, I arrested your brother for that crime," he said, still looking at her closely. "Why do you think of that now?"

She looked down at the dirty waters languidly flowing below Holborn Bridge. "So much muck and so many ill-smelling things have passed beneath us."

"It is rather rank here, is it not?" he said, wrinkling his nose, when the wind brought the smell of the river to them.

Lucy smiled and looked away. "My words may sound odd. But verily, I have seen so many terrible things these last few years. We all have." He waited while she gathered her thoughts. She looked back at him, gripping his hand more tightly. "But you, Duncan—you have been like this bridge. Supporting me. Keeping me away from those terrible things that flow all around us. Keeping me on my path, as it were." She laughed a little.

"Ah, Lucy," he said, reaching his hand out to caress her cheek. "I could so easily say the same of you." He leaned closer and kissed her, a long kiss that set her pulse to racing. For a moment, her confused heart was at peace. There was no worry about where she belonged, she knew.

When the wind blew again, he hopped off the stone railing. "Shall we go?" he asked, putting his hands around her waist to help her down. Rather than letting her go as she expected, however, he kept his hands there and kissed her again, this time with more fervor. When the wind blew a third time, they broke apart, laughing.

As they walked hand in hand back across the bridge, Lucy could see a field of flowers ahead of them. Spring had finally come to London after the very long hard winter.

"Perchance, we will hear tell of a cow with two tails," she said, giggling, as they passed some animals in a pasture. "Master Aubrey might be pleased for a true account of a most monstrous birth."

Duncan hugged Lucy to him. "I have not your words, but I do like your stories."

"That is good," she said, looking up at him. "I think we have many more stories before us!"

HISTORICAL NOTE

In researching this book, I spent a lot of time thinking about the interplay of science and faith in seventeenth-century England, and what those practices meant for healing and medicine. I tried to pay attention to the complex relationships between physicians, surgeons, and apothecaries, and their attitudes toward well-known herbalists like Nicholas Culpeper and famous quacks like Valentine Greatrakes, although I simplified the roles that each group played in the healing process for the sake of the story. Similarly, physicians at this time did not all adhere to the same set of beliefs; for example, my physicians hold with the ancient theory of humors but are also knowledgeable about William Harvey's discovery of the circulation of the blood, although the latter may not have been widely known in 1667.

I also tried to be as accurate as possible about the seventeenth-century medical awareness and understanding of hysteria, epilepsy, and traumatic memory loss, which are all conditions that I ascribed to Octavia Belasysse. Epilepsy, the "falling sickness," was well known, and all the remedies that I describe for its relief can be found in seventeenth-century medical treatises. Several of the tracts I refer to, such as Drage's *Daimonomageia*, are real, although

I simplified the language to make it readable for the modern audience. Likewise, my description of Bedlam came from a number of firsthand and historic accounts, although I had to guess at some of the architectural features. Certainly the methods for keeping the inmates under control varied throughout the seventeenth century, but the abuses, such as tying the patient down during fits, have been well documented. While there were reforms throughout the seventeenth century, true humanitarian reform of the asylum did not begin until the nineteenth century, and arguably the mid-twentieth.

Lastly, I did draw on one true story to frame the overall backstory. There really was a historic figure named Henry Belasysse who, along with Lord Buckhurst (Charles Sackville), was involved in the manslaughter of a tanner whom they had mistaken for a highwayman in Waltham Forest. They were indeed pardoned by King Charles II, and Henry Belasysse became an MP for Great Grimsby in 1666. However, the rest of the story is completely imagined by me, and should be not taken as true.